## "You want an affair,"

he questioned, hoping he'd heard her right.

"I never wanted a sexual relationship with any man. Until you," she admitted, shooting him an embarrassed glance coupled with a sweet smile.

"What about your husband?"

A shadow crossed her eyes. "It wasn't there."

"What wasn't there?"

"*It.*" She drew a breath, glanced down at her forgotten glass and took a swallow of brandy.

He swept his hand across her cheek, feeling the silk of her hair through his fingers. "But it's here now."

"Ty...don't ever lie to me. If I keep thinking I know what I'm doing, then I'll be okay. But I can't fool myself. I don't want to be reckless and blind, too."

Her words were urgent, tense. Ty thought of his secret. The future opened up with blinding clarity. He would lose her. Lose Nathan. Lose everything. He couldn't chance it.

Dear Reader,

Welcome to **Silhouette Special Edition** . . . welcome to romance. Each month, **Silhouette Special Edition** publishes six novels with you in mind—stories of love and life, tales that you can identify with—romance with that little "something special" added in.

This month, **Silhouette Special Edition** has some wonderful stories on their way to you. A "delivery" you may want to keep an eye out for is *Navy Baby,* by Debbie Macomber. It's full steam ahead for a delightful story that shouldn't be missed!

Rounding out October are winning tales by more of your favorite authors: Tracy Sinclair, Natalie Bishop, Mary Curtis, Christine Rimmer and Diana Whitney. A good time will be had by all!

In each **Silhouette Special Edition** novel, we're dedicated to bringing you the romances that you dream about—the type of stories that delight as well as bring a tear to the eye. And that's what **Silhouette Special Edition** is all about—special books by special authors for special readers!

I hope you enjoy this book and all of the stories to come.

Sincerely,

Tara Gavin
Senior Editor

# NATALIE BISHOP
## Romancing Rachel

*Silhouette Special Edition*

Published by Silhouette Books New York

**America's Publisher of Contemporary Romance**

SILHOUETTE BOOKS
300 East 42nd St., New York, N.Y. 10017

ROMANCING RACHEL

ISBN: 0-373-09700-X

First Silhouette Books printing October 1991

Printed in the U.S.A.

**Books by Natalie Bishop**

Silhouette Special Edition

*Saturday's Child* #178
*Lover or Deceiver* #198
*Stolen Thunder* #231
*Trial by Fire* #245
*String of Pearls* #280
*Diamond in the Sky* #300
*Silver Thaw* #329
*Just a Kiss Away* #352
*Summertime Blues* #401
*Imaginary Lover* #472
*The Princess and the Pauper* #545
*Dear Diary* #596
*Downright Dangerous* #651
*Romancing Rachel* #700

## *NATALIE BISHOP*

lives in Lake Oswego, Oregon, with her husband, Ken, and daughter, Kelly. Natalie began writing in 1981 along with her sister, Lisa Jackson, another Silhouette author. Though they write separate books, Natalie and Lisa work out most of their plots together. They live within shouting distance of each other and between them have published over thirty Silhouette novels. When Natalie isn't writing, she enjoys spending time at her mountain cabin at Black Butte Ranch, where she catches up on her reading.

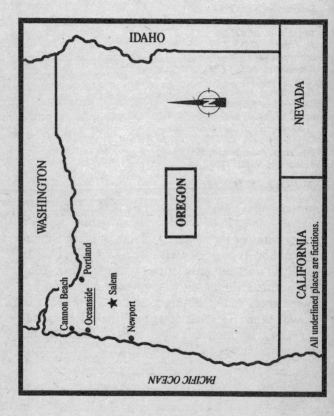

IDAHO

NEVADA

WASHINGTON

OREGON

CALIFORNIA

All underlined places are fictitious.

Cannon Beach

Portland

Oceanside

Salem

Newport

PACIFIC OCEAN

N

## Chapter One

"I have a fifteen-year-old son," Tyrrell Rafferty III repeated slowly, his gaze fixed on the man seated on the opposite side of the dusty steel desk.

"That's right." With an affected clearing of his throat, the man swiped at his knife-creased pant legs and worriedly eyed the dust motes swirling vigorously in the small breeze Ty had created as he'd strode through the trailer to his chair.

Ty ignored the man's discomfort. He glanced down at the business card he'd been handed. Donald M. Davis, Attorney-at-Law. Julia's attorney. He hadn't thought about Julia in . . . well . . . about fifteen years.

"Julia Williams told you that she had a son and that I'm the father," Ty tried again, convinced there must be some mistake.

"Julia Williams-Hunt. Yes. She wanted me to deliver this package to you." Davis grabbed the slim alligator briefcase sitting beside his chair, clicked it open and slid a manila folder across Ty's desk.

The thin walls of the trailer reverberated from the steady pounding from outside. Posts were being driven through earth to bedrock. Rafferty Construction Company never stopped. Seven days a week. Day or night. Ty made sure of that.

"She's married now and living in London," the attorney went on as Ty opened the folder. "But when the boy's adoptive father died, she wanted to make sure—"

"Adoptive father?" Ty cut in. "She gave the child up for adoption?"

"Mrs. Williams-Hunt was only eighteen when her son was born. She felt it was the best thing for the child."

Ty's lips curved dryly. "If Julia was eighteen, *I* was eighteen."

"Yes?" he asked, clearly missing the point.

"She would have told me."

Davis straightened, affronted. "You don't believe me?"

"No."

"Mrs. Williams-Hunt is worried about the boy and wants you to make certain he's being well taken care of," Davis continued intractably, a note of disgust entering his voice.

"I'll bet." Ty was unmoved. He was both amused and irritated by the disapproval emanating in tidal waves from the attorney. It wasn't difficult to read Davis's mind. He'd expected something more from a Rafferty. He'd expected a plush office, a battery of secretaries, an appointment list made out for six months in advance.

Instead he'd found Ty, a normal contractor except for one small detail: Tyrrell Rafferty III had inherited the entire Rafferty fortune in bulk.

Which was exactly why he'd been slapped with a paternity claim.

Julia wasn't the first to threaten Ty with a lawsuit by a long shot. Although this one was perhaps the most ingenious. You weren't born as wealthy as the Raffertys without somebody trying to grab a piece of the financial pie.

And women were the worst. He'd dated one little gold digger less than a month before she'd slapped a mental abuse suit against him, claiming untold damages. Mental abuse? For taking her out to dinner and to the symphony? Unbelievable! And he'd barely spoken two words to her, anyway. He hadn't had to; she'd done enough talking for both of them.

What, in God's name, was mentally abusive about *that?*

And then there'd been the woman who'd called herself his wife and demanded half the Rafferty fortune. True, they'd had a brief, rather lukewarm affair, instigated primarily by the woman in question. But his *wife?* Where had that delusion come from?

Both matters had been resolved by Ty's lawyers. Both women had gotten their greedy little hands on a bit of Rafferty money—settlements being far less costly than long, drawn-out court battles. It was all part and parcel of being a member of one of Portland's wealthiest families. Ty was used to it by now, even though the Rafferty name might not be as well-known as some, mainly because Ty's grandfather and father, Rafferty I and II respectively, had been like Ty in one respect—they all zealously guarded their privacy and tried to keep their considerable financial fortune under wraps.

But there were those who seemed to have a nose for money and an unerring accuracy in zeroing in for the kill. They were the ones who penetrated the Rafferty shield.

Like Julia Williams-Hunt.

Donald M. Davis cleared his throat, his glare replaced by studied indifference. Ty's cynicism had been noted, and

Davis was changing tactics. "Perhaps if you examined the information I've presented you . . . ?"

Ty shrugged in agreement. It was possible Julia's paternity claim was legitimate, after all. She and Ty had been classmates at an exclusive private school. Julia had been wild. Ready for anything. And Ty had been . . . well . . . eighteen. But Julia had never told him she was pregnant. He hadn't seen her since the summer following graduation. Why wait fifteen years?

Impatiently he glanced down at the papers inside the folder. One was a brief letter from Julia, introducing Donald M. Davis, and reiterating her claim that one Nathan Stone was Ty's biological son. Another was an address in Oceanside, Oregon—the residence of the boy in question. Attached to it was another detailed report on Nathan's adoptive parents, Richard and Rachel Stone. Richard Stone had died of congestive heart failure last November, and Rachel worked at Neptune Travel Agency in Oceanside.

Lastly, there was a photograph of Nathan. It had been taken from a distance through a telephoto lens, but it gave a sharp profile of the boy. A chill swept over Ty. The kid *did* look a little like him. That chin and nose were pure Rafferty. The arrogance stamped across the boy's mouth had Ty rubbing his own jaw, as if to wipe away similar traits. Coincidence? Undoubtedly. But who believed in coincidence these days?

"What does Julia expect me to do?" Ty asked flatly.

"Take care of him. Make sure he's all right financially and emotionally. After all, his adoptive father just died."

Ty slid the attorney a look. Make sure he's all right financially. Well, sure. What else? Closing the folder, he leaned back in his chair, stretching his jean-clad legs across the top of the dusty desk.

Davis responded with a disapproving look. "Excuse me, Mr. Rafferty," he said in a stab of honesty, "but you're not quite what I expected."

"I know." Ty grinned, a megawatt smile that invariably dazzled though he didn't strive for the effect. He didn't look like a multimillionaire. Far from it. Although his father and grandfather had cultivated a discreet and aristocratic Rafferty image, Ty had bucked convention from the first. He couldn't content himself with a being a real estate mogul; he needed to actually *do* something. So he'd fired all the levels of managers between him and the construction workers and had dug in. Now, though he still had foremen working for him, he could generally be found on one job site or another himself.

The trailer door banged open. Big Jim Carlson stopped short, rain dripping from the bill of his cap and mud clinging to his boots. "Oops, sorry. Didn't know you had company, Ty. We got some problems with the concrete crew."

"I'll be right there. Mr. Davis was just leaving." Ty rose from his seat, and Donald M. Davis reluctantly got to his feet.

"What should I tell Mrs. Williams-Hunt?" he asked at the door.

Ty glanced outside, grimacing at the leaden Oregon sky. "That I'll look into the matter."

"When?"

"When I'm good and ready."

After Davis left and the problems with the concrete crew were resolved, Ty pulled Big Jim aside. "I'm going to be gone for a couple days. I've got something I've gotta do. You take care of things, okay? I'll call in and give you a number where I can be reached."

"Okay." Big Jim eyed Ty curiously. Ty rarely took time off. In fact, Big Jim couldn't remember a single time when his boss had left work early for anything except business.

Ty didn't notice how Big Jim stared after him as he jumped into his black Porsche 911 and wheeled from the site. His mind was already one step ahead, planning. He drove by rote toward his home perched on a cliff above the Willamette River, but at the last moment made an illegal U-turn and headed back toward city center and the parking lot of the U.S. Bank Tower. He arrived just before six o'clock—just before Gerald Raintree, Ty's personal attorney, normally left work.

Watching the elevator indicator lights flicker, Ty waited impatiently until the lift smoothly settled onto the fifteenth floor. He practically bounded out of the cubicle into the elegant, black-carpeted hallway, striding rapidly toward the double doors at the end of the hall. Gerald was a personal friend, one of the few Ty had kept since college, and he was also one of the best attorneys around.

"Hello, Mr. Rafferty." Gerald's secretary gave him a friendly smile of recognition as he strode through her outer office. She was just locking the drawers on her desk.

"Is he still here?"

She nodded. "Go right on in," she told him. There was no need to stand on ceremony where Ty was concerned. Their friendship superseded regular business protocol.

"Hello, Rafferty," Gerald greeted him without looking up from his monthly calendar. He flipped several pages, made a note, then added, "You're right on time. I was just heading out for a cold martini before Elizabeth meets me for dinner. Join me?"

"No, thanks. I need some help."

"Really?" He sounded bored, but he leaned back in his chair and plucked a paper clip from the solid teak holder on his desk, waiting expectantly. "Can I offer this help over a drink?" He pulled the paper clip apart then sailed it over his desk into the wastecan across the room, one of his favorite pastimes. His accuracy never failed to impress Ty.

"Well..." Ty was anxious to get cracking on this Nathan Stone thing, and he could see where a round of martinis might delay his trip to Oceanside. But he also needed advice. "All right."

He followed Gerald into a quiet bar across the street where they were shown to a back booth against the far wall. Gerald ordered them both martinis and proceeded to savor his as Ty related what Donald M. Davis had told him about Julia Williams-Hunt's paternity claim.

"Is there some reason you suspect this is more than the usual wolf-crying?" Gerald asked, all but smacking his lips around the pimiento-stuffed green olive. Gross things, Ty thought in disgust, wishing he had a beer.

"It's possible the boy's my son," Ty said, explaining to Gerald about his long-ago relationship with Julia Williams-Hunt. "We weren't exactly religious about adhering to birth control, if you know what I mean."

"So, you think there's a chance she's telling the truth."

Ty shook his head in part bemusement, part exasperation. "The boy looks like a Rafferty."

"You've seen him?"

"A picture. It gave me a strange feeling. Made me want to know more."

"I see." Gerald lifted two fingers, silently ordering two more drinks from the waitress passing by, oblivious to the fact Ty hadn't touched his. "I take it you plan to see this kid for yourself."

"Something like that."

"And then what?"

"I'm not sure." Ty watched the waitress set two more martinis on cocktail napkins in front of them. "If he's my son... if there's *any* chance he's really mine..."

"Uh-huh," Gerald encouraged.

"God, I don't know! Then I want to be his father, I guess."

"Ah." The knowing tone of Gerald's voice irritated Ty, but he forced himself to wait patiently while Gerald tested his new drink. "You want my advice?"

"I suppose so."

"This Mrs. Stone—what's her first name?"

"Rachel."

"Right. Rachel. She's the boy's legal guardian?"

Ty nodded. The waitress was hovering nearby. Feeling her eyes on him, Ty glanced her way. She smiled. He recognized that look instantly. It said, "I'm interested. How about you?"

"Could I have a draft?" was Ty's answer, and she nodded, smiling uncertainly, unsure what to read out of that simple request.

"Let's play this out to its logical conclusion," Gerald said, bringing Ty's attention back to the problem at hand. "You believe you could be the boy's father. Let's take it a step further. Let's say, in fact, that you can *prove* you're the boy's biological father."

"All right," Ty said shortly. "Go on. I'm Nathan's father. And . . . ?"

"And nothing. Rachel Stone is still the boy's legal guardian. Period. You're a stranger. You have no rights."

"No rights!" Ty snorted in disbelief. "Oh, come on! As Nathan's father I'd have as many rights as this Rachel person does."

Gerald shook his head. "Not necessarily."

Ty barely noticed when his draft arrived. The waitress hung by their booth for a few moments, but when Ty never even looked her way she disappeared in a huff. "Are you saying that if I could prove—*prove*, mind you—that I'm Nathan Stone's biological father that I still wouldn't have any rights?"

"That's correct."

"Impossible!"

"His adoptive mother has all the rights."

"I don't believe you!" Ty almost laughed. "She's not even a blood relative."

"It isn't a matter of who's related more closely to the boy. It's a matter of who's best suited to raise him. Rachel Stone has been his mother for how long?"

Ty shook his head in exasperation. "All his life, I guess."

"Then how do you propose to take her son from her? You're showing up way too late on the scene."

"I didn't know he was my son!"

"That doesn't alter the present," Gerald argued. "*She's* the boy's mother. She's the one with all the rights." Seeing Ty's thunderous expression, he lifted his palms and added, "I'm just warning you, okay? The situation's entirely hypothetical, anyway."

With an effort, Ty calmed down. Gerald was right about that, but it nettled him no end that if—*if* Nathan turned out to be a Rafferty there would be nothing he could do about it. "It's probably another scam, anyway," he muttered, downing half his beer.

Gerald sipped his martini thoughtfully. "A piece of advice, Ty—tread softly. I don't believe in long shots, but once in a while they happen. If Nathan's your son, you're at a disadvantage. This Rachel Stone person holds all the cards. I wouldn't confront her with the possibility that you're Nathan's father just yet. Go see the kid. See what you think. Then come back to Portland and we'll talk. Don't let on about who you are and what you want, because if she thinks there might be a chance she could finagle some Rafferty money—"

"I hear you." Ty lifted a hand to stem the inevitable lecture on protecting the Rafferty fortune. "I'll just go take a look. I need the break, anyway."

"Good."

Ty grimaced. "But you know, Gerald, if I thought for a minute that Nathan was really my son..."

The attorney gave him a sharp look.

"I'd go grab him and to hell with the courts."

"That's just what I'm afraid of, Ty. For God's sake, don't be an idiot. If you go to Oceanside and tell Rachel Stone who you are and why you're there, you're leaving yourself wide open. At the very least she could extort money from you to allow you to see her son. You'll do more damage than good."

"Fine. Great. Then what do you suggest, oh wise one?" Ty demanded sarcastically.

Gerald downed the rest of his drink. "Don't tell her who you are and what you want. Just look the situation over. The boy probably isn't yours, anyway, but if he is—" he plucked the last olive from his glass, chewing on it thoughtfully "—we've got a hell of a custody battle on our hands."

Outside the gray, shingled cottage, a stiff morning breeze rattled the one manzanita tree and sent the tire swing into a slow, gentle spin. Rachel, who a moment before had been admiring this very view, now stared across the kitchen table at her son, trying to hide her shock.

"What," she asked in a deceptively mild voice, pointing toward Nathan, "is that?"

Nathan glanced up from his bowl of cereal, his gaze centering guiltily on the finger Rachel had leveled directly at his left ear. "Oh, that." He self-consciously touched the piece of string hanging from a newly pierced hole. "Matthew's girlfriend did it."

"Matthew's girlfriend pierced your ear? With a needle and thread?"

His angular cheeks tightened. Swift, sullen anger altered his expression, pinching his lips. He nodded shortly.

Rachel fought back the urge to clap her hand to her forehead in exasperation. Nathan, fifteen last April, was fast becoming a problem she didn't know how to deal with. What had happened to the sweet, happy, funny boy she'd raised since he was seven? Gone was the optimistic child and in his place was a stranger. A teenager, she reminded herself. That dread creature that erupts somewhere between twelve and eighteen and makes everyone's life hell while he bumps awkwardly along the path to adulthood.

"I hope you've used alcohol to keep it clean," she said casually, fighting back a dozen screaming objections clamoring to be voiced. You couldn't alarm teenagers. One false move and they went crazy. At least that was her impression these past few months.

"Yes, Mother," Nathan said in a thoroughly nasty voice.

Rachel sipped from her coffee cup. She had to remind herself that there was more at work here than just out-of-balance hormones. Nathan's father had died six months earlier, and though his death had been anticipated—Richard Stone had fought heart disease for years—Nathan still hadn't adjusted to the loss.

Neither had Rachel, but the pressures of raising a son who was more than half her age had kept her from dwelling on, or examining closely, her own feelings.

Now, however, she turned her gaze back to the manzanita tree and the gray ocean beyond the cliff—and thought of Richard. He'd married her for selfish reasons. He'd wanted a mother for his son after the death of his first wife. Rachel, twenty at the time, had been thrilled that the older, more sophisticated Mr. Richard Stone, computer salesman, should be interested in her. She hadn't realized at first that Richard was lost without a woman only because he needed someone to take care of Nathan. She'd foolishly assumed he'd been swept off his feet by her, Rachel Stone, his travel agent.

Rachel grimaced in remembrance. Well, she'd been less than honest about her feelings, too. Richard, nearly twenty years older than herself, had been something of a father figure to her. She'd deceived herself into believing what she felt was love, when in fact it was only her need to fill the void left by her own parents' deaths when she was just a small child.

However, it was her loneliness that had made her unusually empathetic to Nathan's feelings. Put up for adoption by his teenaged mother, then suddenly losing his adoptive mother, Amelia, the only mother Nathan had ever really known, in a car accident, *then* having been left in the care of a father who really didn't know how to show his feelings... Well, by the time Rachel appeared on the scene, Nathan Stone was shy, withdrawn and had the look of a child just waiting for life's next blow.

Rachel had lost her heart to him instantly.

Nathan must have felt her stay would be temporary, too, because at first he'd resisted her attempts at friendship. But he quickly realized Rachel was a friend worth having and, to her delight, it didn't take long before Nathan responded to her openly and without reservation. His uncomplicated love helped push her own growing problems with Richard aside and made the intervening years bearable.

Hearing his chair squeak, she glanced back and couldn't help wishing for that uncomplicated time again.

"Gotta go," Nathan mumbled around a last spoonful of cereal. Flinging his black hair out of his eyes, he muttered, "I'm gonna be late getting home tonight."

"How late?"

He shrugged. "Don't know."

"Where are you going?" Rachel asked sternly. Nathan was notoriously poor at letting her know his plans. The fact that he'd actually *elected* to tell her he would be late sent Rachel's motherly radar into overdrive. What was up?

"To Matthew's."

"For another pierce job? Oh, good. I can rest easy now."

Throwing her a look, he slung his backpack over his shoulder and banged out the front door.

"Wait!" Rachel cried, following after him. "For Pete's sake, Nathan, don't be so touchy. It would just be nice if you *asked* now and then, you know?"

Nathan swallowed whatever sharp retort he was thinking of flinging at her. "Can I go to Matthew's?"

Rachel groaned inwardly. "Go," she said, throwing an arm out dramatically. "Have a good time. Live it up. Just call me and let me know when you'll be home, okay?"

"I'd like to spend the night there," he said slowly, "if it's okay with Matthew's mom."

Rachel regarded him unhappily. Her opinion on this issue apparently didn't count. "If it's all right with Matthew's mom," she agreed. Hurt, she watched him trudge down their rain-puddled lane toward the highway and the bus stop. He was as changeable and stormy as the ocean beyond.

She was at her wit's end to know how to deal with him.

Dashing the remains of her coffee down the sink, Rachel grabbed a piece of cold toast and headed for the closet. Another morning in the Stone household, she thought with uncharacteristic despair as she held the toast between her teeth and shoved her arms through the sleeves of her jacket. A fight with Nathan, a race to her job and a constant worry over bills.

Richard Stone had left the world with a small life insurance policy that had barely covered the doctors' bills their medical insurance hadn't. Rachel, skilled only in the romantic and extremely low-paying job of a travel agent, had gone back to work with a vengeance—fueled by an underlying desperation. Even so, she was behind in all manner of bills. She hated answering the phone at night, knowing it would be some mock-pleasant voice pleading for money. She couldn't bear to think of how long she'd let her credit card bills lapse. Nathan's orthodontist probably thought she'd been relocated to another planet.

Driving to work, she unscrewed the sunroof on her miniwagon, glorying in the feel of the wind ruffling her auburn hair, her anxieties quietly and firmly stowed in that portion of her brain reserved for such things. She turned her thoughts to the day ahead. The travel business was hectic, exciting and fraught with daily crises. The perfect antidote to a lonely home life where the one person she loved most of all seemed to have turned against her.

Shaking her head to rid herself of troublesome thoughts, she said aloud, "Well, look on the bright side. It can't get any worse."

Abruptly a strange grinding noise sounded from somewhere under the hood of her car.

She groaned aloud. Apparently it could.

"Mr. and Mrs. Thompson are already here!" Shawna said in a stage whisper as Rachel entered the office. She pointed one long purple nail in the direction of Rachel's work space. Above the partition Rachel could see Mr. Thompson's gray hairpiece and the top of Mrs. Thompson's chic black hat.

"I would have been here fifteen minutes ago," Rachel said with a sigh, "but my car's acting up again. It started making horrible noises. I was afraid it was about to die, so I babied it here, driving about twenty miles an hour the whole way. Have the Thompsons been waiting long?" she asked, grimacing guiltily.

"Not too long. I got them some coffee."

"Thanks."

As she crossed the room, Rachel thrust the problems of her car and Nathan firmly to the back of her mind. "Hi," she greeted the Thompsons cheerily. "You're sure early on the scene this morning."

Tommy Thompson leaned back in his chair and slid a mischievous grin at his wife. "We're tired of waiting for spring to come to Oregon. It's June and you'd never know it. We want to leave for New Orleans tonight."

"Tonight?" Rachel repeated in amazement, pulling out her chair and turning on her CRT. The computer, SABRE, was on-line with American Airlines and recorded flight data on all airlines.

"As soon as possible," Karen Thompson agreed. "I can't wait to drink mint juleps in some real sunshine!"

"Sounds great," Rachel said, fighting back a twinge of envy. "Do you want to stay in the French Quarter?"

"Yes. At the Royal Sonesta."

Rachel made the booking while the Thompsons held hands and grinned at each other. They were like two kids doing something outrageous and a little bit naughty. Rachel felt a pang of regret, remembering her own marriage had been so very different.

"I've just got to wait for the hotel confirmation," she told them, pushing a button to start the ticketer. The familiar screech, thunk and grind of the machine sounded in the other room as the Thompsons' airline tickets began printing out.

A movement near the door caught Rachel's attention and she glanced upward, over the top of her terminal. A man was talking to Shawna at the reception desk.

He was the kind of man who deserved a second look even without his air of purposeful neglect. He wore a dark brown leather bomber jacket and a pair of jeans so worn the material was white around the edges of the wallet stuck in his back pocket. His hair was midnight black and long, catching on the back of the jacket's collar. In profile, his chin was strong and covered with dark stubble, his nose hawkish, his brows stern. She frowned, thinking he seemed familiar.

Shawna pointed in Rachel's direction and the man looked swiftly her way. Rachel's heart jerked. He was here to see *her?* Quickly she dropped her gaze to the screen, but not before a pair of dark, assessing eyes imprinted themselves on the back of her mind.

"Okay, there's your confirmation number," Rachel said. "I've given them your credit card number and guaranteed your reservation for late arrival."

"Thank you," Tommy said emphatically as Rachel headed for the other room to rip their tickets off the ticketer. The man in the bomber jacket hung back, waiting for her to finish, but his eyes followed her every move. It made her distinctly uneasy.

Five minutes later the Thompsons were on their way, giving Rachel a wink of shared excitement. "Have a great time," she told them, then turned questioningly to the man who now waited next to her computer.

His hands were in his pockets, and he was scowling. Rachel's eyes met his warily as she sat down in her desk chair. "Can I help you?"

"Are you Rachel Stone?"

His voice was deep and raspy. It somehow fitted with the rest of him. "At your service," she said with a smile, waiting for him to state his business.

He hesitated for several seconds before pulling out a chair with the toe of one dusty lizard-skin boot. With a sigh he sank into the chair as if his back hurt and stretched his legs out until the tips of his boots almost touched Rachel's sandals. He seemed to deliberate for a few moments, as if he weren't quite sure how to approach the issue on the forefront of his mind. Finally he said, "I'm thinking of taking a trip."

"Where to?" Rachel asked in a friendly tone.

"I don't know. Somewhere it doesn't rain so much."

She chuckled. "Phoenix? Miami? The French Riviera?" With a start she realized he was watching her very closely, as if checking for flaws. It was unnerving. Remembering how he'd specifically asked for her, she questioned, "Why did you want to know if I was Rachel Stone?"

He shrugged. "Someone told me you were the travel agent to meet in Oceanside."

"Who?"

"I don't know his name. I met him on a plane trip east."

"What's *your* name?"

He pressed his lips together in a way that reminded her strongly of someone else. "Ty Rafferty."

The strong, silent type, she thought. "Do you need some time to pick a destination, Mr. Rafferty?"

"Maybe," he murmured.

"Let me get you some brochures."

As Rachel walked through the archway into an alcove filled with file cabinets, Ty let his gaze cling to her every move. He was shocked. *This* was Rachel Stone? Mother of a *fifteen-year-old* son?

She returned with a thick pile of colorful brochures, handing them to him as she resettled herself in the chair. Ty stared at her—he couldn't help himself. She had a pair of the most gorgeous, thickly lashed hazel eyes he'd ever seen. For a moment she stared right back, a slight frown puckering her brow.

Could he have made a mistake? he wondered in amazement. Rachel Stone was nothing like he'd imagined. She was too damn young, for one thing! Her husband had died of heart disease, for crying out loud. Ty had assumed the man must have been on the downside of forty at the very least. This *girl* couldn't be more than twenty-five, could she?

The office phone rang, breaking the spell. "I'll let you look those over," she murmured, turning to her computer.

"Thanks."

"Rachel! It's for you," the garishly made-up receptionist called out. "Want me to take a message?"

"No, I've got it, Shawna," was Rachel's answer as she picked up the receiver, cradled it against her neck and began asking questions of another apparent client as her fingers dashed over the keyboard, calling up amber numbers and letters, which Ty recognized as airport city codes and flight itineraries.

Ty was dazed. There had to be some mistake. This woman was not the mother of a fifteen-year-old son, adoptive or otherwise. He stared unseeingly at the brochures, realizing he was going to have to make some kind of travel plans now that he'd embarked on this strange way of introducing himself.

He hurt all over. He hadn't gotten away from Gerald until ten o'clock, and by the time he'd arrived in Oceanside it was nearly midnight. It hadn't helped that every damn motel on the coast had flashed No Vacancy in pink, blue or green neon at him. He'd had to sleep in the Porsche.

Running a hand experimentally over the stubble on his chin, he shifted uncomfortably. Sleeping in the car might have worked when he was twenty, but at thirty-three it was cruel and unusual punishment. He felt dirty and cramped and out-and-out cranky. Not the best circumstances to be facing Rachel Stone, but when he'd driven by Neptune Travel on his way to find a washroom, he'd decided to take care of business first.

Now, with Ms. Stone looking fresh, lovely and completely in control, he wished he'd rethought that plan more carefully.

At that moment she glanced back, raising her brows questioningly. Ty smoothed his hands down his jeans, frowning at one of the brochures as if he couldn't make up his mind. He hadn't known what he was going to say to her when he saw her. Before talking to Raintree, he'd envisioned a meeting where he laid out the facts as he knew them and let her make of them what she would. But now, with the thought that Nathan might be his son becoming, for some inexplicable reason, more believable to him, he couldn't take chances with the truth. Not if he wanted to steal Nathan away from her.

"How about L.A.?" he suggested as Rachel finished her current booking and swung around in her chair to face him. She really had a fantastic pair of legs, Ty thought, his gaze sliding over trim calves and a sexy pair of ankles to the straight denim skirt, which just touched her knees.

She smiled, pink lips curving into a grin. "L.A. it is. It should be nice if you can stand the smog. Which airport? Los Angeles, Orange County or Burbank?"

"Just send me to LAX," he muttered, referring to Los Angeles International Airport.

"Round trip from Portland?"

"Yeah."

"If you're flexible on the dates I can try for a discount fare. Midweek departures and returns are the cheapest."

Ty blinked. He generally traveled first class with nary a thought toward saving money. Amusement brought an ironic smile to his lips. Was she always so conscious of her customer's pocketbook, or was it just his scraggly appearance that had prompted the question? "Let's go the cheapest," he said.

"When were you thinking of departing?"

"The last week in July," Ty said off the top of his head.

She swung back around, her hands flying over the keyboard. Ty's gaze lingered on her thick, luxurious tresses. Her hair was a burnished auburn shot with gold highlights. He felt an almost irrepressible desire to bury his hands in her hair and crush that mane beneath his fingers, wondering if it would feel as velvety as it looked.

Good Lord.

"I can get you out on the twenty-fourth," she said dubiously, "but I can't get a return flight until August."

"Great."

The look she slid from beneath thick lashes said she wondered why he was being so agreeable. "It'll still be two hundred and eighty dollars," she apologized. "That's a nonrefundable fare out of Portland. If I book it, you have to pay now and there's no changing the flights."

Since Ty had no intention of actually using the ticket, he said, "No problem."

She punched several buttons, then waited, her hands poised over the keyboard as the computer apparently took the booking. "Address and phone number?"

Ty hesitated. He didn't want to give out more information than he had to. It wasn't impossible that she'd heard of the Raffertys even in podunk Oceanside, Oregon. "You really need all that?"

"For the invoice, yes." She eyes him speculatively. "And how would you like to pay for this?"

There was no way to continue his evasiveness without fueling her curiosity. "American Express."

Her brows shot up and she sent him a thoughtful glance. She hadn't counted on that one. Given the way he looked, he could scarcely blame her.

"I need the number and expiration date."

He lifted his right hip to reach into his pocket. Her gaze flicked downward toward his upraised crotch then abruptly turned back to the screen again. Removing his gold card, he held it out to her. She glanced down at it.

"Tyrrell Rafferty III," she read slowly. Ty held his breath, half expecting her to let out a gasp of recognition.

But all she said was, "Do you want your full name on the ticket?"

"Ty'll do."

Her fingers flew rapidly across the keys. He heard the whine and thump of a machine somewhere behind him and glanced over his shoulder toward the back of the room. Rachel handed his card back, then smoothly slid from her chair and headed in the direction of the noise. A light, sweet perfume trailed in her wake. Ty drew in a lungful, supremely conscious of the evocative scent.

He frowned, annoyed with himself. So she was an attractive woman. He knew lots of attractive women and this one was thoroughly "hands-off." His thoughts turned to Barbara, and he felt an unwelcome pang of guilt. He always felt guilty when he thought of his fiancée. After all, he'd offered to marry her and she'd accepted. No one had held a gun to his head. He should be looking ahead to their wedding, planning a future together, counting the moments until they both said "I will." Instead, he spent nearly every waking moment working—or at least he *had* spent nearly every waking moment working until yesterday when he'd broken routine and gone off on this wild-goose chase.

What the *hell* was he doing here?

He had a sudden image of Barbara hearing for the first time that he had a fifteen-year-old son. Her mouth was an O of disbelief and horror. For a moment he tried to make the picture work. He, Barbara and Nathan.

It defied the bounds of reality. He couldn't imagine Barbara taking time out from the Junior League to mother a teenager.

Rachel returned, stuffing the ticket into a ticket jacket. "There you are, Mr. Rafferty," she said, handing it to him.

"Thanks." He shoved the ticket into his back pocket.

"I'm glad my mysterious friend mentioned me to you," she added.

Ty hesitated, meeting her gaze. For a moment the truth nearly choked him. He wasn't good at deception.

But he was even worse at losing anything that really mattered to him.

"Me, too," was his ironic answer, and he headed for the door before his need for honesty won the struggle over his need for caution and wisdom.

## Chapter Two

Rain blew in fitful bursts as Rachel dashed toward her station wagon. Climbing into the driver's seat, she brushed drops from her thick auburn hair, then twisted the key in the ignition. The engine ground and sputtered. Rachel groaned. She'd gotten so caught up in work she'd forgotten about the situation with her car. "Come on, baby," she muttered, gently turning the key once more, hoping against hope the damn thing would just start.

"Come on. Come on," she coaxed, pumping the gas.

The engine chugged and ground, gasped, then miraculously caught hold, sounding as if it couldn't make up its mind whether to work or not. Just get me home, she silently begged. She would deal with the car tomorrow, but it was too dark tonight.

Friday-afternoon traffic had turned Oceanside's sleepy main street into a snarl. Rachel's house was only five miles away and it never took long to get home even in traffic, but tonight she was worried the car would give up on her.

She drove out of the parking lot, past the McDonald's and Safeway, down the main street and through two traffic lights, and hit the outskirts of town just as a torrent of rain pounded down, blurring her windshield. She bit her lip. Twice before, when rain had been this intense, the car had stopped running. Some kind of short in the electrical system had been the guess from a garage mechanic named Gordy. But since the car started when it dried out, Rachel had let the problem exist. Now, however, with the engine barely turning over, she knew she was going to have to bite the bullet and take care of all the little wagon's problems as soon as she possibly could.

She edged the car behind the rest of the traffic, biting her lip, her eyes glued to the side of the road for the two small reflectors on white sticks that marked the long, rutted driveway leading to the Stone beach cabin.

Within a mile of the driveway the wagon coughed and died. One second she was gently guiding it forward, the next she was coasting. "Great!" she muttered in distress, pulling over. It was only seven o'clock, but the sky was dense and gloomy, pouring cold, relentless rain from a black cloud cover. Rachel stared through the windshield at the headlights glimmering in a snaking trail down the coast road. Facing her, heading north, the lights were an endless white blur; southbound, the taillights pulsed bright scarlet.

She hoped some Good Samaritan would stop to aid her.

Inhaling deeply, she climbed out of the car. There was a flashlight in her glove compartment for all the good it would do her. She knew nothing about engines, or any part of a car, for that matter.

Headlights appeared behind her car. With soaring hope she glanced back, hearing gravel crunch beneath the tires of the new arrival. Help was here! She squinted in the bright glare of twin beams of light as a huge, cold raindrop skittered down the back of her neck.

Hunching her shoulders, she hurried toward her rescuer. The door opened, clicking on an interior light. The silhouetted figure climbing out was amazingly familiar. Rachel stopped short, staring at the man who was now slamming his car door behind him and thrusting his hands into the pockets of his dark leather bomber jacket.

"Mr. Rafferty?" she asked in disbelief.

"Looks like you ran into some trouble," he answered by way of a greeting. Rain collected in crystal jewels on his dark hair, dampening the shoulders of his coat. "What happened?"

He didn't seem in the least surprised to see her. "My car quit running," Rachel said, gesturing helplessly. "I think it's on its last breath."

"Want me to take a look under the hood?"

"You know anything about cars?" She was already one step toward her glove compartment and the flashlight.

"I know they have four wheels and an engine."

Was he joking? She certainly hoped so. Climbing inside the passenger door, she grabbed her flashlight from the glove compartment and slipped it out the window to Ty's waiting hands. Then she leaned over the driver's seat and scrunched down to unlatch the hood. Unable to reach the lever, she muttered furiously beneath her breath, inching over the bucket seats until her fingers connected with the handle. "Okay," she called, yanking hard to pop the hood. A dull thunk sounded as the latch released. Struggling upward, she looked through the streaming windshield to Ty's blurred form just as he thrust his fingers beneath the wagon's blue hood, releasing the catch. Rachel scrambled from the car.

"See anything?" she asked, ducking her head against the deluge as she looked at the mysterious wires and hardware beneath the hood. When Ty didn't immediately answer, she turned her gaze on him. Rain was running in rivulets down his temples, and a drip was forming at the end of his hawkish nose. She lifted a hand to brush it away, catching herself at the last moment, shocked by the idea of such simple intimacy.

"Hmm." Ty leaned forward, the flashlight's circle of illumination moving gently from place to place. He seemed oblivious to her presence. Straightening, he clicked the light off.

Rachel stared up at him, bewildered. "Well?"

"It's not working."

Her jaw dropped. Then she laughed. She couldn't help herself. Ty Rafferty was certainly a master of the understatement. "I know it's not working. Do you happen to know why?"

A ghost of a smile crossed his lips. "There's something wrong with the engine."

"Really." Rachel was sardonic. She sighed, mentally cursing the carburetor, the differential, the water pump, the battery and the faulty electrical system. If she could have thought of any other part of the car she would have cursed that, too, but her limited knowledge of automobile engines had come to an abrupt end. Unfortunately, she didn't have the money to repair the station wagon no matter what was wrong with it.

"Actually, I'd guess it's the alternator," Ty added.

"The alternator? Is that expensive to fix?"

"That depends on how much money you have."

"What if you don't have *any* money?"

He swiped at the raindrops slipping off the tip of his nose before he closed the hood and tested to make sure it was fully latched. "Then it's expensive to fix."

He handed her the flashlight. Despair filled Rachel's heart. She turned away, needing a moment of private thought. How would she ever afford to fix the damn thing?

"Can I give you a lift?" he asked quietly.

Rachel's gaze swung back to him. It seemed too providential that he'd just happened to be right behind her this evening. "I guess I should count myself lucky that you happened to be driving this way tonight." Her tone was full of unasked questions.

Ty sucked thoughtfully on his bottom lip—a curiously sensual gesture. His dark eyes met hers, and goose bumps stood out on Rachel's skin. For just a moment, she thought he was on the verge of revealing something, but then he said, "I was leaving the Safeway parking lot when you turned onto the street in front of me. I knew it was you, so when you pulled over I stopped to find out why."

"Oh."

Rachel was almost disappointed. Neptune Travel was practically right across the street from Safeway. Meeting Ty again was just a coincidence. A fortunate one, as it turned out.

"Well, let's get out of this rain. I live about a mile from here," she said, grabbing her purse and locking the wagon. "If you wouldn't mind...?"

"I don't mind."

He drove a black Porsche 911, the interior of which smelled new and clean. It seemed so absolutely opposite of the man who owned it that Rachel couldn't help wondering about this mysterious Tyrrell Rafferty.

"I've never seen you before. Do you live around here?" she asked.

"Portland," he answered curtly, switching on the ignition.

"Just vacationing, then?"

"Mainly."

"Is this your car?" she asked. She laughed, embarrassed. "I don't mean to be nosy. It's just...well, it's a nice car," she finished lamely, feeling like an idiot.

He turned his head to really look at her. His eyes were the deepest, darkest brown she'd ever seen, almost black, and once again she felt an uncomfortable sense of déjà vu. He reminded her of someone, but for the life of her she couldn't figure out who.

"It's a nice car," he agreed, his voice dry. "And it's mine. I didn't steal it, if that's what you're thinking."

Rachel groaned on a laugh. "I'm sorry."

"No problem."

Ty was astounded that she'd fessed up to what was truly going through her mind. What other female would? And so engagingly, at that! The way she'd scrunched up her nose in embarrassment had been downright sexy.

"As long as I've got one foot in my mouth, I might as well stick the other one in." Her mouth curved in the most enticing way. "What do you do for a living, Mr. Rafferty?"

Ty dragged his gaze from that pink crescent to the rain-swept road ahead. "I—er—sell real estate." Actually, he developed real estate, but since he sold it also, he figured it counted, and it didn't sound quite so grand somehow to admit you were a salesman.

He'd shocked her. He could read it on her face. Her expressions were so mobile and open that he couldn't believe she had a deceptive bone in her body.

"You *sell* real estate?" she repeated. "Like in houses?"

"Not residential. Commercial. Like in buildings."

"I thought all commercial real estate agents wore three-piece suits and belonged to Rotary and talked about either the stock market or the next big deal that was coming down."

Ty laughed aloud. Rachel Stone was a surprise. A very, very pleasant surprise. "Who says I don't?" he asked, glancing at her from beneath his lashes. Her gaze was fixed magnetically on his smile. He heard her draw a slow breath.

"Well, maybe you do," she answered skeptically. "It's just that you look like..."

"Like?" he prompted.

"Well..." She squirmed.

"Well?" Ty waited. He'd wiped the smile from his face when he'd seen her focus on it. Arrogant vanity at its worst, he supposed, but he'd found a smile was the quickest form of seduction. For him, at least. And he did *not* want to seduce Rachel Stone. Nor did he want her to want to be seduced.

Rachel glanced up at him, her thoughts paralleling his, had she but known it. She hadn't been ready for that smile. It was brilliant, packed with blatant sexuality. And she hadn't even recovered from the nerve-tingling jolt of his laughter before she'd gone gaga over a set of white teeth! "Turn here!" she burst out, spying the white markers.

Ty jerked the wheel, his leather jacket creaking seductively as the Porsche bumped onto the rutted lane. Rachel grimaced. "Sorry. I wasn't paying attention."

Rocks scraped the 911's underbelly. Rachel groaned inwardly. She should have warned him about the dangers of her driveway. She knew how men were about their cars.

But he didn't comment. He just guided the powerful vehicle down the road and into the gravel driveway Rachel indicated, pulling to a stop in front of her cabin. His dark gaze fastened on the small house as if he were fixing it in his memory.

Rachel drew a long breath and exhaled it slowly, following his line of vision. One of the shutters hung drunkenly; the other was missing altogether. The gutters, choked with leaves, poured rainwater down like a pitcher, and the front door's paint was chipped and marred where Rex, Nathan's German shepherd, scratched and whined to get in every night.

"I've been meaning to paint it," Rachel murmured, seeing her home through his eyes. Just slightly run-down. Just slightly overgrown. Just slightly... short of money.

"Is that your phone?" he asked.

Over the beat of the rain she hadn't heard a thing. Now she picked up the faint, soft jingle of the kitchen phone. "Oh, God. Yes. I hate it when this happens. I never know whether to hurry up and risk bumping a shin, or just let the damn thing go."

"Answer it. I'll wait."

Wait for what? Rachel wondered, stepping lightly over the rain puddles and around the back to the kitchen, where the phone sounded louder. Hurriedly she stuck her key in the lock, twisting frantically, laughing and muttering and practically forcing the door open by sheer strength. She half ran, half slid across the floor, catching the receiver on the fly. "Hello?" she gasped breathlessly.

"Mrs. Stone?"

"Yes?"

"This is Officer McMurtry down at the station. Your son, Nathan, is with me. I'm sorry to bother you, ma'am, but he's been arrested for shoplifting. We'd like you to come down and pick him up."

## Chapter Three

"Shoplifting?" Rachel repeated blankly. *"Nathan?"*

"That's right, ma'am. From Tennyson's Coast-to-Coast store."

Rachel was stupefied. She felt her world grind to a halt. She couldn't think. There had to be some mistake. "Are you sure it's my Nathan Stone?"

"He gave us this number, ma'am."

Shoplifting. Rachel opened her mouth, but for several seconds no sound erupted. Finally a strangled, "I'll be right there" passed her lips.

She hung up, staring down at the receiver as if it had suddenly sprouted poisonous tentacles. Nathan had been caught shoplifting. He was at the Oceanside police station at this very moment. Why? *Why?* A burst of anger fired through her. How could he do such a thing?

The back door squeaked on its hinges. Rachel choked out a startled gasp and whirled around, her heart thudding. Tyrrell Rafferty stood in the doorway.

"Oh. Hi. It's you—Mr. Rafferty," she gulped on a short laugh, having completely forgotten him. She'd forgotten something else, too, she realized with an uncomfortable pinprick of awareness. She didn't have a car to pick up Nathan.

"What's wrong?" Ty asked, his voice sharp as his gaze raked Rachel's white face.

"It's Nathan. My—son. He's been..." She choked, embarrassed to be revealing to a virtual stranger something so highly personal.

"He's been *what?*" Ty hissed, grabbing her arm, hard.

His touch jerked Rachel back to her senses. She stared down at the tanned fingers tightened around her flesh. "He's been arrested for shoplifting."

"Shoplifting?" A series of emotions crossed Ty's chiseled face, none of which Rachel could readily identify. For three beats of Rachel's hammering heart he said nothing else. Then, as if rousing himself from the compelling force of some inner tableau, he asked roughly, "Where is he?"

"At—at the police station. Oh, God. I don't have a car, and I can't—"

"I'll drive you."

"No. No." Rachel pulled away from his now unresisting hand, waving him away. She wanted to run to the bathroom, break down and cry in frustration. But she couldn't. She *had* to pull herself together.

"I'll take you to the police station. We'll get your son, then we'll call a towing company and have them pick up your car."

"But I—"

"Don't argue. In fact, don't think," he added. When she didn't respond, he surprised her by touching her once again, dropping his hands on her shoulders and giving her a gentle shake. "Just get going. There'll be more than enough time to straighten the rest out later."

Rachel nodded dully, pushing open the back door and walking blindly through the rain to his car.

The Oceanside police station was a cheery redbrick building with white-trimmed wooden windows spaced on either side of the door. A pair of black, wrought-iron street lamps flanked the lowest cement step, giving the building the appearance of a Hollywood movie set, so perfect was its symmetry and small-town design.

Rachel barely gave the place a passing glance. She hurried up the front steps and into the fluorescent lighting of the central room. Bedraggled as a drenched alley cat, her face pinched with concern, she was at least more in control now. Twenty minutes had helped her get a grip on herself. If Nathan had actually shoplifted, she would show no mercy. Rebelling in the form of ear piercing was one thing; stealing was another. The courts would mete out his punishment and she would stand by it, no matter what it was. She fervently hoped it would be strong enough to make him think twice next time.

She was conscious of Ty by her side. He'd barely said a word during the drive into town. Later she would have to thank him properly for, as she saw it, help above and beyond the call of duty. Right now, however, there was no time for thoughts of anything but Nathan.

The tall, heavyset man with the weathered-looking face seated on the bench next to the front desk turned out to be Officer McMurtry. Rachel read his identification pin and introduced herself at the same moment he got to his feet.

"I'm Rachel Stone, Nathan's mother," she said, then added awkwardly, "This is Mr. Tyrrell Rafferty."

The officer shook their hands gravely. A detached part of herself made Rachel wonder what Ty was feeling about being involved in this little drama. "Nathan's waiting in a detention room just down the hall. Thought I'd leave him alone a few minutes so we could talk."

"Was he—er—by himself when this happened?" Rachel asked, perching anxiously on the edge of the green, vinyl-covered bench Officer McMurtry had just vacated. Ty moved to her side, protectively, Rachel thought. She shot him a glance. His expression was dark, neutral and tense, as if he were controlling himself with an effort. "You don't have to stay," she said softly as Officer McMurtry settled his substantial bulk beside her.

"You'll need a ride home," was Ty's terse response.

Rachel turned toward Officer McMurtry.

"Nathan was with a couple of friends," he answered her. "Matthew Dayton and Jessica Roberts. They were in the process of stealing a cooler and some miscellaneous items when they were caught. The owner, Mr. Tennyson, has been robbed and vandalized by teenagers repeatedly and is pressing charges."

"Is this Nathan's first offense?"

The question was from Ty, snapped out like the crack of a whip before Rachel could make any comment. When Rachel nodded, he told the officer flatly, "Tennyson's overreacting. Nathan's underage. This is a pretty minor offense. It'll go nowhere in court."

"I'm sure you're right," the officer allowed. "But Nathan will still have to show up next week and face the judge."

Rachel felt as if she were losing control. "I'd like to see him now," she said woodenly. *And wring his neck!*

"Come along."

Officer McMurtry led the way down the hall. Rachel didn't expect Ty to follow, but she was mistaken once again. He seemed to hesitate for a moment, then he strode after them, his long legs catching up to Rachel in a matter of moments.

Nathan, who had been sitting in a chair in the middle of a small, sterile-looking room, his hands dangling loosely between his knees, looking as morose and lonely as any lost little boy would, visibly brightened as Rachel appeared in the doorway. Then just as quickly a shadow crossed his face and he lounged back in the chair, affecting a nonchalant who-gives-a-damn pose that both filled Rachel with despair and set her teeth on edge.

The boy's gaze flicked past Rachel and landed on Ty. There was an electric moment that Rachel subconsciously noted. She half turned, but then was distracted when Officer McMurtry said, "Your court date's been set, Mr. Stone. Your mother can check you out and then we'll see you next week."

"Sure." Nathan lifted his shoulders uncaringly.

"A piece of advice, son," he added, holding the door open with his solid bulk, his gaze ironic as it followed Nathan's progress to the hall. "Change the attitude. The way it is now will only make matters worse."

"I don't even know what to say," Rachel declared as soon as they were out of earshot of the policeman. "Shoplifting? *Stealing?* My God, Nathan. This isn't like you!"

Nathan regarded her sullenly as they walked toward the central processing desk. "Who's he?" he demanded, jerking his head to include Ty.

"The man who made it possible for me to come get you tonight. You might have spent the night in jail if Ty hadn't offered to bring me here. The car broke down," she added by way of explanation. "Mr. Rafferty got me home in time to catch Officer McMurtry's call."

"The car broke down?" Nathan repeated, aghast. "What happened?"

"It just died," Rachel answered. A bad feeling was unfurling inside her. *This* was what Nathan chose to fix on? The car. "Ty thinks it's the alternator."

Nathan's gaze narrowed at her mention of Ty's first name. Rachel hadn't consciously switched; it had come with the recognition that this formality was totally inappropriate considering the circumstances.

"Oh, great!" Nathan's mouth grew sulky. "That's just great. Now there's no chance I'll get my permit. We don't even have a car!"

"Nathan!"

"You probably did it on purpose," he grumbled. "You don't want me to ever drive."

"That's enough," Ty said in a quiet voice. "You want to pull this kind of stuff on your mom, do it later. Let's take one step at a time."

Rachel was so hurt and upset she could scarcely find her voice. And she was embarrassed that Ty had to be witness to this unattractive side of her son. "Stop being so selfish," she managed to get out. Turning blindly to Ty, she said, "I haven't really said thank you, yet. Thank you, and I'm sorry."

"No problem. Let's just get out of here," Ty answered, his dark eyes carefully assessing Nathan.

There were forms to sign and initial, a series of steps that Rachel could scarcely remember later. What she did recall was the way Nathan ignored both her and Ty. He spent the time staring down at his beat-up Nikes and looked unrepentant. Rachel had to fight back the impulse to apologize for his behavior to every clerk and officer of the law she encountered. She wanted to yell that this was a mistake. This wasn't like Nathan. But they wouldn't have believed her, anyway, nor would they really have cared. Only Rachel ached over the fact that her wonderful, tender, once-gentle son was acting like a horrible monster.

The ride home was accomplished with even less conversation than the ride to the police station. The rain had stopped, but drops still streamed across the windows of Ty's Porsche. Nathan had made no comment on the car, though Rachel knew any vehicle as classy as this one usually sent her son into orbit. But Nathan, true to his new, selfish and apparently martyred self, remained hostile and aloof the entire drive.

At the house Nathan practically climbed over Rachel in his hurry to get out of the car. Watching him slosh arrogantly through the rain puddles, soaking his shoes and the legs of his jeans, never looking back, Rachel felt an unbearable unhappiness engulf her. She swallowed, following behind him, turning her face into the cool wind drifting over the cliffs from the ocean, closing her eyes. She fought back the urge to cry.

Ty caught up with her on the cracked bottom step outside the back door. "How sharper than a serpent's tooth is an ungrateful child," he quoted wryly. "Or something like that."

"He's not normally so awful," Rachel heard herself say. "But there's no denying he's been awful tonight," she admitted with aching honesty.

"It sounds to me like he and his friends were planning a party."

Rachel nodded. The miscellaneous items Officer McMurtry had mentioned had turned out to be plastic cups, a cigarette lighter and candy bars. It was the candy bars that Matthew had casually removed from the counter that had alerted the clerk to the fact the three of them were shoplifting. When they'd then strolled as bold as you please through the front doors, the cooler held between Matthew and Nathan as if it were their own paid-for, personal property, the clerk had called Mr. Tennyson, and Tennyson had grabbed them all, bellowing furiously, and subsequently phoned the police.

Rachel had been appalled by the three kids' nerve. Even the clerk's testimony to Officer McMurtry when he'd arrived on the scene that their knees had been collectively shaking the whole time hadn't helped vindicate them in Rachel's eyes. She should be grateful, she supposed, that at least there was *some* guilt going on inside Nathan's head, but good God! Whatever had possessed him in the first place?

"I can't believe it," she murmured now. "I really can't believe it."

"Hmm." Ty was gazing thoughtfully at the back door. "Do you need anything else?"

"What? Oh! No. Thanks, by the way. For everything. I know it's inadequate. You've been more than terrific. If there's anything—"

"Forget it. I was glad to help. What about your car?"

"Oh. I'll call Gordy, my husband's mechanic, to come pick it up. Don't worry." Rachel closed her own mind to the thought of what the bill would be. No need to panic yet.

"So you're okay?"

He framed the words in a question, and Rachel nodded emphatically. "Thanks again," she said.

A square of light glowed in the dark night. Nathan's bedroom window. She would wait for morning to have the emotional battle with Nathan, she told herself fiercely. She was too angry and hurt to handle him tonight.

"I'll call you tomorrow," Ty said by way of an answer, his gaze on the patch of yellow illumination. Abruptly he turned back toward the Porsche.

*I'll call you tomorrow?*

Rachel wondered why Mr. Tyrrell Rafferty seemed to have appointed himself her special protector. She listened to the throbbing purr of his engine as he backed down the long driveway to the street and decided it was another question that would just have to wait to be answered in the light of day.

Ty had never felt so god-awful and confused in his entire life. It was an eerie feeling. Downright creepy. Nathan Stone looked and acted just as he had when he'd been a mixed-up, self-centered fifteen-year-old. It was enough to give a guy delusions of fatherhood even without Julia's testimony to the same.

He drove to an oceanfront bar, a little hole-in-the-wall whose stained cedar walls had weathered to a dirty tannish brown and whose creaking sign read Barnacle Bill's. Inside it was like any other dive one could find in any rural town in Oregon: glowing beer signs, scarred tables and chairs, patrons tuned in to whatever sports program happened to be on TV that day, waitresses with either friendly smiles or bored attitudes.

The one that helped Ty fell into the latter category. "Can I getchu somethin'?"

"How about a draft?"

She didn't even answer, just walked away. Ty focused on the fishing net draped over the ceiling in a vain attempt at authentic decor, and wondered how thick the dust was furred on the rope. At least a quarter of an inch. Maybe half.

Damn it all! Why did the kid have to look so much like him?

The beer arrived with a *kathunk* on the table and without benefit of a coaster. Ty swallowed half down and wiped his mouth with the back of his hand.

It had been impulse that prompted him to follow Rachel from the travel agency. He'd been sitting in his car, brooding over how youthful she'd looked, when he'd seen her drive in front of the Safeway lot. Her passenger window was rolled halfway down, even in the rain. He'd recognized that mane of fabulous hair and had switched on his ignition before he fully considered what he was about to do.

Half a mile down the road he'd asked himself what the hell he thought he *was* doing! Following some woman because she might be the mother of the boy who might be his son? The whole thing was totally nuts!

Instead of turning around he'd let himself keep going, and then she'd suddenly veered out of traffic and eased to a stop. Naturally, he'd pulled up behind her. And naturally he'd offered to help.

And Rachel Stone had affected him mightily. The scent of her perfume was magnified by the rain. She looked even younger, if that was possible, than when he'd met her at the travel agency scant hours before. Her hair was long and wet, her skin pale and glowing in the deep darkness, her blouse sticking to her skin, outlining her shape. Like some long-slumbering beast, his senses stirred to life in spite of who she was, in spite of what he wanted from her, in spite of—everything.

He'd been aware of the soft curve of her breasts, the hugeness of her eyes, the seductive pull of her quick sense of humor, the underlying desperation of her situation. He'd wanted to do more than lend a hand with her car. He'd wanted to discover a reason to stay with her a little longer. He'd wanted...well, admit it, Rafferty. He'd wanted *her*.

And then the opportunity had presented itself. She needed a ride. She needed a shoulder to cry on, so to speak. She needed someone strong to help her do battle with the Oceanside police because *her* son had been caught shoplifting.

Ty shook his head, then leaned it as far back on his neck as he could, thrusting both hands in his black hair, squeezing his eyes shut. If he'd met Nathan on the street, not knowing who he was, would he have noticed the resemblance? Probably not. It was there. Plain. But you had to be looking for it. You had to know.

His chest tightened in something like pain. He'd bet money Nathan was his son. Julia hadn't been lying. Yet it couldn't be. It just couldn't! How could fifteen years pass without a man knowing he'd fathered a child?

And Rachel? Jeez Louise. Where the hell did she fit into this bizarre nightmare? Why did he have to actually *like* her? Why did his libido—which had seemed to be at an all-time low ever since his engagement to Barbara, he admitted with a guilty inward wince—choose this particular woman to have a sudden resurrection over?

In his mind's eye he saw her run from the car to answer that ringing phone. He'd followed her, reacting on impulse, something he rarely, if ever, did. And then he'd overheard the gist of her conversation and had simply stepped in to take charge. She'd let him, albeit reluctantly. What choice did she have? And though she undoubtedly felt he'd gone a bit far with the white-knight bit, she'd been too distracted and upset and desperate to stop him.

The situation had given Ty an unexpected boost in his bid to see Nathan. The shock of their first meeting swept through him again, jolting him anew. God. It was like looking in a mirror, a reflection of himself. Nathan's bad attitude only intensified the resemblance; Ty was enough of a realist to remember how *he'd* acted at fifteen when confronted by authority.

"Want another?"

Ty opened his eyes to see the bored waitress. "Sure." While she went to refill the order, he tossed back the rest of his beer, then turned the empty glass between his palms, frowning down at it. Let's get smart here for a moment, Rafferty. Think it through. You don't need the complication of a teenager no matter what the situation. Barbara will never understand or accept an illegitimate Rafferty. A son. One as volatile and ready to explode as a box of TNT.

One who could very well end up being the Rafferty heir.

Ty swore pungently beneath his breath. What a mess!

Yet...yet...

Inside himself there was something new. An excitement. An eagerness. A desire so intense it pumped his heart, swelled his chest and turned his brain to mush. He *wanted* Nathan to be his son. Wanted it more than he'd wanted anything in his life. Wanted it more than Barbara, and the Rafferty name, and the almost narcotic addiction to success.

He wanted it enough to make him vulnerable. Wanted it enough to make himself prey to anyone who understood it and found a way to use it against him. Wanted it enough to pay Rachel Stone any figure she could name, if she ever discovered the truth....

The beer was delivered more quietly this time—slid across the table as the empty glass was plucked from between his palms. The barmaid was smiling at him, but Ty barely noticed her. Realizing this, he purposely focused on her, irritated that he could remember practically every damn pore of Rachel Stone's skin, yet this woman—who was really quite pretty—hadn't made the slightest impression on him except for her persona of perpetual boredom.

"Thanks," he said.

"My pleasure."

Ty drank slowly, forgetting the barmaid even before she turned away from his table. He concentrated instead on his reaction to Rachel. With determination, he turned his attention inward, laying bare his insupportable feelings for Rachel, knowing his only defense was absolute, total and ruthless examination of this weakness. If Nathan turned out to be his son, and if getting custody was only through Rachel, then he had to shore up his emotional walls now, immediately, for they were crumbling around him, his body responding like a sailor on leave with the first beautiful woman who crosses his path.

Ridiculous. Ty Rafferty, who was used to getting what he wanted, wasn't going to let a temporary attraction to Rachel Stone undermine him. So she was reasonably attractive. Reasonably intelligent, too. So she had a sense of humor and a deficit-ridden bank account. So what? She was a woman, first and foremost, with a woman's basic avaricious nature. They were all that way. He'd realized it years before and in all this time nothing had convinced him otherwise. Therefore, she was merely an obstacle to what he truly wanted: Nathan.

Feeling more like his old self, Ty decided on the best course of action. He would call Raintree in the morning and have him follow up on Julia Williams-Hunt. If there was any chance that Nathan wasn't his son, he wanted proof. He already had papers suggesting that Nathan was indeed a Rafferty, although Julia had neglected to include a copy of the boy's birth certificate. The only real proof of parentage would be a blood test, and follow-up DNA testing would prove the case once and for all.

If he was any kind of prophet at all, he already knew the truth, anyway. Nathan Stone was his son. The tests would merely bear him out.

But he was getting ahead of himself. He couldn't do anything until Rachel Stone knew what it was all about. And he couldn't tell her the truth without risking a hell of a lot more than he was willing to.

So what was the answer?

Stay in Oceanside and get to know Mrs. Stone better.

"Excuse me," Ty said, waving the barmaid toward him with his now empty glass. "I need a place to stay tonight. Something nice. Got any suggestions?"

She screwed her face up, as if the process of thinking was both new and painful. "The Wavecrest's really nice, but really expensive." Clearly she felt it was out of his range. "You could try it," she said dubiously, eyeing him. Ty had cleaned up today, but he was pretty rain drenched and mud spattered now. He supposed her opinion was justified. "If that doesn't work, there's the Sea and Be Seen Motel."

"You're kidding."

"Uh-uh." She shook her head, smiling again, the gist of the conversation already lost to her as she focused on Ty in an entirely different way.

"I'll keep it in mind," Ty said dryly, tossing some coins down on the table, and headed for the pay phone in the back of the room.

He had a sudden vision of Barbara learning he was staying at the Sea and Be Seen Motel and he threw back his head and laughed.

"Okay. All right. Mr. Tennyson is an old grouch and everyone hates him. Even *I* don't like the man very much. But you'd better believe I would never steal from him," Rachel said in a voice just short of pleading. "In fact, given the way I feel about him, I would do everything in my power to *stay out of his way!* Your lack of remorse is really scary, Nathan. Don't you even feel the least bit sorry?"

Nathan wouldn't meet her eye. He sat at the kitchen table, wrapped in layers of anger that were covering up layers of fear and inadequacy. At least that was Rachel's hopeful assessment. At this point she didn't know what was going on with him. Maybe he really didn't care that he'd been shoplifting.

"I feel sorry—that I got caught," he admitted at length.

"Oh?" Rachel's patience was razor thin. "That's it?"

Nathan snorted. "We were just trying to get him. Y'know? He's a jerk. He called the cops on Tommy Athers! Said he was loitering, and the cops came and forced Tommy to leave the store." Nathan flung dark hair off his forehead. "All Tennyson did was screw himself out of a sale. Tommy was going to buy a knife before Tennyson tossed him out!"

"Well, I'm sure sorry Tommy didn't get to buy his weapon," Rachel said in a voice laced with sarcasm.

"Real funny, Mom. You're just *so* funny."

"We're talking about you, Nathan, and the fact that you stole something that wasn't yours. I don't care what Mr. Tennyson's like. He could have three ears and raise cockroaches and I still wouldn't care. You stole from him. He has a right to call the police. And you're in trouble.

"I'm not sure where to go from here," she continued when Nathan didn't respond. "What kind of punishment is suitable? If I thought you felt even a smidgen of remorse I would help you, but you don't care, do you? You don't care that you were arrested for stealing."

Nathan slouched down into his chair until his chin practically rested on his chest. Rachel sighed. "I wish Richard were still alive. I could use some guidance here."

"Is that the only reason you want him back?" Nathan sneered. "Because he could deal with me better than you?"

"No, Nathan. I—"

"Well, I don't care that he's dead. *I don't care!*" He thrust back his chair with such force that it clattered to the floor, lying crookedly on its side like a wounded soldier. Moments later his bedroom door slammed shut behind him. Only anger and confusion and hurt remained in the room, making Rachel feel as if Richard's death had been her fault.

She swallowed, feeling overwhelmed. *I will not fall apart,* she scolded herself. *I will not.*

The phone rang, and Rachel picked up the receiver by rote, still staring blankly down the hall at the spot where Nathan had disappeared into his room. "Hello."

"Mrs. Stone?" a tight, unfamiliar feminine voice inquired.

"Yes?"

"This is Madeline Dayton, Matthew's mother. I want you to know that Matthew's told me everything that happened, and I hold your son completely responsible. Matthew's never done anything like that before, and since he and Nathan have become friends, Matthew's grades have slipped and he's been skipping classes. I'm not allowing Matthew to see Nathan anymore," she went on, just in case Rachel had missed the meaning of this conversation. When Rachel, too stunned and choked up to answer, remained silent, she went on sanctimoniously, "I hope you're the kind of parent who'll recognize the problem and deal with it accordingly. Otherwise, I'm sorry to say I believe Nathan's heading for serious, serious trouble."

The nerve of this woman! Rachel had been near tears, but suddenly she was so furious she could scarcely see straight. "Thank you so much for your unbiased opinion, Mrs. Dayton. I'll make sure Nathan understands exactly how you feel."

She slammed down the receiver. The phone slipped off the edge of the counter and smashed into the floor, sending a broken piece of plastic sailing across the floor straight into Rex's food dish.

Rex immediately went to investigate the morsel, snuffling the plastic. With a groan of misery and disbelief, Rachel leaned against the refrigerator, closing her eyes and clenching her fist. *It'll be funny tomorrow,* she told herself. *I'll laugh till I cry.*

Belatedly she remembered her doctor's advice months ago, when she'd felt as though she couldn't go on another day. It was before Richard's death, when the weight of his illness and the guilt for not loving him had made every movement feel as if it was in slow motion. "It's depression," the doctor had told her, and then had gone on to prescribe pills and a daily exercise routine. Rachel had chucked the pills, but had begun running. Not every day. She simply didn't have the desire. But every few days. And eventually it helped.

She needed help now before she totally lost it with Nathan.

Dragging out her running shoes, she banged the soles together over the back porch, knocking sand from between the ridges. She glanced at the sky. Overcast. She couldn't see the beach from her ridge. Fog lay like a soft velvet blanket, obscuring the coastline.

Rex lolled across the muddy driveway. Spying Rachel dressed for a run, he leaped eagerly to his feet.

"In a minute," she told him, yanking her laces with more force than was really necessary.

Deciding to tell Nathan her plans, she headed in the direction of his bedroom. Nathan's door was firmly shut and she could hear the faintest sound of music. He had his headphones on.

Banging on his door, she yelled, "Nathan! Can you hear me?"

No answer.

She twisted the knob and shook the door. It wasn't locked. She didn't allow locks. But she wasn't going to just throw the door open without alerting him. That would be an invasion of privacy.

"What?" he finally yelled.

"I'm going for a run."

His answer was a grunt of acknowledgment. She almost yelled back that his attitude had better improve, but decided it would only worsen the situation.

Her thoughts in turmoil, she headed for the back door, spied the breakfast dishes heaped in the sink and decided to wash them first. The judge would be lenient with Nathan. That was good. She, on the other hand, had to be tough. That was bad. She'd never been great at being tough with her son. She was a pushover where Nathan was concerned and had been since the first time she'd laid eyes on him.

Fresh anger surfaced. How could he do this to her? *How?*

*I don't care that he's dead. I don't care!* he'd screamed, the words cutting through Rachel's soul.

Her chest expanded with anguish. Nathan was hurting, badly. No matter what he said, he felt Richard's death like a tearing wound. Whereas she had felt relief—relief that the agony and pain were over—Nathan felt out-and-out grief. A grief that, unfortunately, he didn't know how to vent.

Should she try to talk about it? Open the lightly scarred wound and draw out the poison? Rachel chewed on her bottom lip. If the situation were reversed, she wouldn't want Nathan—or anyone, for that matter—to try to make her reveal her feelings. She would want to handle the pain alone. Completely alone.

Just as she turned to the back porch, Rachel heard the throb of a powerful engine approaching. Changing direction, she walked to the front door and peered through the beveled panes of glass set in a trio of tiny windows. A black Porsche was sitting in her driveway, next to the weed-lined front walk.

*I'll call you.*

Tyrrell Rafferty had apparently meant he'd call in person.

"Oh, my God," she murmured, instantly aware of her appearance.

Quickly she brushed at her hair with her hands, smoothing wisps back into the loose ponytail. What did she look like? She was in yesterday's jeans, for God's sake! And she hadn't bothered to put on a lick of makeup.

Good grief, she thought to herself in disgust. What was she worried about? She didn't care what Tyrrell Rafferty III thought of her as a woman. The last thing she wanted in her life these days was a man. She'd lived through one uncomfortable marriage and had learned the devastating truth about herself: she didn't enjoy sex. That was okay. Her reasons for falling in love with Richard in the first place were muddy and unclear. A father figure. A friend. Not really a lover.

She didn't want *any* man as a lover. Too much trouble. She'd seen her friends—Shawna, in particular—tie themselves in knots over men only to be left high and dry when the love affair ended. Most often it seemed the ending was over another woman and the man in question terminated the relationship without so much as a by-your-leave. In that respect Rachel had considered herself lucky: she'd been married to a faithful man who'd believed he loved her, even if his idea of love wasn't quite hers, even if she couldn't quite return that love in the way he wanted and expected.

She wrinkled her nose at the memory, guilt rearing its ugly head. No. Men weren't part of her game plan, no matter how good-looking and sexy they were. *Especially* if they were good-looking and sexy! Tyrrell Rafferty III qualified in every respect. But she wouldn't get involved with him. No way, nohow.

And she had to make that perfectly clear.

No time like the present....

## Chapter Four

"Hello." Rachel stepped onto the front porch to greet him. From somewhere behind the house she heard a wild, frenzied barking. Rex, unable to meet the stranger, was frustrated beyond bearing. "Watch that first board," she added as Ty approached. "The bottom step has a tendency to slip."

"Thanks for the warning."

His low voice reminded her of her own advice. There was something too inherently sexy about him. She had to be careful.

Gingerly mounting the steps, Ty was suddenly standing right beside her, his tall frame towering over hers even though she wasn't a particularly small woman. Strange. She hadn't experienced this feeling of being dwarfed yesterday, but today his lean male body made her feel tiny and vulnerable in comparison.

"Thought I'd drop by and see if you needed anything," he said, his gaze probing past Rachel to the interior of the house, "since you don't have a car."

"I called Gordy last night and got his answering service, but he phoned back this morning. He took the car to his garage in Oceanside. I'm awaiting the final verdict." She wrinkled her nose.

"Expecting the death sentence?"

"Something like that. Would you—like to come in?" She wished she'd spent more time picking up papers, plumping pillows and generally making the place presentable this morning. Not that she really cared what he thought, she reminded herself sternly.

"I don't really have anywhere I have to go," she stated as he stepped into the front room. "And anyway, if I need to get somewhere in a hurry there's Nathan's bike."

Ty stood in the center of the room. Rachel was supremely conscious of the slipcovers she'd purchased at the local variety store in an attempt to cover her garage-sale furniture. It wasn't that they looked so terrible. It was that they fairly shouted how much she was struggling to make ends meet.

She had to remind herself that her financial situation could hardly mean anything to him.

"So this Gordy knows his stuff? He'll give you a fair estimate?"

Rachel nodded. She really didn't want to think about the cost of repairing her car right now. "He's not a bandit. Not like some of the others, anyway."

Ty shot her an appreciative glance, and Rachel looked away. He liked her. She could tell. But she knew next to nothing about him and that was—good.

"Can I get you something?" she asked, hiding her growing nervousness. "A cup of coffee, or a soda? And thanks again, by the way, for being my white knight last night.''

''Aiding and abetting damsels in distress is my specialty,'' he responded dryly. ''Coffee'd be great, if you've got it made.''

''It's instant.''

''Close enough.''

Rachel poured water into two cups and put them in the microwave, her birthday gift from Richard three years before. She was exceedingly conscious of Ty behind her, standing in the kitchen archway. It bothered her, this sensitivity to him. But then, it was perfectly normal, she rationalized. How often had she had an attractive male in her home? Since Richard's death—not even once.

''If I believed in fate, I'd think we were destined to keep running into each other,'' she said without thinking. Then, realizing how that could be misconstrued, she added quickly, ''I mean, we meet at the travel agency and then, boom—you're there when I need you.'' When he didn't say anything, she laughed nervously. ''Never mind. That sounded stupid.''

''No, it's all right. Seeing you again was—opportune,'' he admitted.

''How long do you plan to stay in Oceanside?''

''Oh, I don't know. A few days.''

''And then back to commercial real estate in Portland.'' Rachel handed him a cup of steaming instant coffee.

''Yep.''

''Be careful, it's hot.'' She smiled. ''Do you talk more when you're in the midst of a major deal?''

''Nope.'' He grinned.

Rachel's gaze flicked to that sexy mouth, then she looked away. ''So what do you do when you're not selling real estate or vacationing in Oceanside, or flying to Los Angeles?''

He glanced past her, through the window in the center of the back door to the porch and cliff's edge beyond. "Just work some more, I guess. Is that mammoth beast yours?"

Rachel's gaze followed his, to where her driveway petered out into crabgrass. Rex's rope was stretched all the way from the porch to where the dog lay across the rutted lane, his brindled coat dirty and wet, his tongue lolling out of the corner of his huge, smiling mouth. He was completely oblivious to the mud and water surrounding him. Spying Rachel, he thumped his tail, sending water spraying in ten different directions.

"He's Nathan's," Rachel explained. "I don't know what's with him these days. He barked when you first got here and then that was it. He used to be a terrific watchdog. The kind that would raise the roof with his barking and growling. I swear I lost friends because they were sure he was going to tear them limb from limb whenever they dropped by, but now he's not like that."

"What happened?"

"I don't know," Rachel mused. "Ever since Richard, my—er—husband, passed away, Rex has been just plain weird. It's like he makes his own decisions on who to bark at."

"Maybe he misses your husband," Ty suggested, watching her mobile face closely.

"He didn't even like Richard." She swept him an ironic glance that could have meant anything. Ty was intrigued. "But now it's as if he's picked up on Nathan's feelings and doesn't know how to act." She inclined her head. "It's worse now. He's started charging some strangers. We have to keep him chained when he's outside, which is where he wants to be all the time, even when it's pouring down rain. I can't take him running with me anymore," she finished wistfully.

Ty slid a glance over her sweatshirt and jeans. "Is that where you were going before I showed up?"

She nodded. "I've got to change my jeans, but yes. Since you're here now, I'd just as soon have coffee first," she said, taking a swallow of hers as if to drive the point home.

They sipped in silence for several minutes, the only sound the hum of the refrigerator and the slow drip of the kitchen faucet. When Rachel couldn't stand it any longer, she burst out, "Nathan's in his bedroom. We sort of had it out this morning over what happened last night."

"So, what was the upshot?" Ty asked casually.

Rachel took another small swallow, still waiting for the coffee to cool. She was embarrassed to talk about Nathan. Embarrassed for Nathan. "He isn't exactly reacting like I'd hoped," she admitted with some reluctance. "In fact, I'd have to say he's downright unrepentant."

Ty turned his gaze toward the small hallway that led to the bedrooms. It was strange how much he already knew about her life, Rachel reflected as she slid him a look through the screen of her lashes. She knew next to nothing about his. All she had to do was ask, she supposed, but some protective part of herself was afraid to know too much about him. There was an intimacy involved with sharing parts of your life with someone, an intimacy she was desperately trying to avoid.

He moved his shoulders as if his muscles hurt. His leather bomber jacket creaked appealingly. He'd changed his shirt in favor of a less wrinkled one, and this pair of blue jeans seemed to sport fewer holes. His boots were mud spattered, probably from walking up her driveway, but his beard stubble had been smoothly shaven. Over the aroma of the coffee she caught a trace of his cologne, deep and smooth like the taste of rum, and she inhaled a gulp of coffee, scalding her tongue.

She was instantly furious with herself.

"You all right?" he asked as she sputtered and choked.

"I'll live," was her dry answer.

"Let me get you a glass of water."

Before she could protest he'd crossed to the cabinets and pulled open the one nearest the sink, unerringly finding her glasses. Rachel cringed inside as he turned on the faucet— the one that dripped incessantly no matter which way you turned the darn thing to shut it off.

She didn't know a lot about Mr. Rafferty, but the casual use of his gold card had convinced her he was definitely on a higher economic plane than she was. His air of purposeful neglect had to be an affectation.

The country mouse and the city mouse. She'd never been so self-conscious of her financial situation in her life.

"Here," he said, handing her the glass. She took several long drinks, more for something to do than because she needed them now.

"You didn't have to stop by and check up on me, you know." She smiled to make sure he knew she didn't mean any offense. "You've already done more than any human being should have to. I can't thank you enough for taking me down to the police station. In fact, if there was some way I could repay you . . . ?" She trailed off, expecting him to quickly disabuse her of any obligation. Instead he hesitated, and Rachel gained the impression that he was weighing her offer carefully. Her antennae went on alert. Just how well *did* she know this guy? Good Lord, he could be Oceanside's answer to Jack the Ripper, for all she knew!

You idiot, she berated herself instantly. Nobody who looked like Ty Rafferty was that hard up. She wouldn't believe it.

His dark gaze caught hers, and whatever he read in her face must have registered, for he said drolly, "All I was wondering is if I could talk you into lunch. No strings attached." He smiled faintly. "After your run."

Rachel relaxed. "I'm sorry, I had a late breakfast, but thanks, anyway."

A blast of music sounded from the other room. Nathan fiddling with his stereo. Ty stood silently, his hands pushed into his pockets, his face a study in neutrality. Just what did he want really, Rachel wondered. She could almost swear that now, since she'd outmaneuvered his last stratagem, he was searching for another way to prolong their relationship.

What on earth for? He might like her a little bit, but she didn't kid herself that he'd really fallen for her. He hardly knew her.

*What do you really want, Mr. Rafferty?*

As if he'd somehow heard her thoughts, he smiled, this time with less wattage but still devastating effect. "Then how about dinner? Or, if there's no chance for that, just a walk along the beach."

Time to set the ground rules, Rachel thought. "I don't know," she murmured, shaking her head. "I'm not really... interested in meeting new people right now. It's only been a few months since my husband died, and I'm...well, I'm—not interested," she finished lamely, blushing furiously.

He stared at her with what she was sure was amusement. "You mean, you're not interested in *me?*"

Rachel's embarrassment grew. "I'm not interested in a relationship. Any relationship."

"And going out to dinner constitutes a relationship?"

"Please, Mr. Rafferty—"

"It was Ty at the police station," he reminded her.

"I know I sound completely weird, but I'm too tired and too busy to add even one more thing in my life. It's like the whole balance is upset. I'm afraid it'll all come tumbling down. I can't—afford it."

If she'd had any doubt that she had come off sounding like a complete basket case, Ty's dark, assessing gaze killed it instantly.

"Well, believe it or not," he drawled, "I'm not exactly in the market for a torrid affair myself. I just thought a farewell dinner might be in order. I was thinking of asking Nathan to join us, if he will," he added as an afterthought.

Rachel died a thousand deaths. What the devil was wrong with her? How had she misread him so completely? Had her own feelings of attraction been so magnified and intense that she'd made herself believe he felt the same?

"I—don't know," she said, feeling her face burn with embarrassment. "Sorry I sounded like such an idiot. Let me talk to Nathan." She turned wide hazel eyes up to his, opened her mouth to say something else, then just groaned and shook her head.

Ty watched her walk from the kitchen and down the hall, conscious of that thick mane of auburn hair swinging gently behind her, strands of burnished red and brown wisping at her lobes. His eye recorded the swell of her hips encased in faded blue, the jeans not too tight, but tight enough to give him the general idea of body shape—as if there were any chance on God's green earth that he'd missed it yesterday, he reminded himself.

He was annoyed at her attempts to shove him out of her life before he'd made any progress whatsoever. Annoyed, and yet her words had grabbed him deep inside. She'd thought she'd come off like an idiot when in reality he'd heard her fears of being alone, of single motherhood, of what life held in store for her as clearly as if she'd listed them one by one.

Damn, he didn't want to like her that much.

She returned several minutes later, her expression apologetic and faintly distressed, her jeans exchanged for black sweatpants. "He's not really in the mood to go any-where."

He fought a smile. Her statement of the obvious was accomplished with a wrinkling of her nose. A habit, he guessed.

"Do you have any children?" she asked suddenly, so suddenly that it took Ty's breath away. He shook his head, and Rachel sighed in equal parts exasperation and love. "I wish I had the magic answer for motherhood. I'd make a fortune!" In the next moment she headed for the back door. "I'd like to run, if you don't mind. We can negotiate on dinner later."

"I'll walk you down to the beach," he answered quickly, afraid she might somehow try to disengage herself from him. He was having a hell of a time as it was, racking his brain for some excuse to attach himself to her.

She glanced back, shooting a disparaging look at his boots. "The path I take is wet and slippery. Beware."

"I never choose the easy road."

"Neither," she said under her breath, so faintly that he had to strain his ears to hear, "apparently, do I."

The beach was shrouded with distant gray vapor. Distorted figures of beachcombers moved from the fuzzy edges and grew clearer as they approached. Ty, his eyes fastened on the spot where ten minutes before Rachel Stone had magically disappeared into the fog, reluctantly moved his gaze to the older couple walking arm in arm along the water's edge, watching their progress as they poked with a stick at the flotsam left in the wake of the last wave.

He was sitting on a damp piece of driftwood, the cold steadily creeping into his bones. He disdained running, opting instead for hard, solid work, yet right now he would have traded in his three-hundred-dollar boots for a pair of dime-store sneakers without a thought.

He wanted to be with Rachel.

No. He wanted to be with Nathan. He wanted to convince himself the boy either was, or wasn't, his son.

Ty slowly twisted his neck from side to side, wishing he'd had a better night at the Wavecrest. He'd tossed and turned and apparently fallen asleep in an uncomfortable position, because the crick in his neck was killing him.

He snorted. He'd survived a night in the Porsche with no serious ill effects. How come he felt so rotten today?

Barbara.

He'd called her the night before. She'd been alternately piqued that he'd "deserted" her and avidly curious at his reasons for doing so. So curious, in fact, that Ty had simply ceased explaining rather than reveal enough for her to get her churning little mind set on the right path. The last thing he wanted was Barbara finding out his true mission. God knew what she would do.

She'd next accused him of acting just like a Rafferty, her favorite line whenever Ty chose to close her out. Tyrrell Rafferty II had been a virtuoso at playing the strong, silent type; Ty's mother had said so, loudly and frequently, to whoever would listen, including Barbara.

Ty had gone to bed in the narrow room, blanketed by a feeling of uneasiness and pending disaster. Barbara's nosiness irritated him, and even his lie that he was staying at the Sea and Be Seen Motel, and her nearly apoplectic reaction, hadn't made him feel any better. He wanted to be away from her, he realized. Away from everything she represented. He realized he didn't love her. He shouldn't have proposed to Barbara in the first place, and then he shouldn't have compounded that mistake by letting this engagement drag on.

He knew why he'd asked her to marry him. His father had been dying and his last wish was to see his only son settled. Married. On the path toward respectability. Ty, for the only time he could remember in his entire life, had acceded to his father's wishes. Barbara was the daughter of his father's best friend, Myron Pendleton, and Ty had dutifully asked her to marry him three days before Tyrrell Rafferty II had peacefully died in his sleep, a victim of pancreatic cancer.

Becoming engaged to Barbara had effectively ended the reckless days of Ty's youth. Only his need to keep his own business, separate from his Rafferty inheritance, attested to his independent streak. Though she didn't say it, Ty knew Barbara thought the construction business was just a passing phase. It didn't fit with the Rafferty image of making money the old-fashioned way: inheriting it.

Ty sighed, irritated with himself. Why had he ever thought the marriage might work? Now he had the unenviable task of telling Barbara the engagement was off, that it never should have happened and that he didn't love her.

And if he survived her wrath, he still had to deal with his sister and his mother—rabid tigresses when it came to doing the right thing.

It was going to be ugly.

Ty focused on the older couple strolling aimlessly along the curve of the sea. The woman's elbow was tightly clasped through her husband's, her other hand lying fondly atop his bent arm. One couldn't miss the affection between them. They looked as though they'd felt the same way for years.

That's what he wanted. Affection. Someone who would look at him with affection rather than . . . what? What *did* Barbara think of him as a person?

Uncomfortable in this uncharacteristic self-awareness, Ty stretched out his legs, angling his head skyward, stretching the tight, pulled muscles on the left side of his neck, wishing Rachel would reappear. He could systematically pull out his feelings and examine them, but he rarely second-guessed himself or changed his mind or admitted fault. But he'd made a mistake with Barbara. His reaction to Rachel was proof of that.

*And what about that reaction, Rafferty?*

Ty shook his head. He felt like a fool, forcing his company on her. It wasn't in his nature to be such a groupie, and had it not been that he needed to learn more about Nathan he would have already left Oceanside, Rachel Stone and the whole damn mess behind him.

It wasn't that he was interested in Rachel, he told himself sternly. Barbara might not be the woman for him, but neither was Rachel Stone.

His mind's eye recalled the way she looked in those jeans. Maybe he was kidding himself. Maybe the main reason he'd stayed an extra day wasn't because of Nathan. Maybe it was because he enjoyed the company of a woman who was warm, intelligent, uncomplicated and completely in the dark as to who he was and what he stood for. Maybe he just needed someone like Rachel to pull the veil from his eyes about Barbara. He'd known for months he couldn't marry her, but had been too busy and self-absorbed to do anything about it.

Now he would. As soon as he got back to Portland. And then . . . ?

He wasn't sure how to handle this Nathan thing. In the back of his mind, stirring like the smooth circles of liquid in a cauldron, was the plan that he could use Rachel in his quest to learn if Nathan was really his son or not. She was an attractive woman with a sense of humor and an independent streak he couldn't fail to notice. She was also intrigued with him. He'd seen it in her eyes when she thought he wasn't looking. *She* was looking. Looking at him.

She was also afraid of getting involved with a man, afraid of being hurt. That's what she'd really been saying when she'd professed to not wanting a relationship. She was alone, and vulnerable, and she got to him. Got to him more than he wanted her to. More than he could afford.

Slipping his fingers beneath the damp sand, he scooped up a handful, clenching it in his fist. Women fell for him. It was a fact. Sure, most often they knew who he was first so the outcome was inevitable, but Ty was enough of a realist to fully understand the opposite sex's attraction to him. It went beyond money and name in some cases.

So, how difficult would it be to make Rachel Stone fall in love with him?

He grimaced. It could be very difficult. Then again . . .

He had to leave Oceanside this evening or tomorrow morning, but he could be back by next weekend. Better yet, Thursday. The date scheduled for Nathan's court hearing. But he had to come up with some other excuse, so why not have it be that he was wildly attracted to Rachel Stone herself? It wasn't even much of a lie.

Ty thrust aside all the automatic protests forming inside his head and forced himself to concentrate on the plan.

Big Jim could handle things at the construction site. Ty was due some time off, anyway. Long overdue, in fact. He would tell his sister and mother that he was thinking of buying some property on the coast, and then he would deliberately set about romancing Rachel.

Meanwhile, he could work on getting to know Nathan better. The kid was heading for trouble with a capital *T.* If there was any chance that boy was really his son, he wanted custody. Right now. Before the situation got worse.

And the only way to do that was to get closer to Rachel.

Ty's conscience smote him briefly. When she found out why he'd sought her out, which was bound to happen eventually if he wanted proof Nathan was his son, she would hate him for using her.

He thought about that for some moments, his eyes focusing on the spot where he felt she would emerge from that misting wall of fog.

Well, it couldn't be helped. And it didn't matter, anyway, because as soon as she learned he was wealthy things would change. Rachel Stone would turn into the kind of woman he loathed most: cool, brittle, scheming and grasping. That's just what money did to women.

No, the plan was a good one, and it had its side benefits, also. He liked Rachel, actually looked forward to being with her and she liked him, no matter what she said.

*And what about going to bed with her, Rafferty? What are you going to do about that?*

He couldn't go that far, he told himself quickly. No woman would ever, *ever* forgive that. But then he thought of her in her jeans, and a hot wave of lust brought goose bumps to his flesh.

He'd cross that bridge when he came to it.

Rachel panted, her breath feeling like dry ice as it cut through her lungs. She slowed to a fast walk, realizing belatedly that it had been a long time since she'd run this far, this fast.

The fog was beautiful, like soft gray velvet. It surrounded her as she moved and gave her a comfortable, safe feeling.

Which was just as well, because Tyrrell Rafferty was rapidly making her feel *un*comfortable and *un*safe. She was no expert on men, but she understood human nature pretty well, and she knew his interest in her was totally out of character. When he'd come to the travel agency he'd been restless and careful. When he'd stopped to help her he'd been taciturn and careful. And when they'd gone to pick up Nathan he'd been concerned and careful.

Now, today, he was more relaxed, but he was still careful. What did he want from her really?

She stopped and bent over, resting her palms on her knees, listening to her uneven breath and her pounding heart. She knew now what Richard Stone had wanted: a wife and a mother for his son. Rachel had thought she'd wanted the same and she'd stepped into his sheltering arms as naturally as sunlight sparkled on water.

Only she hadn't loved him and he hadn't loved her. And she hadn't enjoyed sex, and only Nathan had kept the marriage relatively happy.

Straightening, Rachel squinted toward the sun, white and brilliant above the cloud cover. She refused to dwell on her mistakes. And she sure as hell didn't intend to make another one.

She ran the last few yards with a black-and-white dog by her side, the latter having slipped his leash and having the time of his life jumping in and out of the surf, barking, then racing like mad to catch Rachel. He came skidding to a halt beside Ty, barked wildly several times, then turned into a turning, wiggling mass as he shook water from his fur.

"Sorry!" Rachel shrieked on a laugh as water rained down on them both.

"No harm done." Ty's amused gaze settled on the dog, which was barely more than a pup. "Who's your friend?"

"I don't know. I just found him down the beach, or more accurately, he found me. He's got a collar." Beads of perspiration clung to her forehead and she swiped at them with her sleeve.

Ty rose from the driftwood and Rachel stepped back automatically, a little overwhelmed by his superior height. The puppy growled threateningly, planting all fours stiffly, as if getting ready to pounce.

"You seem to make a habit of picking up protectors," Ty drawled.

She laughed. "Relax, dog," she scolded. "That's not a way to make friends."

The puppy wouldn't take his eyes off Ty. At Rachel's voice he wagged his tail slowly several times, but he wouldn't give up his vigil no matter what.

"I'm offended," Ty said, reseating himself on the driftwood.

He didn't sound offended. He sounded amused. Rachel, determining it was high time she figured out what really made this man tick, settled herself on the other side of him. There was about twelve inches of driftwood between his hip and hers, all that she could manage, since she was teetering on the end.

"Tell me more about Tyrrell Rafferty III," she suggested, mopping her brow once again.

"What do you want to know?"

The puppy, responding to Ty's outstretched palm, moved slowly forward, still growling. He wanted to be petted so badly his skin shivered and wiggled. But he was afraid of Ty.

"Have you ever been to Oceanside before?"

"No."

"What made you choose it for a vacation?"

His attention had been focused on the now scampering puppy, but he turned to look at her. He had beautiful eyes, Rachel thought inconsequently. Dark brown, almost black, with thick, straight lashes. "I'm combining business with pleasure. Looking at beachfront property."

"Really?"

"Uh-huh." He shifted so he could follow the zigzag course of the puppy as it barked and chased the waves, finally connecting with a young couple who scolded it severely for running off. The hip that had been inches from Rachel's touched hers for a moment, before she carefully moved away.

"Beachfront property like mine?" she teased. Her house above the beach, though possessing a spectacular view, was in sad need of serious work. There were hundreds of other homes that had better views, hundreds of other homes that required less money to fix.

He smiled. "Actually, yes."

"I don't believe you're serious, but if you are, I'm sorry. I couldn't sell my house even if I wanted to. It's really all I've got, and Nathan needs some stability in his life right now. I guess I don't have to tell you," she added, feeling a twist of pain in her chest. "You were there last night."

"Has Nathan been causing you trouble all along, or is what happened last night something new?"

"Well, he's never committed a crime before, to my knowledge, but things changed—Nathan changed—after my husband died."

"When was that?" Ty asked, although he already knew the answer.

"Six months ago. He'd battled heart disease for years. He finally lost."

"And how are you coping with his death?"

The question was quiet. He was still focused on the puppy who was now following on the heels of the young couple, looking completely penitent. An illusion, Rachel suspected, letting her gaze roam over Ty's profile. "I'm doing better than Nathan."

"You seem kind of young to have a son Nathan's age."

"He's my adopted son. In fact, my husband and his first wife adopted Nathan when he was a baby. Richard's first wife died when Nathan was five. I met Richard not long afterward. I was in college."

"Ahh," he said, as if she'd cleared up some mystery for him.

"Richard was twenty years older than I was," Rachel went on, gauging his reaction.

"You were in love with him."

Rachel was taken aback. "I—yes—I was."

"You don't sound sure about that." He angled his head, turning his attention back her way. His gaze was lazy and casual.

"It's all very complicated. I don't think I was really looking for marriage when I met Richard," she admitted. "But I wanted . . . someone. And I fell in love with Nathan on the spot. He was so adorable. Loving and giving and just this perfect child. No one would have been able to resist him. I wanted to be his mother so badly." Rachel sighed. "And later, when he'd throw his arms around my neck and tell me he loved me, it was all worthwhile. Everything."

Silence rained down upon them. Rachel supposed she should have been embarrassed for blurting out her feelings, but she just felt numb. Numb because things had changed so drastically between her and the son she loved.

"You make it sound as if your marriage wouldn't have lasted if it hadn't been for Nathan."

"I got married for a lot of reasons, most of them wrong. Nathan was the one right one. Look, I don't want to give you the wrong impression. Richard was good to me. But there's a big gap between a twenty-year-old girl and a forty-year-old man, and we didn't bridge that gap very well." Her gaze swept downward, to the grains of sand dusting her thighs. "At least, I didn't," she admitted. "I didn't love him as much as he loved me.

"I don't know why I'm telling you all this," she continued. "We were talking about your reasons for being in Oceanside."

"Yes." He hesitated. "We were."

"So, you're looking at beachfront property. For resale?"

"No, I'm actually in the construction end of real estate. We're putting up a shopping center in Beaverton right now, and there's a condominium complex going up along the Willamette, just south of Portland." Ty rubbed his jaw, wondering how far to go with his yarn. "I was thinking of building a resort here in Oceanside."

Rachel looked at him as if he'd lost his mind. Ty wondered if he had. Even with the information she'd given him, information he was absorbing like a sponge, he couldn't get his mind off the appealing curls that fell across her forehead, clinging to her damp skin. He was achingly conscious of the rise and fall of her breasts, the soft mounds lifting and falling beneath her sweatshirt. Hell, she wasn't even wearing anything remotely sexy!

His plan to get to know her was already growing complicated. The sex thing was getting in the way, even if it was all one-sided. His side. He couldn't tell if she felt anything for him other than a mild interest.

"What kind of resort?" she asked. "The Wavecrest is about the only thing we've got that could qualify as a resort. Oceanside isn't exactly a thriving beach metropolis."

"Nothing huge. I don't think the area could support it."

"You're right about that. In the winter the Wavecrest is half empty all the time. You've got to make your money in the summer."

"So, how does the travel business do in the winter?" he asked.

"So-so. Not as many people come, but the residents do like to leave."

She smiled. He was getting used to that smile. There was a dent in her left cheek. Not quite a dimple. Just a small spot that cried out to be kissed.

He sucked in a sharp breath. This woman was completely off limits.

"You're not being completely straight with me, are you, Mr. Rafferty?"

"I'm not?" He stared at her.

"If you were really here scouting out real estate, you wouldn't have involved yourself in Nathan's and my problems like this. Nobody's that much of a Good Samaritan, and besides, you don't even fit the part."

"What do you mean?"

She laughed, embarrassed. "I don't want to sound ungrateful, but you seem to be kind of uncomfortable around me. Like this isn't your usual thing. I get the feeling that…"

"That?" he prompted in a low voice, uncertain he wanted to hear her views.

"Oh, never mind." She smiled and shook her head. "I'm going to say something I'll regret if I'm not careful. Something stupid and hurtful when all I really feel is gratitude, and that's what I should be doing—thanking you for all your trouble."

"You've already thanked me more than enough."

"I don't know what I would have done if you hadn't come along and—"

"Rachel."

His use of her first name stopped her midsentence. That, and his authoritative tone. A tone meant to capture her attention. She gazed at him inquiringly.

Ty took the plunge. "The reason I'm hanging around you is because I want to get to know you. I can't put it any plainer. I have to go back to Portland tonight, but I'll be back on Thursday."

"Thursday?"

"Nathan's hearing. I'd like to be there, and don't ask me why because I don't have an answer for you. And I hope I can find a place in Oceanside to build a resort, because it would give me an excellent opportunity to see you more often."

Ty's mouth was dry. He couldn't remember the last time he'd been so plain with a woman. Except that it was all a cover-up for his real purpose, he reminded himself with an unwelcome pang.

"Well," Rachel said, nearly speechless.

Ty grinned. "So, what do you think of that? Does that come too close to your definitions of starting a relationship?"

"I think so." Her eyes were huge.

"Does that mean if I come back on Thursday you won't see me?"

"No...."

"Are we still on for dinner tonight?"

"Mr. Rafferty—"

"Ty," he said firmly.

"There's only two things I really want out of life," she said with that slicing honesty Ty was quickly growing to both admire and fear. "One, I want Nathan to be happy. I want to be a good mother and make sure he gets on the right track and stays there."

"What's two?"

"I want to make sure I don't make another mistake." She rose to her feet, dusting off her clothes, refusing to meet his eyes as Ty pushed himself upright.

They were alone in the misting fog; not another soul was visible. He wanted to lift up her chin with his hand and...what? Kiss her?

She looked upward all on her own, her lashes raising to reveal eyes as clear and pure as a mountain brook. "I don't know you very well...Ty...but one thing's certain—if anything happened between us, I'd be the one to lose out."

"You don't know that."

"Oh, yes, I do." She headed for the path, adding over her shoulder, "Men aren't high on my list of priorities, and

I'm keeping it that way. I'm going to have to cancel on dinner. If you come back Thursday..."

"Go on," he said, disappointed.

She glanced back and threw him a smile. "I don't know. It's crazy. I hate to admit it, but I'd be glad if you came with me to the hearing. Does that make me really lousy? Because even though I don't want to get involved, I'd like you to be there...?"

Ty caught up with her. She had no idea of the gift she'd given him. Gently swiping sand from the curve of her cheek with his thumb, he said, "No. That makes you honest."

## Chapter Five

The Rafferty family residence was an imposing mansion located in Portland's West Hills. It wasn't Ty's home; he'd moved out years before and now lived alone in a renovated house overlooking the Willamette River. But his mother and sister still lived in the dwelling that had once been described as "one of the premier Portland manors." It had been built in the 1890s by a renowned architect who'd also designed many of the public buildings, including the famed Portland Hotel. It was literally worth millions; its location, impeccable upkeep and sweeping grounds enough to make sightseers ooh and aah and developers drool.

Ty scarcely gave the place a glance. He screeched to a halt in the curving brick drive, slammed the door and strode rapidly to the pristine white portico supported by twin Doric columns. The home was Georgian-style—big, square, white with evenly spaced windows across its front.

He jammed his finger on the bell, faintly aware of the delicate scent of roses as a gentle counterpoint to the damp odor of June rain. Inside, chimes rang musically. Footsteps sounded. Mary, the housekeeper, opened the door.

"Well, goodness! Hello, Mr. Rafferty," she greeted him, unable to hide her surprise.

Ty hid a smile. Even he couldn't remember the last time he'd been here. "Hi, Mary. Is Mother here? Or Kathleen?"

"They're both in the dining room."

"Thanks."

He strode across Italian marble squares of black and white, his mother's choice. Personally Ty had preferred the white oak parquet, but who was he to stand in the way of blatant, frivolous Rafferty spending? Both his mother and sister had been left substantial incomes. How they chose to spend those incomes was their business.

He stopped at the arched entry to the pale pink room. His mother sat at the end of the graceful table, his sister on her left. They both looked up at his appearance.

"Good God, it's my brother," Kathleen said, pausing with her water glass halfway to her lips. She turned to the elegant, silver-haired woman beside her. "What do you suppose he wants?"

Sybil Rafferty gave her a look of pained tolerance. "Tyrrell. What a pleasant surprise," she said with genuine pleasure. "Would you like something to eat? Mary? Please set another place beside me."

"No, thanks, Mother." He was already feeling stifled and impatient. "I don't have a lot of time. I just wanted to tell you something before you heard it elsewhere."

"What?" Her pleasure dimmed.

"I've broken my engagement to Barbara."

Kathleen groaned, throwing her napkin on the table and scooting back her chair. "Wouldn't you know, Father asks you one thing—*one thing*—and you can't do it."

"I wasn't in love with her," he said for his mother's benefit. "I couldn't go through with it."

"How's Barbara taking it?" she asked, looking distressed.

"She's accepted it."

His tone must have given him away, for his mother murmured, "Oh, Ty," as if she'd been there to witness the scene that had ensued. Barbara had *not* taken the news well. Breaking off with her had been singularly unpleasant. She hadn't liked hearing that he didn't love her, that he never had, that he never would. He hadn't liked having to tell her. But the worst of it was that she hadn't believed him. She'd insisted there was more than enough still between them for a successful marriage.

Eventually he'd convinced her he meant what he said. Barbara had then flown into a fury of such immense proportions that Ty was actually taken aback. He'd never suspected her capable of any deep emotion, but the fiery rage she'd hurled at him had made him realize he'd been mistaken. Beneath a veneer of intellect and an awesome amount of cool sophistication, there apparently beat a heart of passion. A passion he hadn't known she possessed. Could he have been that wrong about her? Did she really care about him?

She'd answered him even before the thought had fully crossed his mind. "I'll be a laughingstock, you bastard!" she'd choked in her rage. "Can't you see what will happen? *Can't you see?*"

Now Kathleen's society-minded brain hit on the same issue. "It'll be in all the papers. Before the day's through we'll have reporters calling and God knows what else. Barbara's parents are going to be really unhappy," she predicted.

An understatement, Ty thought, but it couldn't be helped.

"Sit down, Ty," Sybil pleaded, pulling out his chair.

He reluctantly complied, slouching down in the seat. He didn't know what possessed him to thwart all the conventions of wealth, but he couldn't help himself. He didn't want to help himself.

Seeing the image of himself in jeans and a black leather jacket, slouched in the Louis XIV chair, made him think of Nathan. How would *he* like it?

"So where have you been the last couple of days?" Kathleen asked. "That foreman of yours is either dull or rabidly loyal."

"He's loyal."

"He wouldn't tell me a thing."

"Why were you looking for me?" Ty asked.

"Because I thought you were getting married in a couple of months and I wanted to discuss the wedding with you!" Two spots of color entered her cheeks. "I thought we were having it here."

Ty regarded her skeptically. "We never set a date."

"Maybe you hadn't, but Barbara had. She was determined to march you down the aisle by the end of summer. I thought it was a good plan."

"Kathleen," Sybil reproached.

"Well, he's thirty-three and playing tractors with some guy who calls himself Big Jim, for crying out loud! It's time he did something responsible."

Ty held his tongue. He'd had so many arguments with Kathleen that he just couldn't stomach another one. His mother frowned at her. "You're not married and you're older than he is," she pointed out.

"But she has been married three times before," he put in helpfully, unable to resist one little jab.

"Ty—" Kathleen began, but Sybil quickly cleared her throat.

"Would you like me to call Myron and Claudia?" she asked her son. "Maybe it would help."

"Do whatever you like. Barbara knows, that's what's important. I've got some other things to take care of, so I won't be able to stay."

He got up from the chair, kissed his mother on the cheek, pretended to quail at the steely look in his sister's dark eyes, then left them to the rest of their breakfast.

His next stop was Raintree's office.

Gerald was in a conference, and Ty ended up waiting nearly an hour before the attorney could spare him ten minutes between appointments. Wasting no time, Ty gave Raintree his impressions of Nathan and Rachel Stone as soon as he was admitted into the lawyer's sumptuous office. When he was finished there was momentary silence as Raintree methodically unbent a paper clip and flipped it expertly into the trash can.

"The boy may look a lot like you. He may even act like you, but it's not enough proof," Gerald finally said, his gaze meeting Ty's.

"I'd like to see Nathan's birth certificate with my own eyes," Ty answered. "See if it's at least possible I'm his father. I just can't trust the information Julia gave me."

"I can get a copy of the certificate," Gerald said. "But what then? What if the dates and information mesh?"

"If Nathan Stone is my son, I want him."

Raintree sighed at Ty's implacable tone. "And Rachel Stone, the boy's mother?"

"I'll fight her for custody."

"Then you'd better get your boxing gloves on because it's bound to be a helluva battle."

All the way to the construction site the image of Gerald Raintree dolefully shaking his head haunted Ty. He specifically hadn't told Gerald his alternative plan, the one where he made Rachel fall in love with him. Gerald would have a fit, and Ty wasn't interested in listening to the lawyer list all the reasons why romancing Rachel would be a mistake. Ty knew it was a mistake, but if the only other choice was a bloody custody battle, one Gerald felt certain he would lose, why shouldn't he take the risk? He had nothing to lose and everything to gain.

*You could lose her trust and the rest would fall like dominoes.*

He sighed as he parked his car in the muddy lot and walked across the rain-washed ruts to the construction trailer. He was walking a very thin line. Winning Rachel, her confidence, her trust, wasn't even the hard part. The hard part would be when she found out the full truth. He was aware how lethal her reaction and retaliation could be. He would lose Nathan totally.

"So you're back, eh?" Big Jim Carlson greeted him as he opened the door. "Got everything done you needed to?"

"Just about. I'll have to leave again Thursday, though. Catch me up on what's been going on around here."

Big Jim scowled but didn't ask Ty about his trip. Instead he got right down to business. "The spreader's broke down, but we're workin' on it. Should be up and runnin' by tomorrow mornin'. We're ahead of schedule at the shoppin' center, so that's good. Ted's been late to work three days in a row, then cryin' about overtime but I took care of it. Now look at these here plans...."

"I've got you wait-listed on American flight 1157," Rachel said into the receiver cradled against her shoulder. "The flight's overbooked and there are seven people ahead of you on the list."

She listened to the squawking on the other end of the line with only half an ear. What was it about some days? She would swear that everybody in Oceanside was in a bad mood.

Rachel glanced at the clock. Nathan's hearing was in two hours. She didn't have time for this. She needed to collect her thoughts, and she needed to make sure Nathan was on his way home from school. Today was a half day, the last day of school, in fact, before summer vacation. That had burned Nathan, too. The fact that all of his buddies were hanging out at the beach for a big party and he had to face the judge. Even Matthew and Jessica were facing the judge on different days and so they, too, would probably be part of the festivities.

*As if it's my fault,* Rachel thought to herself, trying hard to hide her irritation from the insistent complainer on the phone.

Shawna, wiggling her purple fingernails in Rachel's direction, angled her head toward the door. Rachel glanced past the receptionist, her pulse leaping in spite of herself. For one wild moment she thought Ty Rafferty had made good on his promise and returned to Oceanside. But it was Nathan who sauntered past Shawna, his shoulders tucked in protectively, not quite meeting Rachel's eyes as he slouched down in the chair opposite her desk.

Rachel calmed herself down. She really didn't expect Ty to show up for the hearing, did she? He'd probably regretted offering as soon as the words had been spoken.

"Hi," she mouthed to her son with a smile.

"Hi," he answered while she finished her call and replaced the receiver.

"School's out, huh?"

He slouched down farther, if that was possible, stretching his legs out until his decrepit sneakers nearly touched Rachel's shoes. Déjà vu, she thought, remembering how

Ty's expensive boots had nearly done the same thing. Goose bumps suddenly appeared on her arms and she looked at them in mild surprise.

"Yeah," he answered.

Rachel nodded. She couldn't remember the last time he'd dropped by the travel agency, even though he spent a lot of his free time after school with his friends at the row of shops euphemistically called Fun Center right down the street from where she worked.

They really had grown apart, she thought with a squeeze of her heart.

"You need a lift home? The hearing's not for a couple of hours."

"How?" he asked, giving her a rare direct look. "We don't have a car."

"Allison's been a saint," Rachel said, shining a smile on the woman seated at the desk behind her. Allison's answer was to lift her hands in a halo over her head as she talked to whoever was on the other end of her line. "I'm sure she'd let me use her car to take you back," Rachel finished.

"Nah. I'll just go to the Fun Center."

"I don't know if I feel comfortable with that. You need to change into something more respectable than jeans and a T-shirt, and we won't have a lot of time, so—"

"I can wear this," he interrupted.

"I'd rather you didn't."

"Why? So I can impress the judge? Forget it."

"Nathan." Rachel sighed. She was about at the end of her rope. "Look, I've got a couple of bookings to finish, then I can leave. We can take some time to go to the Fun Center first, if you'd like. Grab a Coke or something."

He grimaced, sending a message she couldn't decipher.

"Unless you don't want to be seen with your mom," she suggested lightly. Talking to Nathan these days was like stepping through a mine field. One wrong move and the whole thing could explode in your face.

"Whatever." He picked up her magnetic paper-clip holder, held it upside down and shook it, trying to displace the clips attached to the magnetic ring. "Maybe I'll just walk home."

"It's quite a walk," she pointed out.

"I don't care." Rising to his feet, Nathan started to say something, thought better of it, then finally blurted out, "Matt's mother's got a choke chain on him! She won't hardly let him out of the house."

Remembering her own phone call from Madeline Dayton, Rachel could well imagine. "Well, I'm not surprised."

"How come?" Nathan's dark eyes pinned her accusingly. "What happened? You talked to her, didn't you? What did you say?"

"Look, don't blame me, okay? Mrs. Dayton called me up and told me what a lousy mother I was and what a total screwup you are and how you're traveling the path to ultimate damnation." Rachel's jaw set in recollection. "I was...offended, to say the least."

Amusement lurked in the corners of Nathan's eyes, and he fought a smile. He'd always been bright and quick, and though he and Rachel might not be seeing eye to eye these days, it looked as if he still appreciated her own brand of sarcasm and humor.

"Mrs. Dayton doesn't like me much."

"Oh, really."

"She thinks I'm bad for Matt."

"You don't say."

"She doesn't like Jessica, Matt's girlfriend, either."

Laughter bubbled up inside Rachel. "How many holes did Jessica pierce in Matt's ear?"

"Three," he admitted.

"Good Lord," Rachel muttered in horror. "I would have liked to have been a fly on the wall when Mrs. Dayton discovered that!"

Nathan actually chuckled, heard himself and brought their moment of shared humor to an abrupt end. He pulled his handsome face into its characteristic stony countenance. Rachel could have cried for the loss of the real Nathan, the one who could laugh and joke and not take life so seriously.

Spying the string that hung through his ear, she couldn't help saying, "You are keeping that clean, aren't you?"

"Yeah." He set the paper-clip holder on her desk with a slap.

"You sure you don't want to go somewhere with me?" she asked a little desperately as he turned away.

"I'll see you at home," he muttered.

Rachel stared after him. She should be happy, she supposed, that she'd connected with him at all. He'd hardly spoken to her since the shoplifting incident except for a few choice words about what he thought about Mr. Tyrrell Rafferty interfering in their lives. Nathan had been waiting in the kitchen when she and Ty had returned from the beach, and if looks could kill...

But after Ty left, Nathan had pulled away from Rachel even further. He'd been cruelly blunt and selfish as only a teenager can be, accusing Rachel of never loving his father, an accusation that held enough truth to cut through her like a sharp knife.

Still, dealing with Nathan was almost better than talking to Gordy about the bill on her car. *That* was really depressing. The main reason Rachel hadn't picked up the wagon—with its new alternator—was simply that she didn't have the money to pay for it. She'd had to ask her boss for an advance on her wages, and he was thinking it over.

What a mess. She was glad, in a way, that Ty Rafferty wasn't here to see her at her lowest. She had enough to worry about already.

"Wanna get something to drink?" Allison asked. "You're leaving early, aren't you? Let's go out and get something. You'll need some sustenance."

Rachel spun around in her chair. "What kind of drink did you have in mind? I'm supposed to be at a hearing."

"I was thinking diet cola, but if you want something stronger, I'm all for that. I could use it," Allison added on a disgusted mutter.

"Diet cola sounds great. What's wrong?"

"San Francisco's fogged in and this pea brain over at Central Packaging is fit to be tied. Thinks *I* can do something about it, but that I just won't, I guess, by the way he talks. I was so ticked, I finally told him off."

Rachel glanced around at her, not knowing what to say. Since Central Packaging was one of Neptune Travel's biggest accounts, Allison had taken quite a risk. "What did you say?"

Allison's hair was as black as pitch, pulled straight back from a face that could grace the covers of magazines. Gorgeous as she was, she was formidable and no one much messed with her, clients and co-workers alike.

"I said I would trot right down to San Francisco on foot and start blowing. And if he didn't like that, he could take the train. Men," she added under her breath. "This guy thinks since he got promoted to second vice president of wrapping and strapping, or whatever, that he owns the place. He's got a real attitude."

"I know about attitudes." Rachel signed off her computer and grabbed her lightweight white coat from the closet at the back of the room. Allison, who wore signature black, already had a short jacket on.

They walked out of the building together, heading in silent agreement toward the small café two blocks from the travel agency.

"I think," Allison added on a sigh, holding open the door, "that unless I find a guy who's rich, or as handsome as that hunk who walked up to your desk last week, I'm staying celibate. What's the point? I mean, all you get is grief."

Rachel nodded. So Allison had noticed Ty, too. Big surprise. He would have been pretty difficult not to notice.

*I'm not interested in a relationship. Any relationship.*

Rachel inwardly groaned as they seated themselves at a booth near the front window. Had she really said that? Why had she ever thought Ty might really be attracted to her?

"Speak of the devil!" Allison said in wonder.

Through the window outside their booth Rachel saw Ty, dressed today in a gray suit and tie and looking incredibly respectable and—to Rachel—totally foreign, striding from the travel agency toward the café. He glanced up, his eyes meeting hers, and her stomach fluttered nervously. Her pulse took off at a jagged gallop, heat flooded her face. He'd come back to Oceanside. He'd actually come back.

"Oh, Lord," Allison murmured, her knowing gaze turned on Rachel's mobile face. "He's taken. For crying out loud, Rachel, why didn't you tell me?"

"There is nothing between me and Tyrrell Rafferty," she answered quickly.

"You sure?"

In Allison's tone Rachel heard the unspoken request: Do you mind if I go after him? Jealousy burned through her veins, turning her blush to a crimson wave. Furious with herself, she said lightly, "He's all yours."

"God, I hope so," she declared, her brown eyes sparkling as Ty walked into the tiny café.

* * *

The place smelled like cooked fish and coffee. In Portland it would have been the kind of hangout only drunks or locals would visit. But in Oceanside, where the brine and wind and fog turned even the most chic and sophisticated restaurant into a weathered and slightly weary establishment within the year, every café looked like a truck stop and smelled even worse. Here, run-down was elevated to a fine art.

Tyrrell Rafferty II would be rolling over in his grave, Ty thought with amusement as he stepped inside the place. He glanced toward Rachel's booth, meeting those slightly wary hazel eyes, feeling a pang of... what? Desire? He deliberately squashed the sensation.

Rachel was seated at a Formica-topped table, her chestnut hair pulled into its ubiquitous loose ponytail, her slim figure swathed in a voluminous white blouse and long denim skirt. A white jacket lay folded on the seat beside her.

"Hi," he greeted her, and the frustrations of his trip home slipped away like water over smooth stones.

"Hi," Rachel answered, inclining her head toward the dark-haired woman seated across from her. "Ty, this is Allison Greer. Allison, Tyrrell Rafferty. The Third," she added with a twitch of her lips.

"How is it you know something as intimate as The Third about this man when you profess to hardly know him?" Allison asked Rachel, but her gaze was turned warmly on Ty.

Ty half smiled. He was used to the Allisons of the world. "She reads my credit cards," he commented lazily and, without waiting for an invitation, picked up the jacket and sank into the booth beside Rachel, his thigh resting against hers. "Do you mind if I join you?"

"No." The feel of that hard, muscular thigh lined against hers made Rachel jump. Pinning on a bright smile, she vowed to stop acting like a teenager around him, hoping against hope that he was unaware of her reaction.

Allison lifted one eyebrow, her penetrating look saying she'd noticed even if Ty hadn't. She was wondering where to go from here, Rachel sensed, so with thoughts of proving to her that Ty meant absolutely nothing to her, Rachel said, "Allison's the one to talk to at Neptune Travel. She's been everywhere."

"Is that right?" Ty focused on Allison.

"Well, there're a few spots on the globe I haven't visited yet, but give me time. Do you travel much, Mr. Rafferty?"

"It's Ty. I travel some."

"For business or pleasure?"

"Both. But I prefer pleasure."

The conversation had quickly moved into dangerous areas, Rachel thought. She turned to Ty, intending to ask some inane question, anything to help derail this subtle sex talk, and then realized he was staring at her, not Allison. That last remark had been for her benefit. Her mouth went dry. If Ty noticed Allison's interest—and he'd have to be deaf, dumb and blind not to—he sure didn't act like it. He had eyes only for *her,* Rachel realized with perverse pleasure.

Flustered, she said, "I didn't believe you'd really come back today. Is that suit because of the hearing?"

"Uh-huh."

"You're going to Nathan's hearing?" Allison said, making no effort to hide her surprise.

"Yep."

Allison gazed questioningly at Rachel. Rachel shook her head. There was nothing going on between her and Ty, she answered silently. Nothing. She marveled that Ty could ignore Allison so completely.

Ty had seen his share of women like Allison over the years. Not that there was a thing wrong with her. He'd dated many a beautiful woman just like her. But Allison Greer looked tough enough to swallow glass, and beauty, for beauty's sake alone, didn't interest him. He'd met too many exquisite examples of femininity who, like the invisible man, if ever stripped of their trappings would be discovered to be nothing underneath. Of no substance.

To Ty's way of thinking, Allison Greer would have to prove there was more to her than a gift of nature. Guilty until proven innocent.

And besides, he wasn't interested in her, anyway. He wanted Rachel, for various reasons, not the least being that she looked so incredibly fresh and lovely that he wanted to drag her into his arms and kiss her senseless. Hardly rational, considering the weighty secret he carried. Yet infinitely rational given his decision to win her.

Except it would be truly playing with fire.

"Are you finished for the day?" he asked her.

"Almost. I've just got to make a couple of phone calls, and then I'm on my way to the courthouse."

"Have you got your car back yet?"

"Umm. No."

"I told you, you can use mine," Allison reminded her.

"I'll drive you," Ty said.

"You don't need to wait," Rachel began, but he shook his head.

"It's okay. I've got time."

"You live in Portland?" Allison asked thoughtfully, and Ty favored her with a brief glance.

"In Portland," he admitted in a tone that didn't invite further conversation. But Allison wasn't easily intimidated, and Rachel suspected her pride was bruised by Ty's blatant disinterest in her charms. If the situation was reversed, Rachel would feel the same way. Although she would never have made a bid for someone like Ty in the first place.

"Your name's familiar," Allison mused, a fine line forming between her brows. "I used to have an apartment in Vancouver. Vancouver, Washington," she added so that he wouldn't think she meant Vancouver, B.C. Vancouver, Washington, was just across the Columbia River from Portland. "I'd swear I've heard of you before."

Ty shrugged. "There are a lot of Raffertys in Portland."

"Relatives of yours?" she asked.

"Some."

"Rafferty," Allison repeated thoughtfully, and Rachel felt Ty tense beside her. He was touchy about his personal life. Any time a question was asked, he seemed to really think his answer through and rarely did he offer more than a one-word reply.

"Ready to go?" Ty asked Rachel. He had to force himself not to overreact. It was only a matter of time until Rachel, with Allison's dubious help, connected his name with his family. Though the Rafferty name wasn't as well-known as some others around Portland—names automatically associated with wealth and social standing—it was certainly in the top twenty. If Allison Greer was the kind of woman interested in Portland's who's who—and he'd bet dollars to doughnuts she was—then she was bound to blow his cover to Rachel sometime soon.

He had to tell her first. He had to keep her trust, small as it was. Except that he didn't want to see her eyes glaze over when she understood the extent of his wealth. He didn't want to watch the subtle change in her. He didn't want to witness her latent avariciousness. And he knew it would happen. He'd been there too many times before.

Only Barbara, whose family was as well-heeled as his own, hadn't been affected by his wealth. She'd wanted him for his social standing, not his money. At least she'd been totally honest about that, he thought wryly.

"I've got a diet cola coming, if they ever get to it," Rachel apologized.

The harassed waitress overheard her. "In a minute," she said. "Sorry. You want anything?" she added for Ty's benefit.

He would have liked a beer but the hearing was ahead. "How about a crab cocktail?" he said. It came within the minute along with Allison's and Rachel's sodas, and while he ate he listened with half an ear to Allison's tale of a series of mishaps inflicted upon some client at the agency.

"And that wasn't the worst of it," she said with a get-ready-for-this smile curling her lips. "They had to wait three hours on the plane before the mechanical trouble was supposedly fixed. Then the plane takes off, or starts to. They get barreling down the runway, then whammo! The engines are shut down. Back to the gate for more repairs. Ken Davidson was so furious he called *me* from the Honolulu airport, as if I could do something..."

His mind drifted ahead. He wondered what the judge would say to Nathan today. Realizing how tense he was, he physically tried to relax, but every muscle felt tight as a spring.

"Ty?" Rachel asked, watching him curiously.

"What?" He jerked to attention, uncomfortably aware that he'd missed important parts of the conversation.

"Allison was asking about your plans for Oceanside."

"You're really thinking of building a resort here?" Allison eyed him skeptically.

So the tales of the travel-worn tourist had been forsaken in favor of some more information on the Raffertys. Ty glanced at Allison, sizing up what to do next. The bright tone of Rachel's voice slowly penetrated, and he realized she was trying hard to turn his attention toward Allison and away from herself.

His ego felt the wound keenly. Had he been wrong about the mutual attraction between them? Was he going to have to come up with some other plan?

"Maybe," Ty answered Allison flatly.

"Isn't that a little risky? Oceanside isn't exactly a thriving tourist spot."

"It's very risky."

"Is it a family business?" Allison queried, and Ty's stomach muscles tightened.

"No. It's just mine." And thank God for that, Ty thought. He didn't want to offer more information about the Raffertys than he had to. Luckily the Raffertys—specifically Tyrrell I and II—had only dabbled in real estate. They hadn't been involved in construction at all, so he felt relatively safe.

Allison regarded him stonily. With a faint tilt of her head, she conceded defeat. "Well, back to the salt mines. You know, I think I need a vacation. Sending people all over the world is tiring. Maybe I'll go to Caracas."

"Why Caracas?" Rachel asked with a smile.

She waved her hand airily as she slid from the booth. "I don't know. I'll think of a reason later." She dropped a quick, slanted glance down at Ty, her lips curving. "Nice meeting you, Mr. Rafferty. Take care of our Rachel here."

His opinion of her was immediately elevated. "Will do."

Rachel was caught between horror and embarrassment. She didn't like being handed over to Ty Rafferty's safekeeping. She tried to get to her feet, but since Ty was stretched lazily across the booth, looking for all the world like a content jungle cat and blocking her way in the process, Rachel said pointedly, "Excuse me, Ty, but if I don't get back to work, we'll be late."

"Just a second. I want to talk to you."

"I don't have time right now. And I don't like this," she added seriously.

"Don't like what?"

"This feeling that you expect something from me!"

"Is that what I come off like?" He sounded honestly surprised.

"Yes!"

Abruptly he moved his legs, sliding his lean form from the booth. Rachel scrambled out. Feeling like an overreacting female, she said, "You know, you don't have to come with me. It's ridiculous for you to assume you have to."

"I don't assume I have to. I want to."

"Why? *Why?*"

His jaw worked for a moment, tensing reflexively and relaxing. "Because I want to be with you, and since Nathan's your number-one priority, I want to be involved with him, too."

"What is it about me you find so all-powerful attractive?" Rachel asked sardonically.

"Just about everything, Rachel," he answered after a long, thoughtful moment, and she could tell he was speaking the truth.

The courthouse was hot and stuffy. Ty could swear they had the heat turned up full blast. The dry, musty odor of years of legalities seemed to swirl through the room as Nathan stood in front of the judge, the hem of his too-small sport coat quivering, testimony to his nervousness despite his rebellious slouch.

"I hereby sentence you to one hundred hours of community service, Mr. Stone, and one hundred hours of volunteer work at the store where the crime was committed.

The court will contact Mr. Tennyson and reach an equitable work schedule so you can finish in six months."

"Mr. Tennyson?" Nathan's voice sounded thin and scared in the quiet room.

"Since the crime was committed at Mr. Tennyson's store, the court feels it would be in his interest, as well as your own, to pay for this infraction with your time. That's all."

Nathan turned, white-faced, to Rachel, who was seated on Ty's right. She smiled at him tenderly, rising from the bench and meeting him as he came away from the proceedings. Ty followed them outside to the slightly cool June afternoon.

"I won't do it," Nathan said. "I won't work for that old goat."

"Yes, you will," Rachel scolded, her mouth firm.

"What the hell are you doing here?" Nathan exploded, swinging around at Ty.

"Offering support for your mother."

"Yeah, right. Like you don't have other ideas, huh?"

"Nathan, you're going to work for Mr. Tennyson, or they'll send you to a home for juvenile delinquents. Do you want that?" Rachel demanded. "You owe Ty an apology."

"It's all right," Ty tried to insert, but she whirled on him, all glorious fury, her skin flushed, eyes brilliant.

"It's not all right. It's never all right. Now, apologize, Nathan. Do it."

Ty held his breath. The boy stared at the ground. A sense of being in his shoes crept over Ty, a dull pain of remembered adolescence, the fears, the insecurities, of never knowing how to act and whom to trust.

"Sorry," Nathan mumbled, not looking up. He walked away toward the parking lot and Ty's Porsche.

Rachel, who'd been staring at Nathan, tore her eyes away, concentrating on the row of petunias someone had planted along one side of the courthouse. Tears stood in her eyes. Ty watched her until he couldn't watch anymore. He wrapped his arm around her shoulder and pulled her against his chest, holding her. It was as much for himself as her, but he didn't care.

She inhaled a choking breath.

He smoothed her hair with one hand.

Collecting herself, she pulled away, more in control, though she wouldn't look at him. "I've got to get Nathan home."

"Sure."

He drove in silence, slightly bemused by the fact that this seemed to be his role: chauffeur to the Stones. When the Porsche bumped to a stop in front of their home, he wondered how in hell he was going to prolong this meeting.

"Rachel," he murmured when she would have followed Nathan from the car. It seemed to take all her willpower to meet his eyes. "Would you have dinner with me later?"

"I don't think tonight's a good night."

"Is any night a good night?"

"No," she admitted on a choking laugh.

"I want to see you. I don't want to wait."

"Ty..." she murmured brokenly.

He moved on blind emotion, pulling her into his arms, cupping her cheek with one hand, pressing his lips to hers. She didn't resist, she didn't react at all. His mouth moved hungrily over hers. Blood crashed in his head. He couldn't explain and didn't try anymore. He didn't care that it was wrong. It was right.

But when he tried to drag her closer, crushing her to him, she twisted her chin away. "You're too scary," she managed on a shaking breath.

"What do I have to do to make you want to see me?"

"That's the problem. You don't have to *make* me do anything. I already want to."

"Then let me take you to dinner. Whenever you say," he urged.

Silence stretched between them as she hesitated, then forced a shaky smile. "Give me an hour," she said in a low voice, and Ty could have whooped for joy.

## Chapter Six

Whatever had possessed her? Rachel stared into her closet at the meager assortment of clothes and wondered if her denim skirt might not be the nicest thing she owned. Why had she consented to have dinner with Ty? Hadn't she determined that she wouldn't get involved with him on any level?

And what about that kiss?

Weakness invaded her lower limbs and she sank down on the edge of the bed. Her heart somersaulted in remembered desire. She was nuts, truly nuts. She was an idiot.

"He's dangerous to you," she said softly to the empty room. Muttering to herself, she yanked off her denim skirt and blouse and changed into a pair of tan slacks and matching T-shirt. Nothing fancy, but nice. Just like me, she thought, wrinkling her nose.

Why was he chasing her? There had to be some yet-undisclosed reason. She had nothing to offer him but herself, and he didn't know her well enough to want her for that. She wasn't vain and egotistical enough to believe she could catch his eye—and capture his heart—out of a few chance meetings. So what did he really want?

Loud music throbbed from Nathan's room. Rachel could feel it thrumming inside herself, heightening her senses. She recalled the way Ty's lips molded to hers, and she groaned aloud, covering her face. You know better than this, she reminded herself sternly. You're not even sexually responsive.

*Oh, yeah?* a voice inside her head smirked.

Drawing a deep breath, Rachel expelled it slowly. Okay, that wasn't entirely true anymore. Forcing herself to explore this unexpected—and not entirely welcome—discovery, she closed her eyes. Her skin felt sensitized just at the *memory* of his kiss. She wanted to die of humiliation. She couldn't escape the truth. Ty Rafferty turned her on.

"Oh, brother," she muttered on a choked laugh, jumping to her feet. Inside herself something was awakening and she didn't like it one bit. It scared her. She was afraid of these new feelings of vulnerability and excitement, of wanting the minutes to hurry by until that next time she'd see him, of making her focus on loving a man.

She wasn't going to do it!

After brushing her hair until her scalp ached, Rachel strode briskly down the hall to Nathan's room. She shoved her thoughts aside. She couldn't deal with her feelings about Ty. It was easier to deal with her hardheaded son.

"Nathan! *Nathan!*" Rachel rapped loudly on the door.

The music slowly diminished to dull background noise. "Yeah?"

"I'm going out to dinner with Ty. There's some hamburger in the refrigerator, and some lettuce, I think. I don't have any buns, but I've got bread...."

When there was no answer, Rachel twisted the knob, making a great racket of it to warn Nathan she was entering his room, his privacy, the danger zone.

This must be where cassette tapes and old jeans go to die, she thought, trying to avoid looking at the mess. She gazed instead at Nathan, whose dark eyes were filled with resentment. What now? she wondered, the moment before she realized he wasn't alone. Matthew Dayton—he of the multipierced ear and uptight mother—was sprawled across the floor, eyeing Rachel warily.

Her heart sank. She had heard Nathan let Matthew into the house, but seeing him now made her ask, "Does your mother know you're here?"

"No." His insolence was razor sharp.

"How come I'm not surprised. You'd better call her, because she already let me know she doesn't want you anywhere near Nathan."

"Mom!" Nathan burst out, hurt.

"I didn't make this rule, but I've got to abide by it. Go call your mom, Matt."

"No way," Matt said sullenly.

"Then you'll have to leave." Two pairs of angry eyes fixed themselves furiously on Rachel. Guilt transference. These guys were masters at it. "Go ahead and be mad. Think terrible thoughts about me. It doesn't change the fact that your mother would have a fit if she knew you were here," she said, lifting a palm toward Matt.

"She wouldn't know, if you didn't tell her," Nathan suggested uneasily.

"Oh, right. That's just what I want. To make an enemy of someone I don't even know." She flung out her arm, pointing down the hall in the direction of the kitchen phone. "Go on."

The doorbell rang. "Ty's here," she said, her heart kicking uncomfortably.

"I don't like him," Nathan declared, switching subjects instantly, his expression darkening. "What's he doing here? What does he want?"

"He's taking me to dinner. Come on, Matt. Get a move on."

Matt reluctantly pulled his long legs beneath him.

"I wish he'd just leave us alone!" Nathan yelled, storming to his feet, startling her with his sudden switch to jealous child. She chased after him, but Nathan had already flung open the front door by the time she caught up with him.

"Hello, Ty," Rachel greeted him with false gaiety. She practically shoved Nathan out of the way. Nathan could act like a spoiled brat to her, but she was sick of it in front of Ty. "Come on in." Grabbing Nathan's arm, she squeezed tightly, warning him to behave.

Through the screen, Ty gazed quizzically at Nathan. It was obvious the boy had something to say, but since Nathan seemed to have developed a sudden case of muteness, the two just stared at one another.

A strange déjà vu broke goose bumps on Rachel's skin. She tried to figure it out, but it eluded her consciousness.

Nathan stepped back, arms folded over his chest in silent judgment. With a sigh, Rachel pushed open the door, allowing Ty entry. "I'll just be a minute," she murmured. "I've got some unfinished business to take care of before we go."

Ty nodded, his dark eyes measuring Nathan. "Okay."

Rachel tore her gaze from them to Matt, who was hovering at the corner of the hall, trying to look tough but succeeding only in showing just how uncomfortable he was. His shoulders were slumped forward, his hands were in his pockets, his gaze glued to the carpet.

"Matt, I've got to insist—" Rachel began, but he cut her off.

"All right, I'll call my mom."

"Phone's in the kitchen." Rachel answered. She turned back to Ty. "Do you have some place in mind you'd like to go?"

"Anyplace is fine. You pick." His gaze swept past her to Matt's disappearing figure. In the lull that followed, Rachel heard Matt dial the phone and speak in sullen monosyllables to the person at the other end of the line.

"How about the restaurant at the Wavecrest?" she suggested. "It's good food."

"Is something wrong?" Ty asked.

Nathan snorted but didn't look at either of them.

"No. I've just some arrangements to finalize."

Nathan flung himself onto the couch, glaring suspiciously at Ty. Ty slid him a thoughtful look just as Matt yelled, "Mrs. Stone? My mom wants to talk to you!"

Rachel groaned and closed her eyes. She looked as if she were praying for divine intervention, Ty thought, wondering what crisis he'd stumbled upon. Without a word Rachel headed for the phone. Matt returned to the living room. He and Nathan exchanged meaningful glances, which heightened Ty's curiosity.

"So why're you here?"

Ty jerked around, surprised that Nathan had addressed him directly. "Here in this room. Or here in Oceanside?"

"Here, period."

He shrugged. "A lot of reasons. Why? You got a problem with that?"

"Maybe." Nathan was hedging his bets.

Silence settled while Nathan struggled to find more ways to act tough. Ty could hear Rachel. In a cool, clear voice, she said, "Whatever you want. I'm not interested in arguing with you, Mrs. Dayton. I'll make sure Matt gets home. In fact, I'll ask a friend to drop him off on our way to dinner." A pause. "No, it's no problem. Really."

She hung up before Mrs. Dayton could have responded. Her footsteps sounded across the kitchen floor, then she was gazing silently at Ty, her expression veiled. "Do you mind if we take Matt home on the way?"

"That's fine. What about Nathan?"

"Nathan?"

"Think he'd like to join us?"

"You *want* him to?"

He almost laughed at her disbelief. Walking toward her, he said softly, "Whatever you want. You're the one who's interested in keeping the situation—safe."

Rachel focused on Nathan, who was pretending hard that he hadn't heard a word spoken about him. "I'll ask him. But don't expect miracles."

Then, before Ty could do what he'd been longing to since the moment he stepped inside her house, namely hug her, offer support or touch her in some way, she eased away from him, making it crystal clear that her guard was still up where he was concerned.

Well, he had all evening to change her mind.

Two hours later Ty sat across from Rachel at one of the Wavecrest's restaurant tables that overlooked the ocean. Nathan had refused to join them. *Adamantly* refused to join them, in fact, which was a mixed blessing. Nathan's surly company would have changed the tenor of the evening. Though Ty was anxious to draw the boy out, he was actually happier to have Rachel all to himself.

She sat pensively staring out the window, toying with her food. Her hair was clipped back, and the thin strands of red were heightened by the dim lighting, turning her crown into a dark burgundy flame. Her face was shadowed and thoughtful. She hadn't said more than three words since they'd dropped Matt off.

In fact, the car ride had been accomplished in near silence. Matt had been utterly quiet. The woman waiting for him on the deck of her home in a new development about two miles outside Oceanside looked as if she could eat nails and still be hungry. Spying Ty's car, she strode angrily up to the driver's window. Amused, Ty slid the glass down and lifted his brows expectantly as Matt climbed from the cramped back seat.

Whatever she'd expected, it wasn't him. One look and the woman's mouth dropped open. Then Rachel said in a steely voice, "Was there something you wanted?" and Mrs. Dayton glared at her before turning away.

Now, studying Rachel's troubled features, Ty resisted the urge to cover her hand with his own. Instead, he asked, "What was that all about with Matt's mother?"

She seemed to drag her thoughts back with an effort. "Oh. Matt can't be friends with Nathan. She thinks Nathan gets him in too much trouble."

"Really? She looked like the warm, understanding type to me."

The smile she shot him set his blood racing. "If I knew you better, I'd tell you exactly what that woman is."

"Tell me anyway," he said, intrigued.

"No." She laughed. "Anyway, she's the least of my worries. I've got to get my car back tomorrow and I'm not sure how to pay the bill." Immediately after she spoke, Rachel's face changed. She clearly hadn't meant to say what was on her mind. "But Gordy's got the easy-payment plan," she hurriedly added, trying to keep it light. "And I've been okayed on a salary advance, if I want to take it. No big deal. So how's the crab?"

"Great."

"Are you staying here again?" Her gesture included the Wavecrest.

Ty nodded. "It's not a bad place."

"The best in Oceanside."

"Rachel..."

"Hmm?"

"Do you need a loan?"

Her reaction was cataclysmic. "From *you?*" she demanded, aghast. "No! Absolutely not. I didn't mean to tell you my troubles—they're not that bad. I've got credit cards. I can pay my bills. I pay my own way."

"Okay." He was a little surprised by her vehemence. "But if you need—"

"I don't borrow money, Mr. Rafferty."

Those hazel eyes were full of reproach and anger. Ty's gaze fell to her lips, tight now, but luscious nonetheless. "You ready to leave?" he asked, thrusting his plate aside.

Her food was only half eaten; neither of them had possessed much of an appetite. Rachel nodded and preceded Ty out the door of the restaurant. She waited, shivering slightly in the cool twilight, while he unlocked her door.

"Where are we going?" she asked as they turned onto the street in the opposite direction from her house. Ahead the road curved down around the cliff, offering a glimpse of the ocean.

"For a drive. Is that all right?"

"Sure."

As they headed northward, Rachel stared out the window at the snatches of ruffled white waves and beach that appeared through the trees. Stupid and dangerous though it was, she was glad the evening wasn't over yet. She wanted to be with Ty.

"Rachel..."

The way he said her name was enough to trap her breath in her throat. Glancing his way, her heart jolted at the serious look on his face.

"I haven't been completely honest with you."

Here it comes, she thought painfully, suddenly not wanting to know.

"I haven't told you all that much about myself. In fact, I didn't intend to go into my family history at all, but I'm sure your friend Allison recognized the Rafferty name. It won't be long until she fills you in on the details."

"What details?" Rachel murmured. "I'm not certain I'm ready for some deep, dark secret."

"Well, I don't think it'll be anything that you'll object to." His sardonic tone wasn't lost on Rachel. "There's a little more to it than just commercial real estate. The Raffertys have been around for years. I think they were wealthy even before they planted roots in Portland. They just grew wealthier.

"By the time I arrived on the planet, there wasn't a hell of a lot to do except spend money. My father felt I ought to do just that, but I can't. So I'm in construction."

Rachel didn't immediately respond. She'd half expected something like this, but hearing it made it seem even less real, somehow. She didn't know people like Ty Rafferty. They were out of her experience. "So what are you doing here with me?" she heard herself ask.

He pulled to a stop at a lookout point at the side of the road. Cutting the engine, he half turned and laid an arm over the back of her seat, but he made no move to increase their intimacy. "Damned if I know," he admitted. "I like you. You're not like any woman I've ever met. And I'm . . . compelled to keep seeing you."

"Compelled." Rachel's mouth was dry.

"Yes, compelled."

She choked out a nervous laugh. "And where do you think this relationship could go?"

"I don't know. I'd like to find out."

"Ty, I've already told you—"

"I know. You're not willing to let a man in your life. Why not take a chance?"

She held up one hand, hoping to slow down the thunderous race of her pulse. "No. Wait. I won't believe there isn't some woman in your life. One more suited to you."

"There isn't. I was engaged once, but I'm not anymore."

"What happened?" Rachel seized on this new topic like a lifeline.

"I'd consented to marrying her for all the wrong reasons. Because my father asked me to."

The way he said "my father" pricked Rachel's nerves. There was obviously no love lost between Tyrrell II and III. "And what did your father say when you broke the engagement?"

"My father's dead. Has been for several years. I'm the only Rafferty male left."

"Well, like I said, this is all very interesting, but I don't see where it can have any effect on me."

"Don't you?"

His tone turned silky. Rachel regarded him helplessly, knowing she was rapidly losing control of the situation. "Do you do this often? Pick up women and try to impress them with your money?"

The arrow hit its mark. He flushed. "I've never done it before."

She believed him. Why, she couldn't say, but she knew he was telling the truth.

His gaze slowly swept her face, fastening on her lips. Rachel trembled in spite of her need to remain cool. "I'm way out of my depth," he said softly, so softly she could scarcely hear him.

She eased back, away from his magnetism. "You're not the only one."

"Take a chance, Rachel. I am."

His hand slid up her arm, his other one gently turning her cheek his way until she felt captured, unable to escape the seductive questions in his dark eyes. Her own eyes focused on the sensual curve of his mouth. Heat flooded her at the thought of kissing him. One kiss? What could it hurt? And she wanted that feeling back, to see if it was real or only her imagination.

She moved forward slightly, without conscious thought. Ty's hand cupped her chin, drawing her forward, his mouth unerringly finding hers, moving gently at first, then with increased fervor.

Rachel went limp, both with desire and disbelief. *This* was what it was all about? How come she'd never felt it before? Why had it taken all these years to discover what everyone raved about? Were there other women like herself who never, ever knew? Who lived sane, moderately happy, passionless lives?

"Oh, God," she murmured achingly, tearing her lips from his.

"What's wrong?"

"Nothing. Everything. Oh, God." She laughed, her soul aching.

His arms surrounded her, dragging her close, but the confines of the car prevented an intimacy Rachel was certain she wasn't prepared for anyway.

"I'm a mess, Ty. I've got a life so unraveled it'll never be put together right. I've got a son who's in trouble, a mortgage payment I can't make and a lot of guilt over the way I felt about my husband."

"What do you mean?"

"I didn't love Richard. Ever. Not like I should have. Nathan's the one I loved. And now I see...that...marrying Richard wasn't what I should have done." She swallowed, closing her eyes against his face, his touch, his being. "I should have waited for a man I loved. It would have been different."

"There's nothing stopping you now, is there?" he questioned softly.

"Only Nathan. And the fact that the first man I've been attracted to is—I don't know—a multimillionaire? I'm not Cinderella. This doesn't happen to people like me."

"If I wasn't rich—"

"You'd still be out of my league." Rachel smiled. "And you know it. You've got enough pluses without a fortune to back them up."

Ty frowned. His eyes probed hers as if he found her incomprehensible. He kissed her again. Lightly this time, but with passion still smoldering. Lifting his head, he let his thumb trace her mouth, running the pad of it over her lower lip in a way that made Rachel go weak at the knees. Touching him wasn't working. It made her brain stall. She tried to pull back farther, but his arms tightened, preventing her.

"You sell yourself short," he said in a low voice. "You're beautiful. And though I shouldn't do what I'm doing, I refuse to stop. Immediate gratification. My worst failing. I want you, and I want you now. Believe me, when it comes to women, this isn't like me at all."

The last came out as if he were furious with himself. Maybe he was. Rachel searched her mind for some response, but there was no time. He leaned over her, his chest pressing against her breasts. She made a muffled sound of protest, but his mouth began its magic once more, his tongue slipping between her parted lips, stabbing in quick, lightning strokes against the tip of her own tongue.

Rachel moaned. Her hands slid around his back, encountering rock-hard muscles. Construction. No wasting away. No leading a spoiled, soft life.

His hand slipped beneath her cotton T-shirt, curving around her rib cage. Her heart was beating so hard it sounded like the roar of the ocean in her ears. His fingers cupped the mound of her breast. Her nipple surged forward. She wanted to rip off her clothes and rub her body against his, a thought so wanton and wild and new that it shocked her to reality.

"Ty!" she choked.

"Hmm." His mouth had relinquished hers, his lips grazing the soft skin at her neck, his dark head moving inexorably downward to where his hand molded and squeezed her breast.

"I can't. I can't!"

"Neither can I, in this car," he murmured on suppressed laughter.

"No, I can't at all!"

He raised his eyes to hers, heavy lidded. He examined her closely, searching for answers in such an intense way that Rachel could have been seduced by that look alone. "You're afraid of making love, or afraid of me?"

"Afraid of making love to you."

"Afraid of the—aftermath?"

She felt ridiculously near laughter. Hysterical laughter. "Afraid of the *during!*"

Unexpectedly he grinned, that unfairly dazzling smile that threatened to be the bane of Rachel's sanity. "You're so blasted honest it's dangerous." With a slowness that made her nerves scream, he laid a delicate kiss on her mouth, then moved away, raking his hands through his hair and closing his eyes, gathering his control in a manner that she was coming to know. "But this isn't the time or the place." He started the engine and backed the car onto the street.

At Rachel's door he reached out to touch her arm. "I'm willing to go more slowly, but I'm not willing to give up. Tell me you want to see me again."

She swallowed. "I want to see you again."

"Rachel..."

His urgent tone arrested her as she was stepping over the threshold. She gazed at him, instinctively aware that even though nothing had happened, it would, very soon.

"Take care."

June's rain changed to July's sweltering heat. It rose from the pavement in shimmering waves. It filled the air with hot dust. It settled in Ty's house like a suffocating blanket and made him long for the cool, moist feel of the coast.

The pavement of downtown Portland sparkled, tiny bits of glass worked into the cement creating the illusion of diamond particles glittering against the heat. Raintree's office building was like a refrigerator. Ty actually shivered as he rode up to the fifteenth floor.

"Okay, what?" he asked, striding impatiently across the lush carpet.

"Take a look."

The paper Raintree slid across his desk was a photostatic copy of one Nathan Williams's birth certificate. Dazedly Ty read the names of Nathan's parents: Julia Williams and Tyrrell Rafferty III.

She'd actually written in his name fifteen years earlier, at the time of Nathan's birth.

"It could be fake," Gerald warned.

*"What the hell do you mean?"* Ty thundered.

"She could have written it in to cover someone else. Now it suits her to follow through with you."

"You haven't met Nathan," Ty said flatly. "That boy's my son."

Gerald gazed unhappily at his empty paper-clip holder. "Maybe."

Ty relaxed. "Well, at least you admit it's a possibility. That's progress."

"I think you should talk to Julia direct," Gerald went on as if he hadn't heard Ty. "Forget her attorney. You need to hear it from her own lips."

"Good idea," Ty agreed, surprised at Raintree's change of heart.

"You're a good judge of character, Ty. I don't think you'd let her scam you, no matter how much you want this boy to be yours."

"Thanks for the vote of confidence," he said dryly.

"Her number's in the file."

"What is London? Eight or nine hours ahead of us?"

Raintree nodded. "Call around eleven tonight. You'll catch her in the morning."

"Ty?" Amazement radiated across the transatlantic line. "Is it really you?"

"You're not really surprised I'm calling, are you, Julia?"

"Just a moment."

Her voice was just as girlish as he remembered. He thought briefly of the few weeks they'd spent together and realized he knew next to nothing about her.

She was talking to someone else, her hand over the phone. Ty heard a child's voice answer, then Julia was back on the line. "I have to get my daughter ready for our trip to France," she said distractedly. "My husband isn't here right now. He's . . . not aware."

"Not aware of—Nathan," Ty finished for her when it was clear she was struggling to continue.

Silence. Then, quickly, "That's right."

"Like I wasn't aware of Nathan. Give me a reason I should believe you, Julia."

"Oh, Ty." She sighed heavily, regret echoing poignantly across the line. "I wanted to tell you. I really did. But your father's a very persuasive man."

The hairs on the back of Ty's neck lifted. "My father?"

"My parents cut me off without a penny when they found out I was pregnant. A tough break for someone who wasn't used to living on a budget. But I wouldn't have an abortion. I wanted that baby!"

Her voice had lowered with each syllable. "You gave that baby up," he reminded her.

"He paid me to!" she whispered fiercely. "Oh, my God! My husband's here! I've got to go!"

"Wait, Julia! Who paid you?" he demanded, though the sick feeling in his stomach said he already knew the answer.

"Your father, Ty. *Your father!*"

The line abruptly went dead.

"You really want to fly a kite with me?" Nathan asked, making no effort at all to hide his disbelief and growing horror that yes, his mother was serious.

"Well, I don't feel like listening to rap music, or going down to the Fun Center and wasting money I don't have, or watching girls. It was all I could come up with besides staring at the TV together. Nathan, we've got to get back to basics."

"Great," he muttered.

Rachel, who'd been attempting to untangle the string on the kite Richard had purchased for Nathan when he was eight years old, sighed heavily. "I got the car back, but it pushed my credit limit to the max. I'm two weeks late on the mortgage. If I take an advance at work, I'm just buying time. The crunch is here. Now. I need to talk to someone and that someone is you. We need to help each other.''

Nathan looked alarmed. ''If I didn't have that community service work, I could get a real job instead of cleaning up litter and delivering food to old people who can't get around.''

''Nathan, you've got to pay your dues. And I don't want your money if I can help it. Besides—'' she smiled ''—old people who can't get around need to eat, too.''

Nathan shot her a look.

''Actually, *I* was thinking of getting a second job. Part-time on weekends. Just for a while,'' she continued. ''Maybe six months or so.''

''I'd never see you then.''

Rachel whipped her head around in amazement. She'd been thinking aloud, working through her difficult financial situation. The last thing she'd expected was to hear something human and caring from her volatile son.

''Well, it's true,'' he said defensively. ''You're the one who wants us to do stuff together.''

Rachel smiled. ''We can't do stuff together if we can't afford it. Don't worry. I'll think of something. But for now, are you the least interested in kite flying . . . ?''

His answering look said, ''No, but I'll humor you,'' and Rachel, refusing to buckle under, seized the opportunity and led the way down to the beach. They spent nearly an hour trying to get the kite airborne, Rachel finally giving up in laughing disgust. Nathan seemed more relaxed and, once committed to the job, actually was quite determined to fly the kite. Rachel called encouragement as he raced back and forth, stopping occasionally to patiently unwind the string again, then pounding the sand once more.

It was late Saturday afternoon by the time they trudged up the cliff path again. Rex's barking greeted their ears as soon as they rounded the first bend.

"Someone's at the house," Nathan said.

*Ty.* Rachel knew it as if someone had whispered his name in her ear.

So, apparently, did Nathan, for he turned accusingly her way, his dark hair wind-tossed around his angry eyes. "You invited him back, didn't you?"

"I've never invited him anywhere, but he seems determined to come. And I like him," she admitted.

"Well, I don't. He's got something up his sleeve."

"Maybe we should give him a chance."

"A chance to do what?" he asked softly, and the quality of his voice sent a frisson of awareness down Rachel's spine that bothered her. She didn't like Nathan delving into her personal life. He had no right.

Or did he?

At the crest of the hill, Ty's familiar form came into view. He wore gray denim jeans and his bomber jacket over a white shirt, the darkly tanned skin of his throat contrasting attractively with the crisp white collar.

"Hi," he greeted them, his gaze lingering not on Rachel but on Nathan. "Rex is practically in a lather over me walking across your property."

"He didn't try to attack you, did he?" Rachel asked quickly.

"No, just barked like he was ready to rip out my throat. I stayed to the perimeter of his chain. How's it going, Nathan?"

Nathan stared belligerently at Ty. "Okay."

Ty nodded thoughtfully.

"I didn't know you were coming back this weekend. Did you just get here?" Rachel asked.

"About an hour ago."

They fell in step beside each other on the way to the house, Nathan keeping a good five feet to one side of Rachel and as far from Ty as possible without incurring his mother's wrath.

"Still checking out sites for a resort?"

"Actually, that wasn't quite the truth, either." Ty held the back door open for her, but Nathan strolled over to Rex, patting the German shepherd's head and keeping his back to them.

"You're not looking for beachfront property?" Rachel questioned when Ty was beside her in the kitchen. He was staring out the window, however, his gaze focused sharply on Nathan.

"Not really. The truth is, when I first got here I was looking for something else, and now I think I've found it."

"What do you mean?"

He swept her with a look that was both amused and full of the unfulfilled expectations his kisses had first promised. "I was looking for something...different. Something with meaning in this life. And I'm surprised because I think I've discovered it."

Rachel chewed on her bottom lip. "You mean—me?" she asked a bit anxiously.

He studied her for so long that Rachel's nerves were screaming by the time he crossed the room and gathered her in his arms. "Spend the night with me," he said in a curiously tortured voice.

"I—I can't. I can't leave Nathan...."

"Then be with me for a few hours, at least."

"This is going too fast, Ty," Rachel said a bit desperately.

"It's not going fast enough," he disagreed. The next moment he dropped his arms, shook his head, then raked his hands through his hair, shooting her a crooked, apologetic smile. "Never mind. You're right. My priorities are getting screwed up."

"Your priorities?" She was totally at a loss to understand him.

"Do you want me, Rachel?" he asked suddenly. He was so tense, she realized her answer mattered very much.

"Want you—sexually?" she hazarded, coloring slightly.

"Yes."

She nodded. "But I shouldn't."

He relaxed. "Neither should I."

She was about to ask what he meant, since he was the one hell-bent on starting this relationship, when Nathan entered the room. He glanced wordlessly at the two of them, and Ty said, "I'm taking your mother out tonight. You're welcome to join us, but . . ."

Rachel shot a surprised glance at him, and realized instantly that Ty had calculated Nathan's reaction before ever offering the invitation.

"No, thanks, man. I'm busy." With that he plunked down in front of the set and turned the volume to megadecibels.

"Let's go," Ty said softly to Rachel, and knowing she was taking a risky step into her future, she went to change her clothes.

## Chapter Seven

He was embarking on a dangerous journey. It was lunacy and he knew it, but he'd spoken the truth: he was compelled to it. He wanted Nathan and he wanted Rachel, and some subconscious force insisted he bind them both to him any way he could.

Nathan was tricky. Only time would win him over.

Rachel was trickier. He had to make her want him in every way or she would be his undoing. In the final countdown, she would decide whom Nathan should be with.

Twisting his brandy snifter around in his hands, he glanced at Rachel, who was standing by the balcony rail of his motel room. He worried about her growing silence. At her house it had seemed so simple. He wanted to go to bed with her and damn the consequences. Thoughts of her had haunted him throughout dinner. While they'd strolled through shops and she'd purchased a kite, of all things, his mind was crowded with images of Rachel in his arms, lying naked beneath him on a bed. And when they'd returned to the Wavecrest, to his room, he'd been so certain the evening could have just one ending.

But now...?

They'd been standing on the deck together for three-quarters of an hour while tension had mounted by the second and conversation had stalled. She hadn't touched her brandy; he'd drunk two glasses. She didn't look at him, while his eyes were all over her.

Should he follow his instincts or try to listen to his brain—the one organ that seemed to be absolutely out of commission these days?

Wisps of brown hair shot with red and gold escaped their loose French plait and drifted sensuously along her cheekbone and the curve of her chin. Ty wondered if there was some distinct flaw in his character. The one woman he shouldn't, couldn't have was the one he wanted.

Her arms were folded, the brandy snifter tilting precariously from one hand. "I'm not sure I could survive an affair," she said suddenly, startling him with her objective tone. "I never thought I'd want one, but now that I do, I don't know..."

"You do want an affair?" he questioned, hoping he'd heard her right.

"I never wanted a sexual relationship with any man. Until you," she admitted, shooting him an embarrassed glance coupled with a sweet smile.

"What about your husband?"

A shadow crossed her eyes. "It wasn't there."

"What wasn't there?"

"*It.*" She drew a breath, glanced down at her forgotten glass and took a swallow of brandy.

He swept his hand across her cheek, feeling the silk of her hair through his fingers. "But it's here now."

"Ty..."

"Hmm?"

"Don't ever lie to me. If I keep thinking I know what I'm doing, then I'll be okay. But I can't fool myself. I don't want to be reckless and blind, too."

Her words were urgent, tense. Ty thought of his secret. The future opened up with blinding clarity. He would lose her. Lose Nathan. Lose everything. He couldn't chance it.

She gazed up at him, her long lashes casting shadows on her cheek. His hands cupped her chin of their own volition, his thumbs stroking her skin. He leaned down, and her mouth tilted toward his, soft lips trembling beneath his.

Rachel sensed his reluctance and wondered about it, but it lasted only a second. A moment. Then his arms surrounded her and his chest pressed hard against her breasts. Her heartbeat thudded, drowning her with each beat. His hands slid down her back to her hips. He pulled her against him, and the hard length of him shot showers of desire through her.

She was no novice to sex, but she was a virgin when it came to passion. Dazedly she let him guide her to the bed, lost in a maelstrom of feelings she'd thought only happened to other people.

This is right, she thought, reaching up to bring his head down to hers when she was lying on the covers, Ty bending over her. She felt him grin beneath her lips, grin at her first aggressive move.

"You're laughing," she accused softly.

"You're incredible," he answered, sliding down beside her.

"I bet you say that to all the girls."

"I do," he averred. "But it only works on some."

She was startled by his answer before she realized he was teasing her. He turned her face to his, staring lazily into her wide eyes. "You told me not to lie," he reminded her quietly.

"Have there been a lot of women?"

"Not a one while I was engaged. Not even Barbara. And none since then."

"Barbara? She was your fiancée?"

He nodded.

"How long have you been unengaged?"

He brushed his mouth on hers, lightly, coaxingly. She realized he was giving his answer a lot of thought. "A few weeks."

"A few *weeks?*" She struggled upward, but he simply pinned her to the bed, holding her hands down to her sides, lying atop her, forcing her to meet his gaze.

"After I met you," he admitted hoarsely, and Rachel couldn't believe her ears.

"I don't believe you broke off your engagement because of me! You don't even know me!"

"That's where you're wrong. I do know you. And after one day with you I realized what I'd been trying not to face—I didn't love Barbara. I never did. And I couldn't marry her. Is that so wrong? To face the truth?"

His limbs held hers motionless. Their weight sent signals up her body, sensual signals pulsing inside her. Rachel wanted to keep her head, but she was fast losing sight of why. What did it matter? He was unattached and he was here with her and she wanted him.

"I get the feeling I'm being seduced," she whispered.

"Good." He smiled, then bent down and captured her mouth with his.

There was no more time for indecision. Ty was intent on making love to her, and Rachel felt boneless and weak beneath the onslaught of his kisses. Her desire to touch him overcame her inhibitions, and she slid her hands up his back, tentatively exploring. The confines of his shirt bothered her. She yanked it from his jeans, her fingers delving beneath the cotton to feel taut, smooth skin over fluid muscles.

His tongue found her ear, touching softly. Rachel's blood ran hotly, and she moaned. She didn't want to wait anymore. She wanted it—*him*—quick and fast, and the torment seemed at once too much and too exquisitely painful.

One hand held his nape; she dragged his mouth back to hers. Ty's breathing was fast and ragged. "Rachel," he murmured, pulling back long enough to gather the tail of her T-shirt and pull it gently over her head. She was suspended in a kind of horrified fascination as his dark gaze devoured the mounds of her breasts beneath her bra. One hand covered one breast, pressing hard, but gentle, too.

"Rachel," he said again, as if amazed.

"Make love to me."

Her urgent tone penetrated his own dazed senses. His lips twisted. "Let's do this together," he said softly, and grabbed her wrists, placing her palms flat on his crisp white shirt. "Unbutton my shirt."

With fingers made clumsy by a mixture of panic and desire, Rachel slid the buttons free one by one. With an expertise that troubled her slightly, he unhooked her bra and swept it aside. Then he laid his bare chest down on hers and stared into her eyes, smiling.

A distant part of herself rebelled. This was too easy. Too pat. Ty Rafferty was used to getting what he wanted, and though he definitely wanted her—today, at least—it didn't necessarily mean she should comply. There was no love in that wicked smile. Just an understanding as old as time.

But it was too late for mistakes. He kissed her mouth, stifling protests before they ever fully coalesced inside her. He kissed her neck, and she arched upward, begging for fulfillment in a way she never had with her husband. He kissed her breasts, his mouth closing on each swollen peak in turn, sucking.

"Ty!" she gasped, shocked.

His dark head moved lower. This was new territory for Rachel, and she wound her fingers in his hair to stop him, reacting with involuntary panic.

He shifted atop her, his hands holding her hips tightly against his rigid desire, moving gently in a way that turned Rachel's bones to liquid. Dreamily she waited in a kind of suspended euphoria as he deftly removed the rest of her clothes.

But then he placed her hands on his belt buckle. "Help me," he ordered softly.

Rachel looked at Ty's bare chest. She unbuckled his belt. She refused to listen to the doubts that haunted her like dark shadows. She pressed her lips to the taut muscles of his stomach, and his hands plunged into her hair, holding her still.

"Never mind," he groaned with suppressed laughter. "I don't think I can take it."

Moments later he joined her on the bed, his nakedness wound around her own. This was so different from the almost mechanical lovemaking she'd been used to that Rachel could only stare at him in wonder.

"What?" he asked softly.

"I don't know. This is so—wonderful."

For a moment, in his face, she thought she saw something change. A reckoning overcame him. It was reflected in his dark eyes. And when he next kissed her, it was with tenderness.

The tempo changed, increased. He beat a trail of kisses across her midriff, and this time she shifted to allow him. "You're beautiful, Rachel," he told her. "And warm and responsive. Don't believe you're not."

"I know. I know."

Her whole body felt aflame. His mouth was everywhere, exploring the secret places of her body, stroking and caressing and awakening a strong sexual urge she'd never known existed. Her hands began an exploration of their own, sliding through the crisp dark chest hairs that arrowed downward, her nails biting into the bunched muscles of his shoulders, her fingers instinctively moving downward, caressing him in a way that dragged a shattered gasp from his throat.

Poised above her, Ty's face was dark with passion and harsh with suppressed longing. She closed her eyes, her lips opening against his jawline, against the strongly corded muscles of his neck. Ty moaned softly in his throat, his mouth hungrily searching hers. He lifted her hips, plunged into her in one swift movement. Rachel gasped, shocked. There was neither pain nor embarrassment. Just a thrilling, thrilling desire that had her clinging to him, wrapping herself around him.

And Ty, who had been bent on his own sexual pleasure, and hers, found himself unable to draw out the moment for maximum satisfaction. She'd said she thought she was being seduced, but the tables had turned. Like a teenager with unbridled rampant emotion and enthusiasm, desire pounded in his head, driving him forward, into Rachel, again and again. He groaned, feeling her warmth and gentleness and yes, innocence, surround him, and it was intoxicating. Unbelievable.

He climaxed so quickly it was embarrassing. In a feverish rapture he poured into her, thrusting deep into her femininity. There was no time for Rachel to do the same. He didn't give her time. He simply took what he wanted most, what had driven him crazy since the moment he'd met her, and left her in a state of frustration, her fingers gently stroking his sweat soaked brow.

Ty was shattered. For her, and for himself. What in God's name was wrong with him?

She started struggling gently against his weight. Lifting his head, he gazed down into her beautiful face. "You're heavy," she said, flushing.

"I'm sorry."

"Sorry?"

"Sorry that I didn't give you time. I'm amazed. That hasn't happened to me in years."

Her blank look stopped him short. Balancing his weight on his forearms, he brushed mahogany silk strands away from her face. "You don't know what I'm talking about?"

"Yes. Yes, I do...."

"What am I talking about?"

Rachel inhaled a long, long breath. "You expected something more from me. I hate to disillusion you, but it doesn't happen for me. I thought—"

"You thought?"

"I thought with you it might be different."

Ty's face changed expression. Very seriously he said, "I think it is different already." Rolling onto his side, he pulled her with him, cradling her head against his chest. "No, don't leave," he murmured when she made a sound of protest and tried to get up. "Give it some time. It might be different yet...."

Hours later, Rachel rested her head against Ty's chest and watched a brilliant orange sun sink blazingly into the horizon through the sliding glass door of Ty's room. Her thoughts were far removed from the view. Smiling to herself, she pressed her face into his chest and his arm tightened possessively around her.

He'd been right. It *had* been different. She'd wanted to leave as soon as their lovemaking ended, but he'd insisted she stay. He'd entertained her with stories of his family. His sister, Kathleen, who was from all accounts an incredibly coldhearted bitch with a mind like a cash register. His father, whose obsessive need for power surpassed even that of Ty's grandfather, a known egomaniac. His mother, the only member of his family who received any tenderness or love from his raspy voice. Whether the stories were true or not, Rachel had no clue. But Ty wove them in such a way that she forgot that she was supposed to be embarrassed, or filled with guilt, or dreading the morrow.

And then he started making love to her again. She'd protested at first; she and Richard had scarcely made love twice in one month, never in the space of a few hours. But desire could be an insatiable beast, Rachel learned to her consternation, and when Ty moved within her, intent on making her feel something glorious, something always outside her reach, Rachel found herself gasping and clutching him, trying to pull him deeper inside her until her desperate need to increase their intimacy suddenly brought her to the brink of trembling fulfillment. She cried out in ecstasy and surprise, her legs and arms entwined with his as he plunged deep inside her, probing the essence of her being, and her moans of need were answered by his groan of pleasure.

"Ty," Rachel had murmured over and over again. "Ty, Ty, Ty," and he answered with rhythmic strokes that sent her spinning over the edge into a kaleidoscope of fiery erotic pleasures.

She felt his answer as he drove fiercely into her, his body jerking convulsively from his own pleasure.

"Rachel," he'd murmured shakily, and then nothing more was said for long, long, dreamy minutes as Rachel dared to fantasize having this man fall in love with her. By all accounts he was halfway there. Clearly this lovemaking had affected him as deeply as it had her.

Her moments of delicious introspection abruptly came to an end when Ty suddenly shifted, levering himself onto one elbow beside her. His expression was serious and aloof, somehow. Her heart contracted. Had she misread him? Had she been wrong? Was this only a quickie affair after all?

"You said you didn't want a relationship, but I've got news for you. You're in one."

Relief flooded her. She hadn't been wrong. "Who says?" she teased.

"I says. And I'm not going to let you talk me out of it with some cockamamy story about not being ready for a man in your life. You seemed pretty ready to me," he pointed out with an irresistible smile.

"Yeah, right."

"I've embarrassed you." Ty's smile turned to out-and-out laughter as he pulled Rachel once again half atop his chest. He swept back her hair to look into her brilliant eyes.

"I'm not really embarrassed yet. But I will be tomorrow."

"Tomorrow we'll do something with Nathan. Anything you like. Monday I've got to get back to Portland, but I won't have to stay long."

"Is it really me you come to see in Oceanside?" Rachel asked. "There isn't any other reason?"

His hand was stroking her hair. It hesitated. "No. Why?"

"I find it incredible that you just found me, broke your engagement and now insist we're in a relationship. You're too good to be true, Ty Rafferty."

"Oh, I don't know about that...."

"I do."

And she leaned forward and kissed him, thrilled when his arms suddenly tightened around her as if he were afraid to let her go.

## Chapter Eight

"But I don't understand how that can be," Rachel said in a voice taut with frustration. "The balance is too high."

"Well, that's what our records show," the bank teller answered. "Your balance is six hundred seventy-three dollars and seventeen cents."

A line creased Rachel's smooth brows. She stared across the top of her computer to a poster of the Taj Mahal on the opposite wall. She'd dreaded calling the bank and learning exactly what her balance was, but she'd had to. Her boss had given her her salary advance, and it wasn't enough to solve her problems.

"I'd love to believe you're right," Rachel said into the receiver. "But that balance is about five hundred dollars too high."

"Would you like me to check your last deposit?"

"Yes. Please."

Rachel sighed as she listened over the wire to the hollow sounds of the bank teller pressing computer keys, drawing up Rachel's last deposit. The teller had asked Rachel her mother's maiden name as a means of identification over the telephone, and then given her the startling news that there was more money in her account than there should have been.

"Your last deposit was Friday. Five hundred dollars."

"I didn't make a deposit Friday. *Last* Friday? Three days ago?"

"Uh-huh."

Shawna, spying Rachel's confused face, lifted her eyebrows in question. Rachel shook her head. "There's some mistake. Someone else's money was put in my account. I didn't make a deposit last Friday."

"Would you like me to get the particulars on this and call you back?" the teller suggested.

"Please." Rachel gave her number at the office before hanging up.

Five hundred dollars. What she couldn't do with five hundred dollars! The mortgage payment was late, and it would just about let her squeak through the month without dipping into next month's salary. But she hadn't made the deposit and therefore it was someone else's money, so it was all academic, anyway.

"Hey, are you awake?" Allison tapped a pencil on Rachel's shoulder.

Swinging around, Rachel smiled. "No, I'm dreaming. I'm dreaming I've temporarily solved my financial problems."

"Oh. Boring. I thought you might be dreaming about The Third."

Rachel managed to control the blush that threatened to steal over her face, but not the quirky smile that seemed to constantly hover around the corners of her mouth.

"Well?" Allison asked in a knowing voice, her own lips curving.

"No, this is about money. Not The Third."

"So when's he stopping by again?"

"I'm not sure. Soon. I hope," she added softly.

She'd kept her romantic lovemaking with Ty a secret from her friends, certain if she told them she'd suffer untold embarrassment, or even worse, a lecture on all the whys and why nots about entering into an affair with him. But she had told Allison why the Rafferty name had seemed so familiar to her.

"I knew it!" Allison had crowed. "There was just something about him that gave it away. Rafferty! My God, Rachel! That guy is *rich* with a capital *R!*"

Of course it hadn't done any good explaining that she couldn't care less. Or that Ty's wealth made Rachel feel more uncomfortable than anything else. Oh, sure, it would be nice to fall in love with someone who was more financially secure than Richard had ended up being, but did it have to be *this* much? From what she'd gathered, even without Allison's ecstatic declaration, Ty Rafferty came from the kind of money detailed in prime-time soap operas. It made him that much more unattainable.

Unattainable. And she was in love with him. In love with a man who she was desperately afraid was out of her reach.

"I'd be happier if he was just plain normal," Rachel had muttered to end the conversation.

"You just count your blessings, honey. That guy is wild about you, and it's because he cares. There's no other reason. You're not some exotic socialite with a big bank balance. He doesn't want that. He wants you." She'd shaken her head at Rachel's troubled look. "Stop worrying. Hey, I gave it my best shot and he didn't even see me. Mark my words, Rachel. The Third is serious. Totally serious. And it's *incredible!*"

Incredible. Yes, it was incredible. Rachel had smiled, wishing she could share Allison's positive view. It was amazing, really, that as soon as Allison had realized Ty was interested in Rachel, she'd become Rachel's most ardent supporter in her new relationship. Allison had made it clear that she only wanted the best for her friend. Her philosophy was simple.

"I wasn't his type, that's all. You are."

"How can I be? I'm nobody!" Rachel had protested vehemently.

"You're obviously perfect for him," Allison had answered seriously. "And that's all it takes...."

Now, with last weekend uppermost in her mind, she dared to believe Allison was right. Ty *did* care. He made no secret of it. And he'd spent most of Sunday at the house, trying to draw Nathan out, asking him about his interests, his childhood, hundreds of questions in that slow drawl of his that even Nathan couldn't completely resist. It wasn't an interrogation, it was an honest interest in his life, and Nathan had slowly changed from grunting monosyllables to speaking sentences of five words or more. Rachel had been so filled with a warm glow that tears had sprung unbidden to her eyes. Richard had never been so patient with Nathan. Never.

"Rachel, sweetie," Allison said, shaking Rachel from her reverie. "It's time you lived life for the moment. God knows where this relationship could lead."

"What do you mean?"

"You know what I mean. I mean marriage."

"Oh, Allison." Rachel swung away from her friend.

"Why not? He likes you. It's not impossible. If that's what you want, well then—follow the yellow brick road. And even if it isn't, enjoy the trip."

Rachel shivered. She wasn't going to listen to any more of this. She had her dreams, sure. But she knew better than to expect them to turn to reality.

"Rachel! Line two," Shawna called, holding up two fingers.

"Thanks," Rachel called, punching a button on her phone and lifting the receiver. "This is Rachel Stone."

"Mrs. Stone, this is Sandra, at the bank. That deposit was made into your account at the drive-through window around five o'clock Friday evening. It was all cash."

"Well, I wasn't anywhere near the bank last Friday. It has to be a mistake."

"It was made on one of your own deposit slips, printed with your name."

Rachel's mouth dropped open. "That's impossible. Does the drive-up teller remember anything about the person who made the deposit?"

"No. It was really busy Friday. Cars stacked up all the way to the street for over an hour. Payday, you know. She thought it was a man, though, but she couldn't be sure."

A man?

"Well, thanks," Rachel murmured as she hung up. "I'll figure it out."

"Who was that?" Allison asked, and Rachel swung back around, her nose wrinkled in perplexity.

"Someone deposited five hundred dollars into my account last Friday. A man."

"*Ty?*" she demanded in disbelief.

"No." Rachel was adamant. Ty knew better than to buy her off.

Didn't he?

"It's just a mistake." *But the deposit was made on your personal deposit slip.* "There's no reason in the world Ty would do that. It's too—stupid," Rachel argued aloud. "I told him I wouldn't accept a loan. He backed off immediately."

Allison's brows shot up. "But he did offer you a loan?"

"Ye-e-e—actually, no, not really. He said something about it, but he didn't make an actual offer."

"Well, if he didn't make the deposit, who did?"

"Nobody could have." Rachel thought hard. "Wait a minute. I did toss some leftover deposit slips in the trash can at the bank a few weeks ago. I used my last check and I just chucked the extra deposit slips." She laughed shortly. "I mean, who needs them? I never use them up."

"You actually think someone reached in the garbage and used one of your deposit slips?" Allison's tone was laced with skepticism.

"Well, I'd rather believe that than think Ty was feeding my account behind my back," Rachel answered grimly.

Allison didn't answer, but her feelings were clear on her face. A cold dread crept across Rachel's skin.

The paper clip sailed through the air and missed its target by a good three feet. The corners of Ty's mouth curved in amusement. Gerald must be really upset.

"You're *seeing* Rachel Stone," he repeated. "I'm afraid to ask what that means."

"It means I like her."

"Ty, Ty, Ty." Gerald shook his head and looked slightly sick. "What're you doing?"

"I didn't set out to seduce her, if that's what you're thinking. That's the last thing I wanted. I honestly like Rachel. I enjoy being with her."

"But you haven't told her who you are," he put in quickly.

"You were the one who suggested I don't."

"I know. I know. And I still feel that way." Gerald grabbed another paper clip and twisted it into a kind of lopsided spiral. He gazed up unhappily at Ty, who was standing in the center of his office. "God help me, I'm afraid to ask what you plan to do next."

"Relax, Gerald. I'm just marking time."

"Until...?"

Now Ty frowned, unwilling to delve too deeply into the future. He knew what Gerald was really asking. He knew his friend wanted to know what his intentions were regarding Rachel. Like some overprotective father from another century, Gerald wanted to know if his intentions were honorable.

"I broke my engagement to Barbara a few weeks ago," Ty said.

Gerald groaned. "I read about it in the gossip column. Nice work, Ty."

"Gerald, I couldn't have married Barbara, anyway. It wouldn't have worked," Ty responded tightly. "Nathan, and Rachel, just made me realize that a little sooner than I would have."

"I suppose that should make me feel better, but it doesn't."

"For God's sake!" Ty exploded. "Stop being my conscience, all right? I'm telling you this as my lawyer. I need some advice."

Gerald flipped the paper clip. It pinged against the side of the plastic trash can and landed on the floor.

"What do you think will happen if I tell her the truth now? Legally, I mean?"

"Forget the legalities. That woman is never going to forgive you. Wake up, Ty. You know women better than I do. She's going to come after your hide when she learns you've had an ulterior motive all along. She's going to make certain you never see that boy."

"Not if I can convince her I care about her, too."

"My God. Am I hearing straight? Ty, you'll *never* convince her. Even if it was true, you couldn't convince her now. She's going to know you used her, no matter how you feel."

"What if I asked her to marry me?"

The room was utterly silent. A complete absence of noise. Gerald was a statue, his gaze riveted on Ty's determined face, his own expression frozen in pained disbelief. Ty held his breath, a little surprised he'd spoken his thoughts aloud.

"You think you wouldn't have been able to stand marriage to Barbara. Wait until you're trapped in one with this woman. Because as soon as she knows your real reason for asking her to marry you, she'll make your life a living hell."

"But you think she'll accept my proposal, anyway," Ty muttered, seething inside. He was angry at Gerald. Angry that he was telling him everything he already knew.

"Of course she will. She'd have to be completely indifferent to you to turn you down, and that's not the case, is it? My guess is, from all the things you've purposely left out about you and her and what you're doing together—"

"Gerald," Ty warned.

"She's half in love with you already. Am I wrong?" When Ty didn't immediately answer, he demanded, "Tell me. Am I wrong?"

"No."

"And you can't keep the truth from her forever. Not forever, Ty. Come on, my friend." Gerald climbed out of his luxurious office chair and nabbed his jacket off the coat tree by the door. "I need a drink. And you need some serious waking up."

Ty tossed back the rest of his draft. Talk, talk, talk, talk, talk. He was talked out. And darkly furious—with himself and Gerald. He didn't want lectures. He'd embarked on this course of action with his eyes open. Okay, it mightn't have been the smartest move, but so what? What options did he have?

By the time Gerald finished his second martini, he was more amenable. "So when are you going to pop the question?" he asked, while Ty twisted his glass around and around between his palms, smearing the rings of condensation across the tabletop.

"Well, I'm not certain I am."

"Oh, come on. You came to see me hoping I'd sanction the whole thing."

"No." Ty had had about all he could take. "I came to see you hoping you'd have an alternative. I wouldn't mind marrying Rachel. Whether you believe it or not, I think we could be happy. But I don't know how to bring up Nathan without coming off like a coldhearted bastard."

"You can't. And you know why? Because in the back of your mind you've been planning this all along. You didn't really think you were, but you were. It's natural. And because you know that, you won't ever be able to convince her you care about her. It just doesn't work that way. You've got too much integrity."

"Integrity!" Ty snorted.

"You know what I mean. You won't be able to pull off such a bald-faced lie."

Ty felt a swelling anger. Sometimes Gerald's insights were positively frightening. "From the moment I began to believe Nathan was mine, not long after I met Rachel, I started thinking that there were possibilities there, yes. She's an attractive woman. Very attractive."

"You can't tell me that you would have felt the same way if she wasn't the mother of your son."

"Okay!" Ty glared at him. "You're right. You're right, damn it! Is that what you want to hear? Sure, that had a lot of bearing on my feelings. But if Rachel wasn't close to my ideal of a woman, I wouldn't feel this way just because she was Nathan's mother."

"Are you sure?"

"Positive! The woman makes me feel like a goddamned teenager half the time. It's crazy. The whole thing's crazy! But I want to marry her and I feel like if I don't soon, then it'll all blow up in my face."

Gerald opened and shut his mouth several times, as if further objections were withering on his tongue. Finally, he remarked, "I've gotta meet this Rachel."

Ty relaxed. He hadn't realized how tense he was until this moment. "You will. I'm asking her to come to Portland this weekend."

"And meet the family?" Gerald looked worried.

"And meet the family," Ty agreed.

"Waitress! Another drink."

Rachel was washing the dinner dishes when the phone rang. Before she could dry her hands, Nathan bounded off the couch and swept up the receiver in one fluid movement.

"Hello?" A pause. "Yeah, just a minute. Mom," he called sullenly.

By his tone Rachel suspected it was Ty on the other end of the line. She made a face at Nathan as she took the receiver from him.

"Hello?" she answered.

"Hi," Ty's deep voice responded. "How're you doing?"

"Terrific."

"I've got a request for you. How about coming to Portland for the weekend? I'll come and pick you up after work on Friday."

"I—can't," she said, flustered.

"Nathan can come, too."

"No, Ty. He's got his community service work. And I can't just leave for the entire weekend."

"Why not?" His voice lowered. "Rachel, I want you to meet some of my friends and family."

Panic started somewhere down by Rachel's toes and swept upward, cold and icy. "I'm—I'm not sure," she whispered frantically.

He chuckled. "It won't be all that bad. I promise. How much community service work has Nathan got?"

"Um . . . I think he's just working Saturday."

"I could stay with the Holts," Nathan said without turning around, trying to disguise the eagerness in his voice.

Rachel tossed him a look, her expression wry. He might not want her getting friendly with Ty, but he'd sacrifice this one weekend just to buy himself some freedom. He knew she'd never let him stay by himself.

Rachel considered. Carol Holt would be a worthy guard to keep Nathan out of trouble. Rachel knew her through the school. And the right word placed in Carol's ear would keep Nathan and her son, Anthony, close to home.

But did she really want to meet the Raffertys?

"Rachel?" Ty asked.

"Okay...I could check with a friend of Nathan's and see if he could stay with them."

Nathan whooped with delight. Rachel wrinkled her nose. Had she been that much of a jailer?

"See you Friday," Ty said in his low voice, and Rachel drew a steadying breath as she hung up the phone.

"Just a minute," Rachel warned as Nathan lunged for the telephone. She held her hand over it protectively. "We've got to get some things straight."

Nathan groaned. "Oh, Mom!"

"First, you've got to do that community service work. You know that."

"Yeah, yeah."

"Second, I don't want to hear one negative word. Be on your best behavior. Nathan, this is important."

"I *know!*"

With a shock Rachel realized she hadn't mentioned finding the extra five hundred dollars in her account to Ty. She hadn't really thought about it again since her conversation with Allison.

"What?" Nathan asked suspiciously, watching her face.

"Nothing. I was thinking about something else. I seem to have more money in my checking account than I should," she added absently.

"Really? How much?"

"Five hundred dollars too much."

A grin crossed Nathan's face. "Great!"

"Oh, no. It's not mine. I have to give it back."

"What do you mean?" he demanded. "Give it back to who?"

"Well, I don't know." Rachel's face flushed as she thought of Ty. She couldn't believe he would feed her account, but what other answer was there? She was furious with herself for not bringing it up on the phone, but maybe, she rationalized, it would be better to see his face when she gave him the news.

"Then you gotta keep it," Nathan declared, looking at her as if she were dumb as a rock.

"Oh, no." She shook her head and went back to the dishes. "No, no, no."

"Mom!" Nathan was horrified.

"It's not my money, Nathan! It's someone else's. It's a mistake. If I even used a nickel of it, I would have to pay it back in the end."

"Well, then...well, then...just use it like a loan," he sputtered. "You said we need the money, right?"

"Nathan." Rachel stared at him in shock. "Where did you get these cockeyed ideas? I'm not an opportunist. It isn't my money."

"How do you know? Maybe you made a mistake."

"Someone made a deposit to my account of exactly five hundred dollars. The teller thinks it was a man. *I* didn't make the mistake. This mysterious benefactor did."

Nathan was silent.

"Oh, Nathan..." Rachel sighed. "We'll get through these tough times one way or another. We have a lot more than a lot of people."

"Oh, yeah."

"We do." She drew a breath and turned on the faucet. "Actually, I'm afraid Ty might have made the deposit. Some kind of misguided need to help me out. I already refused a loan from him once. But I've got to give the money back."

"He won't take it," Nathan said in a philosophical tone that had Rachel staring at him. "You know he won't. He won't even admit to it."

"Since when are you such an expert on Ty?"

"If he wanted you to have the money, he's not going to admit to putting it in your account, that's all."

"Well, it's not your problem. I'm sorry I brought it up. We'll figure something out."

"Are you in love with him?"

Rachel's immediate reaction was to deny it outright. But Nathan's voice was quiet, reflective. She couldn't remember him acting this way once since Richard's death. She couldn't afford to brush him off with words he wanted to hear, words that might not be the truth.

"I don't know," she answered honestly. "I do care about him a lot. I don't know what's going to happen. Does that scare you?"

He shrugged. "I don't like him much."

"Would you like anyone I was dating?" she countered with a smile.

Nathan struggled with an answer. "I guess not," he finally mumbled, then quickly left before Rachel could ask anything more personal.

"It's gonna be a scorcher, folks. Temperatures approaching a hundred. That's one-zero-zero. A good day to spend in the river, a backyard pool, your bathtub or somewhere wet. Doesn't really seem like Oregon, does it? If the mercury climbs high enough, we might even break some records...."

Rachel concentrated on the cheery voice emanating from Ty's radio. It helped keep her nerves from stretching to breaking. They were nearing the outskirts of the city, driving east on Sunset Highway to the tunnel. Through the tunnel was the city. One moment you were zipping down the freeway, then darkness, then *bam!* Portland city center. Dropped in front of you like some incredible magician's sleight of hand.

Rachel could feel herself sink backward into Ty's leather seats in preparation. She didn't want to meet his family.

She jumped when his hand stole over hers.

"Relax. It won't be all that bad."

She tried on a smile. "This is my first time for meeting anyone's family. Richard only had a brother left when I met him, and they were estranged."

"You'll get on fine with my mother."

Rachel heard more by what he left out. "You said you had a sister. What's her name?"

"Kathleen."

"Kathleen, right. So how'll it be meeting her?"

"Piece of cake."

"Sure."

The Porsche turned off the freeway and wound over Vista into the West Hills. Rachel was familiar with Portland only from the times she'd come into the city to go shopping. But she knew where the pockets of residential wealth lay. And she knew she was heading into one of the city's toniest areas.

She was not prepared for Ty's home, however.

The lawn looked as if every green blade were standing at attention. The walkway had been acid scrubbed; the rich, red tones of the bricks glowed in the morning heat. The Georgian home was white with dark emerald trim, imposing and grand and somehow silent in its elegant mastery. Beyond, down a grassy slope to the south, Rachel could see a glimpse of the city, giving her a clear understanding of what the views must be like from every window of the place.

She stared down at Portland, smothered in a layer of dense July heat.

Ty's hand was at her elbow. She wanted to run. She was out of her league. As if sensing her panic, his grip tightened slightly. He laughed beneath his breath.

"Rachel, my love. Don't faint. This isn't where I live, you know. This is my mother's house."

"The Rafferty family mansion?" Rachel tried to keep her voice light, but it sounded strained.

"It's just a house."

He rang the bell. Footsteps sounded. The door was opened by a middle-aged woman in a black dress. "Hi, Mary," Ty greeted her easily. "Mother here?"

Mary grinned at him with affection. "In the breakfast room with your sister."

"The breakfast room?" Rachel choked out on a nervous giggle as they followed her.

"They have a great need for affectations," he muttered.

"Ty." She grabbed his arm in desperation at the end of the marble-floored hallway. Mary had disappeared through a pair of impressive double doors to a smaller hallway beyond, but Rachel was loath to follow her. She was panicked, in fact. "How do I look?"

Ty shot Rachel a swift look. Her face was nearly colorless. Her hazel eyes were deep and smoky green and fearful. In a simple white cotton dress and sandals, she looked younger and more vulnerable than he knew her to be. Her mouth was faintly trembling.

He cupped her chin in one hand, increasing the terror in her eyes. She was afraid of being discovered in such an intimate position by his family. He laughed.

"I don't know what's so funny," she hissed.

"Rachel. You're perfect. Keep that in mind all the while."

"Somehow you're not reassuring me."

"How do I look?" he asked with a lazy grin.

Since he was dressed in worn jeans and a dark blue shirt that, though obviously expensive, looked as if it had been a treasured and well-used favorite, she didn't know quite how to answer.

"The only way to deal with pretension is ignore it," he advised dryly. "Drives them crazy."

"Ty, I don't want to be here," she answered urgently.

"It'll only be a few minutes. Just long enough for them to get a look at you."

"Why? *Why?*"

Mary's footsteps were returning. Soon she'd come back through those doors to where they were standing. Rachel jerked herself from Ty's tender grasp, but he suddenly grabbed her to him fully, holding her close, his mouth near her ear.

"Because I want to marry you," he said in a voice so low she could scarcely hear it.

The door opened. Mary studiously pretended not to notice their embrace. "They're waiting breakfast for you," she said. "Go right in...."

## Chapter Nine

"My brother has been extremely mysterious these past few weeks," Kathleen Rafferty said over the rim of her coffee cup. Her eyes, so like Ty's, were alive with curiosity. "We hardly ever see him."

"You hardly ever see me, anyway," Ty drawled, lounging in his chair.

"Not for lack of trying. You're just never around."

"Have you lived in Oceanside all your life?" Ty's mother put in politely.

Rachel drew a breath and turned to Sybil Rafferty. This whole scene was surreal. She could scarcely keep her mind on the gist of the conversation because the undercurrents threatened to pull her under. "I've—um—lived on the coast most of my life. I moved to Oceanside after I got married."

"Ty said your husband died just a few months ago," Sybil said gently.

"About seven months ago."

The conversation lagged. No one really knew what to say. Rachel picked up her water glass with fingers that trembled ever so slightly. Get me out of here, Ty, she thought anxiously. She wasn't certain how much longer she could keep up this facade of sophistication.

Ty's mother was small and neat and filled the bill to perfection of matron of this lovely home. Kathleen, however, was a restless dynamo with a mean tongue. As first impressions go, she made Rachel feel like such an outsider that Rachel's normally ebullient personality seemed to have died a quick death. Rachel was tongue-tied. And bound and determined to keep the topic neutral lest Kathleen should find some reason to attack her. Ty's sister was that kind of woman.

Ty, however, seemed to be supremely unaffected by the whole thing. He wasn't even tense. Rachel had to admire him for that. Within the first five minutes of meeting his mother and sister, Rachel had gleaned a pretty clear picture of what growing up in this environment must have been like. Ty was the rebel. Or maybe he was like his father, whom no one seemed inclined to talk about much. In either case, by accident or design, he didn't fit in at all.

Rachel sipped water, her nerves tingling uncomfortably. Even without the drama going on around the breakfast table, she would have felt strange and disconnected. Ty's softly spoken words rang through her mind: *Because I want to marry you.*

Lord, did he mean it? She was shocked and thrilled and afraid. Afraid because she wanted him to mean it so badly. Yet...yet...how could he? She slid him a surreptitious glance, thrilling to the thought that his man had said he wanted to marry her. *Marry* her!

"Ty says you're a travel agent." Kathleen's voice was carefully devoid of expression.

Rachel met her gaze directly. "Yes, that's right."

"That how you met?"

"Two for two," Ty said lazily, ignoring Kathleen's sharp look.

Rachel's heart fluttered in her throat.

Kathleen examined Rachel so thoroughly that Rachel had to force herself not to squirm under such intense scrutiny. "Frankly, I'm amazed." She turned to Ty. "You've been with Barbara for years, and then to just, I don't know..." She glanced at her mother before asking Ty ironically, "I mean, what did you do, fall in love or something?"

Rachel cringed, setting down her water glass. Her face felt flushed.

"Or something," he agreed blandly.

"Would you like some more coffee?" Sybil interjected hastily to Rachel.

No. She was swimming in caffeine. But she saw the desperation in Sybil's eyes and realized Ty's mother was trying her best to keep the situation from deteriorating. "Please," she murmured. As if drinking coffee were the panacea to all ills, she thought a bit hysterically.

"Well." Kathleen looked taken aback.

"I brought Rachel here so you could meet her," Ty said, watching his mother pour Rachel another cup from the silver pot. "I'm not engaged to Barbara. I'm seeing Rachel."

"How long has this little romance been going on?"

The look Ty sent his sister would have shriveled a lesser woman. Kathleen, however, was made of pretty stern stuff. "I broke up with Barbara because we had nothing in common."

"And you and—Rachel—do?"

For an answer Ty looked Rachel's way, his dark eyes full of warmth and reassurance. Rachel managed to keep her answering smile from shaking. "Yes," he said flatly to

Kathleen, scraping back his chair. "In fact, we have a lot more in common than I do with anyone in my family, including you."

"That doesn't have anything to do with anything."

"Doesn't it?" Ty gazed at her from beneath his lashes.

Staring back at him, her face in profile, Kathleen looked angry and intense and...and...familiar. Rachel was jolted. She felt a stirring inside her, a distant memory of something she couldn't name, a déjà vu. She frowned. What was it about Ty's beautiful, arrogant sister that seemed so significant? Kathleen, feeling the intensity of her gaze, glanced Rachel's way.

"I'm just rather...surprised, that's all." she said with a delicate sniff.

With a sudden grin, Ty said, "Give it a rest, Kathleen," then he walked around the table to lay a kiss on his mother's faintly wrinkled cheek. "See you later. We've got things to do. You ready, Rachel?"

Rachel tried to hide her relief. She slid from her chair. "It was nice meeting you."

Sybil turned slightly troubled eyes from her son to Rachel. "We'll see you again, I'm sure."

"You can count on it," was Ty's drawling answer.

As Ty opened one of the double doors and Rachel escaped to the marble-tiled hall, Kathleen's voice echoed in dismay, "Mother, I think he plans to *marry* that woman!"


"Whoa, wait," Rachel ordered, yanking on Ty's arm as he led her toward the glittering pink stone tower in the heart of the city. "Where are we going now? I haven't recovered from the last meeting. Give me a chance to catch my breath!"

They'd driven straight down the dizzying narrow residential streets outside Ty's family home to Portland's city center. Ty had parked the car in an underground lot and now they were at street level, crossing at the light.

Ty actually laughed. "This one won't be so bad."

"How do you know?" Rachel was highly skeptical.

"Because Gerald Raintree's nothing like Kathleen, who, as you now know, is a piranha in high heels."

"Gerald Raintree?"

"My attorney. And friend."

"Oh, Ty..." Rachel wanted to sink into his arms, squeeze her eyes closed and shut out the real world. She placed her fingers to her temples and groaned. "I don't think my heart can stand another scene like that one."

"Scene? That was normal everyday life at home with the Raffertys."

"You're teasing."

He grinned.

"That smile isn't going to work on me," Rachel warned sternly, but in truth she felt a glow somewhere in the region of her heart. Control, she told herself. Hang on to your control. "Ty, listen. You're moving too fast and making my head spin. Don't I get a say in any of this?"

"What do you mean?"

"I'm a fish out of water here—with your family and friends. You know that. It's plainly obvious."

"You're beautiful and charming and smart. You're not a fish out of water, you're—"

"Are you doing this because you want them to know there's no chance of you and Barbara getting back together?" she interrupted. His expression darkened, and Rachel added in a rush, "It's clear to me they want the two of you back together. If that's why you said what you said, I'll understand."

"What are you talking about?"

"I'm talking about what your mother and Kathleen want," she explained patiently.

"Rachel, what they want and what I want are diametric opposites. And anyway, you're lumping my mother with Kathleen, which isn't fair. She's nothing like Kathleen."

"You're not listening, Ty. Your mother looked concerned that Kathleen might be right about...about you wanting to marry me."

"She's right."

Rachel stared at his chiseled features helplessly. The crowd surged around them, jostling the two of them as they crossed the street. Ty grabbed Rachel's elbow and led her to the corner building.

"Mother only wants me to be happy."

"And you're happy with me?"

Her tentative tone made Ty sigh. "You know I am. Why do I have to have ulterior motives? Can't I just find you attractive and intelligent—and wildly sexy?"

She grinned. "No."

He muttered beneath his breath.

"But I'm willing to go along with things for now," she said softly, touching his arm as they entered the building. For some reason Ty wasn't facing reality, and though Rachel would give almost anything to believe that he did love her, that he did want to marry her, that he did want to live happily ever after, she had to be careful. Proceed with caution. Maybe there was a chance for that, but she didn't believe it had happened already. She was too much of a pragmatist to think Ty had fallen so deeply and completely in love with her.

He'd mentioned marriage, she realized with a funny little twist of her heart. But he hadn't mentioned love.

Ty ushered her inside an opulent office that made Rachel want to pinch herself back to reality once more. A fish out of water? She was a fish in the *desert!* She was as far from home as she could be.

The man behind the desk climbed to his feet and smiled. Rachel shook his hand, but even his smile and warm handshake weren't enough to displace the worry in his eyes. The way his gaze traveled over Rachel, as if he were afraid he might find some serious flaw in her, echoed Kathleen's sharp-eyed inventory and made Rachel's already dry mouth turn to dust.

"Gerald Raintree, Rachel Stone," Ty introduced. "Gerald's an old college friend."

"You're Ty's attorney, too." Rachel dredged up an answering smile. "For the construction company?"

"For anything Ty needs."

"Gerald wanted to meet you," Ty explained. "He thinks I'm getting too serious too quickly."

Rachel glanced at Ty uncertainly, but Ty was eyeing Gerald. Something was going on. And she was the focus of it.

It made her uncomfortable.

"Have a chair, Rachel," Gerald invited with a wave of his hand. "Tell me your life story. I've got at least fifteen minutes before I have to be somewhere."

"Fifteen minutes is about all my life story will take."

"Well, that's fourteen and a half minutes longer than anything interesting in mine," he answered. This time the look he sent her was more relaxed. Had she passed some crucial test?

"I have a son," Rachel said. "From my first marriage. An adopted son."

Gerald Raintree plucked a paper clip from a near-empty holder and mangled the thing apart. With an expert flip he sailed it past Ty to the trash can on the other side of the room.

"A son," he repeated.

In Rachel's peripheral vision she saw Ty shift his weight from one foot to the other. She turned his way, needing encouragement. The corners of his mouth lifted, but the smile never quite reached his eyes. He looked as tightly coiled as a spring.

Gerald Raintree abruptly shoved back his chair. "I can reschedule my appointment. It's almost noon. Let's go have lunch. I know a great place."

"One that serves martinis?" Ty drawled lazily.

Gerald sent him a pointed look as he hustled them both out of the room.

Rachel's uneasiness faded as her lunch with Ty and Gerald Raintree wore on into the afternoon. Gerald had been so tense at first that Rachel had just about decided all wealthy or successful individuals simply didn't know how to relax. But he had unwound after one martini, and though the alcohol certainly was responsible to some degree, Rachel had the funny sensation that he'd also relaxed because of her. Because of who she was. What she was like.

Was he that concerned over his friend's love life? she wondered in amusement. Had he thought her some kind of gold digger? She was surprised anyone would think a man as determined and strong willed as Ty could be duped by a woman. Especially a friend as close as Raintree. Why, then, she wondered curiously, had his opinion so obviously changed about her?

"You know, it's really been pleasant meeting you," Gerald said, as if reading Rachel's thoughts.

"You sound surprised." The corners of her mouth twitched.

"Well, yes, I guess I am. A little."

"You're not anything like Barbara," Ty explained for Rachel's benefit, sending his friend an amused look.

"What do you mean? I liked Barbara." Gerald was affronted.

"You hated Barbara." Ty shared a conspiratorial grin with Rachel. "She drove you wild. You told me a hundred times she would make my life miserable. A thousand times."

"I didn't think you ought to *marry* her, that's all."

The word *marry* hung in the room like the last note of a disturbing melody. Gerald's gaze was centered meaningfully on Ty, but Ty was watching Rachel, studying her reaction.

Marriage, she thought. Marriage to Ty Rafferty. He was half-serious about it. Or maybe he just thought that's what she wanted to hear.

And it *was* what she wanted to hear. She wanted to believe he was so in love with her that marriage was the natural follow-up. Still, she wasn't foolish enough to seriously consider a proposal, was she? She knew from experience that marriage wasn't the be-all and end-all to everything. It was work. Hard work. And it wasn't the kind of decision for her to rush into in any case. With backgrounds as disparate as hers and Ty's, well, the subject shouldn't come up at all.

Except she was in love with him. And he must love her, or at least think he did. She couldn't be completely sure.

Good grief, worrying about it could drive her crazy!

"Marriage," Ty said, drawing out the word. "I'd like to be married."

"Waitress!" Gerald raised his hand. "Another martini over here as soon as possible."

They left Gerald back at his office just as downtown traffic started to heat up. The smell of exhaust trapped within the blazing concrete streets was enough to choke an elephant. Grateful for the Porsche's air conditioning, Rachel sighed in relief as Ty eased the powerful car behind a huge delivery truck and headed south.

"Where are we going?" she asked.

"My place."

Rachel ducked her head. His place. Alone on a Friday evening. She fought back a muffled laugh at the unfamiliar feeling of actually looking forward to sex! She could picture herself alone with Ty in a wide, masculine bed in a room overlooking the river. She'd been picturing it all week.

"Am I through meeting your friends and family for a while?" she asked.

"For the moment. Tomorrow you can meet Big Jim, my foreman at the site," Ty explained with a faint smile.

"And have I passed the test?"

Ty fiddled with the radio. He didn't pretend to misunderstand. "With flying colors. Sorry that Kathleen's such a bitch."

"I got the feeling she was just looking out for your best interests."

"*Her* best interests, maybe. Mine, never."

The Porsche left the city behind and headed down a tree-lined thoroughfare. The Willamette flashed by on the left, bright sunlight mirrored off brownish water in between Douglas firs.

"Why do you try so hard not to fit in?" Rachel questioned softly.

"I don't have to try hard. It's easy. I just don't fit." He slanted her an amused look. "And, no. That's not the reason I'm seeing you. I'm not trying to score points off my family by dating someone they would consider a nobody. Do you seriously think I'm made that way?"

Rachel studied his profile intently. "No."

"Then give it a rest, huh? All I want to do is make love to you. All afternoon."

Rachel half choked. "Well . . . okay," she answered in a small voice.

Ty chuckled richly. "You're too much."

His home was on the cliff above the Willamette. Overlooking the river, it was gray, three storied, with skylights glowing atop a steepled roof. The garage was on the second level, and Ty parked next to another vehicle, a pickup truck, which bore the inscription Rafferty Construction in plain black letters. Ty led her through the kitchen to a smallish living room crowded with richly glowing walnut and cherry furniture—pieces that appeared to be genuine antiques. A spectacular eastern view of the river and the houseboats lining the opposite shore left Rachel in awe.

"Wow," she said under her breath, but Ty was already gone. He'd left her in his quest to find something for them to drink. She could hear him rummaging through drawers in the kitchen, searching for a wine cork. A few seconds later she heard the cork release with a squeaky pop.

Wine. And twilight. And hours alone with Ty.

"Are you hungry?" he asked, reappearing several minutes later with two glasses in one hand, the neck of the wine bottle in the other. A glance at the label told Rachel it was nothing she could ever buy. It was way out of her price range. But Ty held the bottle negligently between careless fingers, as if it wouldn't matter one iota if it fell and broke against the lovely hardwood floor, or spilled on the incredibly lush peach-colored Oriental carpet that spanned the living-room area.

"It's almost as nice as your view," Ty commented, inclining his head toward the slowly moving river beyond as he poured her a glass.

"The house is much nicer." Rachel smiled.

"You're sitting on a prime piece of property in Oceanside."

"Not that prime. The people with money like to buy in a development."

"Not all of them. I wouldn't."

"But you're not in the market for beach property. Or so you said." She leveled him a look. "Or are you?"

Ty laughed, and Rachel once again realized how attractive he was. The man was deadly.

"Stop it. Your property's not the reason I'm seeing you, either. You're just going to have to accept it, Rachel. I like you."

He leaned forward and kissed her lips. Gently. One hand still holding his glass, the other the bottle of wine. It wasn't meant to strike sparks. It was just a beginning. But Rachel's heart thumped heavily and she couldn't drag her gaze away from his when he drew back.

"If you break my heart, I'll never forgive you," she said. There was a soft tremor in her voice.

"If I break your heart I'll never forgive myself."

"Don't fool me, Ty. Let's keep things honest. I can't play these kinds of games. I can't tease about marriage."

"I'm not teasing."

"I know you think you're not, but—but—"

He sighed. "Rachel?"

"What?"

"Shut up." His mouth pressed down on hers, more urgently but with a grin lifting the corners.

"You're moving too fast for me," she mumbled against his warm lips. "Way too fast."

Ty drew back, exhaling heavily. She'd irritated him. "Then tell me how fast I'm supposed to move. Am I supposed to wait six months before I ask you to marry me? Should I mark it off on my calendar and say, okay, today's the day? What does it matter if I ask you now? What difference does it make?"

She gazed at him helplessly. "I might actually believe you if you waited!"

"Why can't you believe me now? I'm not known for making idle promises. You know me well enough for that."

"I don't think you love me," she admitted, though it took every bit of her courage.

Ty set the bottle and glasses on a beautifully carved end table. Rachel held her breath, desperately afraid she was going to hear words she didn't want to hear. He didn't love her, and she was forcing him to either admit that fact or lie.

His gaze moved restlessly over her upturned face. His chest constricted. "Rachel," he said, hesitating. She waited, her cheeks pale, her eyes tortured. "I'm thinking about marriage. It's what I want. Because I'm falling in love with you."

She should have been elated. She should have been relieved. But she sensed he was lying. "You can't fall in love that fast."

"The hell I can't," he growled, capturing her face, forcing her to meet his burning gaze. "My mother fell in love with my father. That fast. From all accounts it was love at first sight."

Rachel shook her head. "If you're trying to make some kind of parallel here, forget it. This is about what you feel, and what I feel."

"I'm telling you what I feel," he insisted harshly. "What isn't there to love about you? You're sensitive and caring and hilarious and beautiful. If my mother can fall in love with my father, who was as unlovable as they come, then I can surely fall in love with you. My father was greedy, selfish and abused his power shamelessly. He tried to run everybody's life. Everybody's. My mother's, my sister's and *mine*." The way he said "mine" sent a shiver down Rachel's spine. There was underlying hostility in his tone, a deep, unforgiving anger. "People fall in love all the time. Most often, it's not with someone as perfect as you. My mother loved my father," Ty went on. "She fell in love instantly. It does happen, Rachel."

There was something wrong here. A lot of words, but something left unsaid. "And you're falling in love with me," she repeated dubiously, meeting his eyes. She couldn't tell what he was feeling. He was adept at keeping his emotions under lock and key.

"Yes," he told her tautly.

Rachel drew a slow breath. It was decision time, she thought with a sense of fate. "I—believe you."

His smile was so full of relief, her lips curved in return. "And I'm nothing like my father," he added with some urgency.

"Well, good." Her smile widened. "Since you didn't paint the most terrific picture of him. Sounds like you're still mad at him."

Ty groaned, squeezing her close, his breath stirring the auburn hair at her crown. "You're not going to psychoanalyze me, are you?"

"No." She laughed, and her laughter sparkled in the quiet room. It made Ty feel alive. More alive than he'd felt in years. There was a part of himself that shied away from the travesty he played. How could he lie so blatantly? It wasn't his way. He recalled the words he'd told her and was shocked by how sincere he'd sounded.

He sure was learning fast, he thought bitterly.

He tipped up her chin, staring down into her glowing eyes with their long curly lashes, marveling at the soft incandescence of her skin. "Now it's your turn. How do you feel about me, Rachel Stone?"

"Oh, no." She tried to turn away, but he wouldn't let her. He held her face between his palms and waited until she was forced to meet his gaze. Wrinkling her nose in that enchanting way, she pretended to be angry but the light in her eyes gave her away.

"No, no, no," she told him, shaking her head. "You're getting too personal."

"I want to get personal."

"Uh-uh."

His palm slid into the glory of her hair. Her mouth curved endearingly. "Play fair, Rachel," he ordered in a quiet voice. "Tell me."

Silence.

"Rachel?"

"I . . . like you, Ty. You know that." She struggled with the words.

"And . . . ?"

"And what?"

"That's it? You like me."

"Well, you told me you liked me," she retorted defensively.

"I also told you I'm falling in love with you," he reminded her gently.

She quirked a brow at him. "If you expect me to say something similar, you've got a long wait ahead of you."

"You're not falling in love with me?"

"If I was, and I'm not saying that I am, I certainly wouldn't tell you."

"Tell me," he ordered again. For some reason he felt compelled to hear it from her lips, even with his own perfidy surrounding him like a dark, choking cloak.

"Ty," she murmured on an embarrassed laugh, shaking her head.

"What are you afraid of, Rachel?" His thumb caressed her cheek, then followed the path of her lips. They trembled beneath his touch.

She shook her head again, more emphatically.

"Say it."

"There are too many problems between us. Big problems."

"Like what?"

"Money."

"Money isn't a problem," he said on a short laugh.

"Oh, pardon me. Not for you, but for me it is. And don't even think about pointing out how if I married you then it wouldn't be a problem for me, either, because it most certainly would be."

"Still afraid I'm going to buy you?" he tossed back, growing impatient.

Rachel sucked in a breath. Good Lord. How could she have forgotten that deposit? "Like with five hundred dollars?"

The blank look on his face couldn't be an act. Rachel knew it instantly.

"What are you talking about?" Ty demanded.

"Nothing." She was so relieved she wanted to laugh. Instead she clung to him, hugging him tightly.

Ty accepted her unexpected change of mood with delight. His mouth lightly brushed hers. "Rachel, I want you. I want to spend time with you. Lots of time. Maybe a lifetime. I want some simplicity in my life. And I want a woman who wants me. Me. Not my money. You're the only woman I've ever met who seems to feel that way. *If* you want me."

She nodded, her cheek rubbing against his shirt, her eyes squeezed tightly shut. "I want you, Ty," she admitted shakily.

He swept her into his arms so suddenly she gasped. His face was dark with passion and some deeper emotion Rachel couldn't quite identify.

Without a word he carried her upstairs to the bedroom loft. Fading sunlight slanted through the skylights. The bed in the center of the room was covered with an Indian print spread. Ty laid Rachel down on it, stretching out beside her.

"I'm glad that's over with," he muttered.

She quirked an eyebrow. "I'm that heavy?"

"A megaton," he agreed with a sexy smile. "No, it's the soul-searching I can't take. For a moment there I thought . . ." He shook his head, ending whatever he might have said.

Rachel ran her fingers over his cheek. Ty grabbed her marauding hand, turning his lips into her palm. "You didn't seriously think I'd be immune to your charm, did you?" she asked.

She felt his mouth curve. "Immune . . . no. But you sure as hell were resistant."

"You incredible egotist!"

He laughed. Brushing back her hair, he let his gaze rove lovingly over her face. "Tell me what you meant by five hundred dollars."

"Oh, it was nothing."

"Come on, Rachel."

"No, it's silly."

"Try me."

Rachel felt more foolish with each passing second. "I found extra money in my checking account. I—I thought you might have put it there. Keeping with your Good Samaritan tactics and all," she added hurriedly.

"I tried to offer you a loan and you cut me off at the knees. You actually thought I would make a deposit to your account without telling you?" He sounded more nonplussed than annoyed.

"I couldn't think of anyone else," she said simply.

"Sounds like a bank error to me."

"It must be," Rachel agreed, eager to change the subject. "Besides," she added impishly, "if Tyrrell Rafferty III was trying to buy someone, it'd be for a lot more than five hundred dollars!"

"You'd better believe it."

His mouth closed over hers, his chest pressing against the softness of her breasts. He wanted to block out everything but the taste and feel of her. Rachel emitted a soft, willing sigh, her arms circling his neck, a smile hovering on her lips.

*If Tyrrell Rafferty III was trying to buy someone, it'd be for a lot more than five hundred dollars.*

A cold chill ran down his arms. Those words on her tongue, innocently spoken, made his lie so much worse. He *was* trying to buy her. Buy her trust, buy her love, buy her! And he was using golden promises and false emotions. Hating himself, he slammed the door on his conscience. He cared about her. Maybe not as much as he'd intimated, but he did care.

Rachel's gaze was sweet and honest. He'd torn away the last shreds of her doubt. Trust shone from her eyes. And love.

Ty felt like a heel.

"I love—"

His mouth swooped down on hers, stopping the words before she could utter them. Rachel melted into his arms, full of peace and joy. His senses stirred at the feel of her limbs tangled with his. A pulse beat at his temple, desire and guilt.

He kissed her long and hard, like a dying man holding on to his last breath. In the final countdown he hadn't been able to hear her utter those three little words he'd tried to force out of her earlier. He couldn't humble Rachel that much.

It would only make the truth that much harder to accept in the end.

## Chapter Ten

Big Jim Carlson was a man after Rachel's own heart. He didn't talk a lot, didn't try to impress. He just worked hard and was as honest as the day was long. He wore dungarees, a hard hat and the kind of serene, amused expression that only came from leading a blameless, uncluttered life. Rachel fell for him on sight, and they established a mutual admiration society almost immediately.

"I think that says something for the type of company I like to keep," Rachel pointed out later on as she and Ty shared burgers in his office trailer over Saturday's lunch hour. "Give me Big Jim over the rest of your family and friends any day."

"That's because there's no pretension," Ty argued. "It has nothing to do with background."

"It has everything to do with background."

"Why are you trying so hard not to fit in?" he demanded, echoing her own words of the night before. "You don't have to like Kathleen, or my mother, to be part of my life.''

"I like your mother," Rachel said quickly.

"Well, I like Big Jim, too. He's completely himself." Ty chewed on his burger, pinning her with those dark eyes that saw everything. "You might like Gerald if you got to know him."

"Gerald's fine. Everyone was great. I just—" She cut herself off, and Ty lifted his brows. Rachel inclined her head. "I don't know. Things are just moving pretty fast."

"Not fast enough for me," he muttered, wadding up the white bag the hamburgers had come in and tossing it in the trash. The look he suddenly sliced her was wickedly sensual.

"What?" Rachel wiped her fingers on her napkin, her own lips curving in response.

"I was thinking about last night."

"Don't," she said on a laugh.

"Why not?"

"Because I don't trust myself around you."

"Really?" He sounded intrigued and delighted.

"And if you aren't careful, I might just throw you over this desk and have my way with you."

He gazed at her in astonishment, and Rachel, who'd never joked with a man about sex before, turned sixteen shades of scarlet. "I'm—sorry. I didn't mean for—"

"Don't apologize. Good grief. I was just amazed that you actually said what was on your mind. I've never met a woman who could before."

Rachel gave him a long look. "You profess to love me and want to marry me, yet you don't know anything about me."

"I'm a quick study." His smile was dangerous.

"I'm sure."

They grinned at each other. Rachel's thoughts flew to their lovemaking of the night before. She was surprised at her shameless wanton ways, surprised and a little delighted. She'd always hoped she was more of a sexual being than her marriage had indicated. Ty had proved her right.

"Let's go home and make love," he suggested, jumping to his feet. He grabbed Rachel by the hand, pulling her out of her chair so quickly that she was laughing, her hair falling out of its ponytail to swing around her shoulders. He buried his hands in it, kissed her curving lips with abandon. Suddenly the door of the trailer cracked open.

"Tyrrell?" Sybil Rafferty asked tentatively.

Rachel wriggled to free herself, mortified. Ty, however, refused to let her go. His kiss, which was more for fun than passion, turned into a loud smack, loud enough for Sybil to hear even if she were stone-deaf.

"Hi, Mother," he greeted her, holding tightly to Rachel and refusing to budge against her desperate attempts to escape.

"Oh, hello, Rachel," Sybil said, smiling worriedly.

"Hello, Mrs. Rafferty." She was going to kill Ty! He knew better than anyone how to make an impossible situation even more impossible.

"What in the world are you doing here?" he asked Sybil pleasantly.

"I was hoping I could talk to you. I called your house but got that answering machine."

"Mother hates the answering machine," Ty explained, finally releasing Rachel, his eyes glowing with amusement at the furious darts shooting from hers.

"I wanted to invite you to come by the house this evening."

Rachel sensed Ty stiffen beside her. "Why?" he asked, his voice turning soft and dangerous.

"I didn't realize Rachel was still here."

"That doesn't answer my question."

Rachel grew distinctly uncomfortable. It didn't take a brain surgeon to decipher Sybil's remarks. She didn't want Rachel around—nohow, no way.

"Kathleen's taken a quick trip to Los Angeles and won't be back for several days. I'd like to spend some time talking with you, if you don't mind," Sybil said a bit primly.

"I don't mind." Ty's gaze was narrowed on his mother's face. He didn't have to tell Rachel how unusual it was for Sybil to request his presence; it hung in the air as if the words had been spoken aloud. "I'm driving Rachel back to Oceanside in the afternoon. When I get back in the city, I'll stop by."

"Thank you, Tyrrell." She smiled at Rachel—a nice smile—then she carefully made her way down the narrow trailer steps while Ty held the door for her.

"So," Rachel said, watching Sybil climb into the yellow taxi that had delivered her to the construction site. "I think she minds you seeing me very much."

He shook his head.

"Why, then, did she make such an effort to insure that you would come by the house?"

Ty didn't answer.

Nathan was already back at the house when Ty pulled into the driveway. Rex barked and jumped in a wild frenzy as Rachel headed for the front door. Taking pity on the German shepherd, she circled around to where he was chained and let him ruin her clothes with his muddy paws as he joyously tackled her.

"Worthless mutt." She laughed, fondly scratching his ears while avoiding his sloppy tongue.

The dog growled menacingly in his throat at Ty's approach.

"Relax, you beast," she scolded.

"I wonder if he'll ever get used to me," Ty said in amusement. He held out his hand for Rex to smell.

Rex eyed him steadily. He gave Ty's hand one snobbish sniff, then crouched down beside Rachel.

"Did you want to come in, or do you have to go right away?" Rachel continued scratching Rex's ears.

"I should get back. But there's something I want to say first." He drew a long breath and gazed out over the cliff to the gray waters of the Pacific. "Give this marriage thing some serious thought. Please."

"I don't know, Ty. We haven't even talked about Nathan, or about where we would live, or anything. There would be a lot to decide, even if we agreed that that's . . . what we wanted," she finished lamely.

"It's what I want. Is it what you want?"

He was coiled tightly, gazing at her with such intensity that Rachel hesitated before answering, afraid he might give her answer more weight than it truly deserved. "It's what a part of me wants."

Ty smiled. "Tell me which part, and I'll work on it."

"Why is it so important to you that I marry you?"

His hand slid around the back of her neck, gently tipping up her chin. He pressed a kiss to her forehead. Rachel felt herself sink inside, loving the touch of his skin against hers. Rex whined worriedly.

"When you find what you're looking for, you know it," he said softly. "I found you."

"And a ready-made family," Rachel was compelled to insert.

His muscles tensed. "Things'll work out, Rachel. Just give it a chance. I like Nathan. Don't worry about that."

And then he kissed her, slowly, with passion and a certain desperation, as if he were deliberately sealing a bargain. Rachel's senses resisted for all of five seconds before her own lips softened, her own arms slid around his back, caressing the hard muscles, her own breath accelerated, reaching a ragged tempo of need.

"Oh, Rachel." Ty squeezed her close. He couldn't get her close enough. A pervasive sense of disaster hung over him. Rex licked his hand, the one wrapped possessively around Rachel's waist, and Ty released Rachel long enough to bend down and show the dog some attention. Then he glanced up at her, feeling her eyes on him. She was chewing her bottom lip.

"What?" he asked softly, sensing her uncertain mood.

"If I wanted our relationship to just continue as it is, at least for now, would you mind very much?"

There were doubts in those beautiful hazel orbs. Worry. "I wouldn't have much choice, would I? If you don't want to marry me, you don't. There's no forcing the issue."

"I would just feel more comfortable if we didn't rush things," Rachel said hurriedly.

"Sure."

"Will I . . . see you soon?" she asked when Ty dusted off the knees to his jeans and turned back toward his car.

"Very soon." He smiled ironically. "I can't seem to stay away."

"Next weekend?"

"If not sooner."

She watched the Porsche reverse down her driveway and turn onto the highway before she returned to the house. Nathan was hovering by the back door. From his anxious expression—and how desperately he was trying to hide it— she figured he'd seen more of their embrace than he'd wanted to.

"So you're home already," she greeted him, glancing down ruefully at her dirt-smudged jeans. "How was the weekend?"

"Good." He hesitated. "How was yours?"

"Good."

"I did my community service work. And I *slaved* at Tennyson's store."

"And how was Mr. Tennyson?"

Nathan snorted.

Rachel grinned. "Think I'll change and take a run."

"Wait."

She glanced up at him in surprise. Nathan was frowning, scowling really. He fidgeted with his fingers for a few seconds, then shoved his hands in his pockets. "Are you— and this guy—getting kind of serious?"

"We like each other," Rachel answered cautiously.

"I saw him kissing you."

Betrayal rang in those few words. And fear. Rachel's heart twisted. "Yeah, well, he's a little more serious than I am, at this point."

"How serious?" Nathan's face was tense.

"I'm not making any major changes right away," she tried to reassure him. It had the opposite effect.

"You're thinking of marrying him!"

Under ordinary circumstances Nathan's jump to his worst possible conclusion would have been normal teenage overreaction. But in this case he was too close to the truth. Troubled, Rachel said, "You know my marriage to Richard wasn't perfect. No marriage is. So before I married anyone, I'd sure take a good hard look at who he was, what he expected from me and what I expected from him."

"He'd want us to move, wouldn't he? To Portland? I'm not leaving Oceanside!"

"Nathan..."

"No way! I don't care how much money he's got! I don't care who he is or anything! I'm not leaving!"

"No one's asking you to leave. You're way ahead of yourself. Ty and I have barely gotten to know each other."

"I'm not stupid, Mom!" he fairly shouted.

"Well, neither am I!" she shouted right back. "Give me a little credit, huh? Just seeing Ty is a big step for me. I hardly know how to react. Yes, I'm attracted to him, and yes, I dream about something lasting, something permanent, and yes, he's asked me to marry him. But I've put him off. I can't just jump in. I've got to think about you, and me, and everything. And I'm not going to make any decision without consulting you first."

Nathan's lips were parted in shock. It was rare for Rachel to lose her cool.

"Isn't it all right for me to have a boyfriend?" she asked.

He looked down at the toes of his dirty sneakers. The sole was separating from the leather. His mouth worked.

"Well, isn't it?"

"I guess so."

Moved, Rachel committed the greatest sin of all; she wrapped her arms around him and gave him a hug. But for once Nathan didn't shove her away. "You want to go running with me?"

"No. Sorry," he added to take the sting out of it.

"You want to have popcorn tonight in front of the TV? We can watch whatever mindless things show up."

"Mom ... ?"

"Hmm?"

She sensed him struggling to get something out. Here it comes, she thought fatalistically. The ultimatum. The plea.

"Did you ask him about the money?"

She blinked. "The money?" This wasn't what she'd expected at all.

"The five hundred dollars."

"Oh." She smiled to herself. "Yes, I did. He didn't deposit it into my account."

"Are you sure?" he asked quickly.

"Pretty sure. Ty thinks it was a bank error."

"Bank error," Nathan repeated slowly.

The turn of phrase on Nathan's tongue did strange things to Rachel. It was exactly what Ty had said. She glanced down at the crown of Nathan's head. His thick black hair stirred uncomfortable embers of something she couldn't quite name.

Sometimes he reminded her so much of Ty it was scary.

As he eased out of her embrace, she wondered if that was one of the reasons she found Ty so attractive. He possessed Nathan's good looks and the best parts of his personality. But Ty was a mature male with a sharp sense of humor and a jaded view of life. Nathan was simply angry at the world.

"If you turn out half as good as he did, you'll be great," she muttered under her breath as she headed for her room to change.

"Huh? Were you talking to me?"

"Yes, and I said you'll be great," she sang out, purposely keeping the fact that she'd compared him to Ty a secret. There were some things Nathan wouldn't ever be able to handle.

They were seated at the butcher-block table in the center of the kitchen. Ty's attitude had nose-dived from interested and slightly wary to downright worried. He hadn't eaten in the kitchen since he was twelve years old. Maybe eleven. His mother had *never* eaten here.

What was this, some kind of latent mothering on Sybil's part? Some attempt at filling in the gaps of the past?

He lifted his gaze to hers. His mother's eyes were a steely gray blue; his father's had been the deep brown, almost black, that he and Kathleen and now Nathan shared. But even though Rafferty genes seemed to dominate when it came to physical appearance, there were traits Sybil possessed that Ty recognized in himself and Kathleen and Nathan as well. The way she skewered him with that piercing gaze was more her side of the family. And right now her determination, though more gentle than his father's had ever been, was extremely lethal. He was in trouble, and she was going to set him straight.

"You broke your engagement to Barbara because of this girl," Sybil said, getting right to the point. Her tone was quiet, almost conversational.

"I broke my engagement to Barbara because I didn't want to marry her."

"Because of this girl."

"Rachel Stone is twenty-eight years old. I'd classify her as a woman."

"Are you in love with her?"

Irritation flashed through him. His mother, of all people, should know better than to press him. She was using Kathleen tactics—a mistake. "Who wants to know?"

"I want to know."

"All right. I find her nearly irresistible." He reached for the wine bottle, ignoring the plate of elegantly displayed fan-tailed shrimp Mary had placed in front of him. "Why are we eating in the kitchen? You never eat in the kitchen."

"I didn't want you sitting fifteen chairs away from me at the dining-room table, as you're known to do."

Ty gulped down half the glass before answering. He resisted wiping his mouth with the back of his hand. "What do you want to know?"

"Are you planning to marry her?"

Ty emitted a bark of disbelief. "This is something new. You, in the role of overprotective mother. You left me alone as a kid. Why now?"

"Because you've never done anything crazy in your life and now you are."

"I've never done anything crazy?"

Sybil Rafferty looked at him in mild annoyance. "Oh, you've been impossible. Always trying to irritate your father and your sister. I've seen it. But you've always done the right thing in the end. Marrying Barbara would have been the right thing—if you loved her. But since you obviously don't, you broke the engagement."

Ty finished his wine and waited. The rebel in him felt like asking for a pad and pencil so he could write this down. Lord, but his mother was acting weird. Another time he might have asked her what she'd been smoking, but he figured tonight she wouldn't see the humor.

"Either you've fallen desperately in love with Rachel Stone or there's another reason you're seeing her."

The wine went down the wrong pipe. Ty half choked. Tears came to his eyes. "You sound like Rachel," he croaked out.

"Tell me the truth, Tyrrell, and I'll leave you alone."

Drawing a breath, Ty rubbed his eyes. When he focused on his mother again, he felt a jolt of shock. She was aging. Deep lines had formed beside her mouth and at the corners of her eyes. She looked dreadfully unhappy.

His revelation must have shown on his face because she sighed. "I'd like to think that one of my children is taking charge of his life. Maybe I've been wrong, but I've always counted on it being you. Kathleen can't stick with anything. She's miserable and will always be miserable unless she learns to like herself a little. But you. You've always gone your own way, made your own life. And you've always done the right thing. For you."

"I'm not sure I'm following this," he murmured.

"Ty, you're so different with this girl. You treat her like she's yours. And how long have you known her? A few weeks. You don't jump like that into a relationship unless there's a good reason."

"So, what do you want me to say? That I'm having an affair? That it'll be over soon and I'll find another Barbara?"

"Don't patronize me. Just tell me the truth. I'd like to think that if you're truly serious about this *young woman*—" she stressed the words slightly, enough to draw a smile from Ty "—that there's some chance you'll be happy. Some chance this marriage will work." She lifted her chin. "On the selfish end of it, I'd like to think I might have grandchildren one day."

Ty stared into his mother's eyes for a long, long moment. He thought of the consequences. Of the future. Of Nathan.

Leaning on his elbows, he clasped his hands together and rested his chin on his fingers. "All right. There's more to it than love."

He saw her steel herself. "What is it?"

"Rachel's adopted son, Nathan."

Confusion entered her gaze.

"He's my son, Mother. My biological son."

There was barely a flicker of emotion in her face as she absorbed the news. She reached for the wine bottle and refilled her glass—to the top. Carefully she lifted the glass to her lips. Ty wouldn't have been surprised if she'd belted the whole thing down in one gulp, but she sipped with extreme delicacy.

"Does he know?" she asked.

Ty slowly shook his head.

"Does *she* know?"

This was tricky stuff. Even his own mother might not forgive him for his deception. "Not yet," he admitted with a grimace.

"So that's what this is all about? You've been romancing her so that you can have your son? Ty," she murmured unhappily, "that's something your father would have done."

"My father's the reason I never knew about Nathan!" Ty snarled through his teeth. "Don't talk to me about him."

"When are you going to tell her?"

Refilling his own glass, he lifted it in a mock toast to his mother. "That's the sixty-four-thousand-dollar question, isn't it? Raintree told me I'd never get custody, so I decided not to let Rachel or Nathan know who I was. And then... and then..."

His mother took a steadier sip of wine. "And then?"

"And then one thing led to another and I thought that if I could get to know her, if she could trust me..."

Sybil Rafferty groaned and closed her eyes. Ty could almost read her mind. She had always harbored great hopes for him, her only son. Though she'd loved her husband, she wanted something sounder, purer, *better* for Ty. Tyrrell Rafferty II had been an unbearable autocrat who'd molded Kathleen in his own image and desperately tried to do the same with his son. Secretly, Ty suspected Sybil had cheered on Ty's own rebellion, and he'd always counted on her to understand him, champion his side.

But Rachel Stone was something else again. Though Sybil would hardly dismiss Nathan, her first grandchild, and the complicated issue of his custody, she wouldn't be happy that Ty wanted to be with Rachel. In fact, she *wasn't* happy. He knew what she was thinking—they weren't suited for each other, she would be out of place in his rarefied social circle, marriages of convenience never worked.

She opened her eyes and drew a breath. "Have you let that poor girl think you're in love with her?"

"Wait a minute. This is a different issue. I care about Rachel. A lot. I didn't expect to, but I do."

"How terribly convenient."

"Look, Mother." Ty rose from the kitchen stool and gave her a perfunctory kiss on the cheek. "Sorry to say it, but you sound a lot like Kathleen. I know what I'm doing. The only serious mistake I've made is not being truthful with Rachel from the beginning."

"That's not the only serious mistake."

"I trust you won't mention this to Kathleen."

She nodded.

Ty strode down the marble-tiled hall, his footsteps echoing hollowly throughout the massive entryway. Rain was gently falling outside, dampening the brick walk. Shoving his hands in his pockets, Ty ducked his head, aiming in the direction of his car.

*Have you let that poor girl think you're in love with her?*

Biting out a string of epithets, he turned his face to the rain. It drizzled softly against his skin, as fine as mist. He'd spoken the truth to his mother. He cared about Rachel. Maybe not love, but damn close enough.

"God," he murmured, the weight of fear pressing down on him like a brick wall.

In a perverse twist of fate all the little lies he'd uttered of love and trust and plans for the future were more truth now than fiction. He loved so many things about her. She was a perfect fit for him. She didn't even care about his wealth. She cared about *him* and was even on the verge of admitting her own love.

How ironic that the main obstacle between them was the one that had brought them together in the first place—Nathan.

And now he didn't know what the hell he was going to do about it.

## Chapter Eleven

The bank manager looked at Rachel as if he had better ways to spend his time than deal with a crazy woman who insisted he remove five hundred dollars from her account.

"Let me turn you over to Yvonne. She can come up with a solution."

Yvonne was the personal accounts specialist. She listened to Rachel's tale with a faint smile hovering around her mouth, as if she were certain that yes, now she truly had heard everything.

"I'll tell you what I'll do. I'll put the money in a separate account. A savings account. We'll leave it there for a few months. I'll have to check our policy, but if we don't discover an error on our side, I'm sure the money reverts to you. It's more yours than ours."

Rachel nodded.

"It's possible someone accidentally deposited to your account instead of theirs," Yvonne said doubtfully. "It'd be hard to make that kind of mistake, but strange things do happen upon occasion. You're absolutely certain no one you know deposited the money?''

"I can't think of one person," Rachel said truthfully.

"A family member?"

"The only family member I have is my fifteen-year-old son. Trust me. If he had five hundred dollars, he'd gallop right down to the Fun Center for a video marathon.''

"We'll see what we can do, Mrs. Stone. Now, just sign these papers.…''

An hour later Rachel was back from lunch and hard at work. Nathan was working off his time at Tennyson's Coast-to-Coast and also doing beach cleanup, his community service assignment. He didn't complain about the cleanup, but working for Tennyson was a test of his rather limited patience. But he was trying hard, and for that Rachel was proud of him. And he'd apparently been doing his work without grumbling, for one of Tennyson's clerks had caught her on the street one day and remarked at what an industrious, handsome, *polite* young man he was.

Rachel had been bowled over. That side of Nathan had been buried so long she'd thought it would never be resurrected! She'd taken heart at this unexpected turn of events. Maybe some good would come out of Nathan's shoplifting. Maybe he would grow up, think about the consequences, become more responsible.

She hadn't broached the subject of Ty with him all week. They'd been enjoying a sort of truce since the last blowup. And Rachel was less tense since she'd paid most of her bills. True, next month loomed like some dark monster, ready to swallow her up at the first opportunity, but until she had to once again ask for an advance on her salary, she was holding her own.

*If you marry Ty, your money problems will go up in smoke.*

Rachel growled beneath her breath, punching the computer keys with more speed and fervor than necessary. The machine beeped at her in outrage. Hieroglyphics appeared on her screen, the blasted inanimate object's own form of swearing.

"Okay, okay," she muttered, slowing her racing fingers. Thoughts of Ty and his wealth made her crazy. She had this dreadful feeling that were she to jump deliriously into marriage with him, she'd be exchanging one impossible situation for another. Why that was so, she couldn't explain. Most other women on the planet would consider his fortune a plus. But it scared Rachel. Terrified her.

He'd called her on Wednesday. The sound of his low, slightly raspy and thoroughly sexy voice had actually raised goose bumps on her skin. Something in her tone must have alerted Nathan to the fact that Ty was on the other end of the line because his head had jerked up, his eyes fixing accusingly on Rachel, his dinner completely forgotten. Rachel had smiled at him, but his expression hadn't changed. By the time she'd gotten off the phone and done her best to appease Nathan, she couldn't remember exactly what Ty had said, but it was something about seeing her over the weekend. And something about making plans.

Wedding plans?

With an impatient sigh, Rachel pushed her tumble of hair back. Her clip had broken, and her ponytail was now a swath of red-brown hair that fell in front of her eyes. Why was she letting this romantic dream play out? Why didn't she tell him she absolutely couldn't marry him? Not now. Not ever. Why did she let him push her forward as if she were tossed and tumbled and shoved by the tide and unable to battle against it?

Because, damn it, she wanted him to convince her he was right. She wanted to believe she could marry him.

She wanted *him*.

Allison appeared from the staff room with two cups of coffee. She held one out to Rachel, who accepted it gratefully. "You look furious enough to spit nails. What's wrong?"

"This damn hair won't stay put!" Rachel bit out, twisting the silken strands into a rope and flinging it over one shoulder where it slowly uncoiled.

"Yeah, right. It's your hair." Allison smiled. "Had a fight with The Third, did you?"

"Way off, Allison."

"Had a fight with Nathan about The Third?"

"We always argue about Ty. No, this is simple disenchantment with the reality of life." Rachel sighed and wrinkled her nose. "You know the old cliché. We're from two different worlds."

"Ahh. Does he feel this way, too?"

"No, he thinks just the opposite. In fact, he's got this idea that all we have to do is walk down the aisle together and *poof!* no more problems."

Allison leaned forward, her dark gaze searching Rachel's face as if she were making certain her friend was still sane. "He asked you to marry him?" she said with rising incredulity.

Rachel groaned inwardly. A part of her had been dying to get this discussion going even though she'd told herself to keep it under wraps. "In so many words."

"Wow." Allison was thoroughly taken aback.

"Why do you suppose he'd do that? What's he thinking of?"

"Oh, come on, Rachel. You don't have to squeak compliments out of me. You know why."

"Yeah? Maybe you could fill me in," Rachel grumbled.

"You're a good-natured woman with a sense of humor and an attractive bod and face. That's what he sees and that's what he wants."

"But *marriage,* Allison. Marriage is so much work."

"You and I know that, but he's never been married before, right?" At Rachel's slow nod, she went on, "He's in love with you, you dunderhead. My God, girl! Go for it!"

Rachel laughed, grateful for Allison's magnanimity. After all, Allison had been very attracted to Ty herself. "You didn't ask me if I loved him."

"I didn't ask you whether the sun is going to come up tomorrow morning, either," she said on a snort. "It's one of those things I just know."

Ty watched his footprints disappear beneath a chilly wave. He'd been standing on the beach for about an hour, watching the sun on the gray undulating surface of the water. The ocean was dazzling today. That was the word. No rain, just bright, dazzling sunlight bouncing off water as far as the eye could see. It almost hurt to look.

The wind was up. The coast was always windy in August. The hottest month of the year, but the wind sent sunbathers scurrying inside. In some ways September was better.

He wouldn't mind getting married in September. At the coast. Maybe a justice of the peace and two witnesses he'd never met before. God save him from a Rafferty wedding with the photographers, the Dom Pérignon champagne, the old ladies bent double under the weight of their necklaces, and the scores of relatives he'd never seen before and suspected were lying about their Rafferty connections, anyway.

If only he could convince Rachel of the same.

Glancing back, he gazed up the cliff to where Rachel's house sat. He could barely make out the roof and chimney. She would be home from work soon. Nathan might be there already. Did he dare visit Nathan without Rachel around? It would be an opportunity to get to know his son—an excellent opportunity—but from what he'd already learned of Nathan's personality, it would be welcomed only on one side. For all Ty knew, Nathan might slam the door in his face.

He smiled at the thought and turned back to the cliff path. He'd used the public access, not wanting to encounter either Rex or a hostile Nathan by acting as if he had a right to be on Rachel's property. But now the thought of talking to Nathan alone was so appealing that he drove straight to Rachel's rutted drive. Rex, who'd been curled up by the back door, came racing out to the length of his chain, barking furiously.

It occurred to Ty that Nathan might not be home. The thought brought both disappointment and relief. Disappointment that he couldn't make some attempt at friendship, relief he wouldn't have to withstand the emotional scene his son would undoubtedly create. His mouth twisted. With a sense of self-disgust he realized that Rachel was his buffer. He used her to help him with his son.

He used her in so many ways.

Drawing a sharp breath between his teeth, Ty fought back a wave of fear. Newly sensitive to his own feelings for Rachel, he was swamped by overwhelming doubts, a sense of vulnerability. He, who had never questioned which path to take, now suffered moment by moment from a desperate certainty that everything he'd done would come crashing down around him.

Raintree's call the other morning hadn't helped.

"What do you want me to tell your mother?" he'd asked in exasperation. "You told her Nathan Stone was your son and now she wants particulars."

His mother's involvement exasperated Ty. "As long as she isn't feeding the information to Kathleen, tell her what she wants to know."

"And how am I supposed to know if she's telling Kathleen?" Raintree had asked in a nasty tone. He was at the end of his rope.

"She said she wouldn't and I believe her. Hell, I don't know," he'd added, giving vent to his frustration. "Tell her I'm taking care of things and don't want any interference...."

The back door slammed with a bang. Ty heard it as he approached the front steps, so he turned and followed the buckling sidewalk around the corner of the house.

Nathan was scratching Rex's ears, staring at Ty's car. Seeing Ty, he scowled darkly, folding his arms over the chest of his black leather jacket.

"Hi," Ty greeted him, secretly amused at the boy's rebel-without-a-cause attitude.

"Hello."

"Rachel still at work?"

"Yep."

Well, this wasn't working. Ty stopped about ten feet in front of Nathan, turning his gaze away from the boy to the view of the distant ocean. The wind fluttered the leaves on the manzanita tree. Several fell to the ground, brown and curled. September was on its way.

"How's it going with Tennyson and the community service work?" Ty asked conversationally.

"What's it to ya?"

The question was practically a squeak. Nathan wasn't half as good at acting tough as he was at looking tough. Ty treated the query like a breakthrough. It was better than being ignored.

"I don't know. I like your mom a lot. I was just interested."

"Yeah, well, you can be interested in her. As for me, stay out of my way."

Ty's lungs felt starved for air. The way Nathan sounded was so much like the way he'd been himself as a teenager that it was almost creepy. How could Rachel not see it? He paused to collect himself before answering. "I'll bear that in mind."

"How come you want to see her, anyway?" Nathan demanded, his courage apparently bolstered by Ty's quiet answer. "She's not your kind."

"My kind?"

"Yeah, your kind, man."

Ty eyed him, and Nathan eyed him right back. "My kind of... woman?" Ty asked cautiously, his moment of uncertainty replaced by amusement once more. The little jerk. Who the hell did he think he was, passing judgment on adults?

"I know what you're doing. I'm on to you."

"Is that right?"

Emotion smoldered in Nathan's dark eyes. "You're using her. You think you can have anyone you want. You think your money will get you anything. And you don't care!"

This was quite a speech for Nathan. And so close to the mark that the hair on Ty's arms lifted. Guilt. It was a physical sensation. "You're wrong. I do care about Rachel. I'm not sure why I'm telling you this, since it's something I'm not sure you have a right to know. It's my business. And your mother's. But I do care. And next time you try to take me on, make sure you've got all the facts straight."

The color disappeared from Nathan's face, leaving it stark white against the black jacket. Ty wanted to reach out and grab him. He was furious. But he wasn't certain whether he wanted to shake Nathan or hug him. And it was a shock to feel so protective. A shock to know he cared enough to want to physically hold his own son.

"You stay away from me," Nathan said, backing up. Rex growled, glancing from Ty to Nathan, unsure what to do.

Good Lord, Ty thought.

The sound of a car's engine interrupted the tense scene. Ty almost gulped with relief. Rachel's wagon pulled up behind the Porsche. She stepped from the driver's seat, taking in the scene in one encompassing glance.

She wore a dress. Dark green blue with a full skirt. It was more a jumper over a short-sleeved white shirt. Her hair was free and whipped wildly in the wind. Her gaze swept from Nathan to rest on Ty. He saw the softening of her expression, and it did wonders for his bruised soul.

Nathan must have seen it, too. He stumbled away without a word. Back to the house. Rex followed, whining, until the chain brought him up short.

"I couldn't remember what day you said you were coming," she greeted Ty, her hazel eyes tinged with sadness as her gaze followed Nathan. "I was sort of out of it on the phone the other night."

Ty couldn't wait. The scent of her was enough to turn a saint into a sinner. He pulled her into his arms and held her tight against his body, smelling the lemony scent of her shampoo, burying one hand in the rich silk of her hair. Rachel let out a squeak of protest. "Let me hold you," he said roughly. "Please."

She instantly stilled in his arms. "What's wrong?"

"Nothing."

A moment passed, and she drew a long breath, sweetly melting into his embrace. "Try again," she said, humor turning her voice to music.

"Have you ever felt like you're never going to be able to make things right? That it's all an illusion, and it's your own fault?"

Rachel eased away from him to look into his eyes. His desperation must have communicated itself to her because her brows drew together in concern. "What is it? What happened?" She glanced swiftly past him. "What did Nathan do?" she demanded sharply.

"It wasn't Nathan. It's just me." Managing a laugh, Ty dropped his arms, running one hand through his own hair. A tremor ran beneath his skin. "I want to marry you, Rachel, and it feels like every moment we delay is making that possibility an impossibility. You don't have to say when, just say you will."

Rachel glanced down at her hands. They were clenched tightly. Her knees were trembling. This decision had followed her around since the moment she'd realized Ty was serious.

*What are you going to say when he demands an answer?*

"Rachel?"

"I love you, Ty," she admitted tremulously. "And I want to marry you."

It was clear he couldn't believe his ears. "Do you mean it?"

"Yes."

He gathered her close with a whoop of triumph. Rachel laughed when he suddenly spun her around. This was so unlike the Ty she knew that she blinked in surprise, feeling as if she were with a stranger.

"When?"

"You said you wouldn't ask me when," Rachel pointed out with a crooked grin. She was feeling better now. Stronger. The decision was made and it was right.

"Okay, okay. I'll leave it for now. But we've got a lot to talk about."

"You said it," she murmured with meaning.

"And Nathan," Ty said, his thoughts clearly running ahead of himself. "Somehow we've got to tell Nathan."

Rachel nodded, fighting back a fresh onslaught of doubts. "How do you think he'll take it?" she asked rhetorically.

The meaningful look Ty slanted her said it all.

Rachel knew exactly what it felt like the moment before an explosion. The air crackled.

Nathan was utterly motionless. Frozen in front of the TV set, his body half-turned to Ty and Rachel, the remote control in his hand. On the TV someone was singing a rap song. Nathan very calmly clicked the television off.

And then the bomb detonated.

"You can do anything you damn well like," Nathan snarled. "But I'm not going. I'm staying here. If you think I'm moving to Portland, forget it. I'll run away first. Why can't you just go have sex and leave it at that?"

"Nathan!" Rachel was horrified.

"Wait a minute," Ty warned dangerously.

"Why the hell do you have to get married? Why can't you just be normal!"

He ran, but Ty caught him by the jacket. Nathan swung at him. His fist connected with Ty's jaw, but Ty flinched at the last second, and Nathan landed only a glancing blow. Nathan's second punch was to Ty's gut, but by this time Ty was on guard. He grabbed Nathan's right arm and yanked it behind his back. Rachel grimaced, anticipating the pain. Unbalanced, Nathan fell onto the couch.

He bounded up as if pulled on a string. Ty took a step back, his hands in front of him in surrender. But the grim set of his jaw said the fight wasn't over unless Nathan gave in.

"Wait. Wait!" Rachel squeezed herself between them. She couldn't get her mind in gear. Every muscle was shaking. "Wait, please!"

"Don't do it," Ty warned Nathan in a voice that was meant to be listened to.

Nathan hesitated.

Ty waited.

Rachel looked from one to the other.

"You owe Rachel an apology," Ty told Nathan. "Either give her that apology or leave the room."

*Oh, no.* Rachel's gaze swung desperately to Ty. This was no good. Nathan never took orders. This was the quickest way to alienate him.

Nathan's eyes narrowed hatefully on Ty. "I don't have to listen to you. You're not my father."

Ty didn't answer. Rachel wasn't certain what to do. Richard and Nathan had never had a scene like this, but then Richard hadn't possessed Ty's forceful will.

Nathan's gaze dropped first. He was coiled so tightly that Rachel prepared herself for another explosion. But then he shoved past Ty and stalked down the hall, slamming his bedroom door behind him in a childish display of total contempt.

"I'm sorry," Rachel heard herself say. She sounded like a child herself.

"Don't be. It's no less than I expected."

She wanted to tell him Nathan wasn't that way. Not really. He was good and lovable and empathetic. She wanted Ty to at least like him a little.

Ty closed his eyes, grimacing. He seemed utterly shaken. Rachel was a bit surprised. She wouldn't have expected him to care so much about Nathan's reaction.

"It's going to take him some time," she explained needlessly and a trifle pathetically.

Ty nodded, exhaling a long breath. "Did I handle that right?" he asked aloud, and Rachel had the peculiar sensation that her answer truly mattered.

"I think so."

"I'd hate to think I was like my own father. I was trying to remember what he would have done in a similar situation. I did try to hit him once, but it's funny, I can't remember how he reacted."

Rachel slipped into his arms, wrapping hers around his waist, touched by Ty's worry over his role in Nathan's life. It made her realize like nothing else had how she'd made the right decision. With an assurance she hadn't felt before, she lifted her mouth to drop a soft kiss on his lips. "You're going to be a good father to Nathan." At the jerk of his limbs, she amended, "A good stepfather. The kid doesn't know how lucky he is."

Ty made a strangled sound. "Rachel, we've never talked about children. About having another child. How do you feel about that?"

"Well, I guess I expected you to want one of your own, if you could have it." She ducked her head, slightly embarrassed. "I mean, it's probably possible for me to conceive. Richard's first wife couldn't, and after he adopted Nathan he didn't want any other children.

"Of course," she added, wrinkling her nose, "after Nathan's last show, I wouldn't blame you for forgoing children. You may never want to experience fatherhood firsthand."

Ty pressed a kiss to her forehead. "You'd be surprised," he murmured. "Just don't change your mind, Rachel. Whatever happens."

"I won't."

"Promise me."

She grinned, loving the sensation that he was insecure and worried she might somehow elude him. How silly. "I promise I won't change my mind. Hell could freeze over and I'd still marry you. I love you, Ty. I think I have from the moment you stepped into my life."

He tilted up her chin, kissed her with suppressed passion, then groaned, rubbing his jaw. "Nathan's got a helluva right cross," he complained.

"You're lucky you got out of the way like you did."

"Let's just hope he doesn't have occasion to hit me again," he said cryptically, and Rachel wondered what he was thinking of.

## Chapter Twelve

Rachel had always run her life in a calm, orderly manner. Monumental decisions were made with care and discretion. They took time. Acting on those decisions also took time. But when Tyrrell Rafferty III made a decision, things started popping. There was no time for second-guessing. He moved fast. So fast that within two weeks he'd convinced her there was no reason to wait to get married.

He wanted a September wedding. He wanted a justice of the peace. The one from Oceanside would do nicely. No, he didn't feel like inviting his family. He would tell them afterward. When Rachel, uneasy, protested, Ty asked her if she really wanted to suffer through the pomp and circumstance of a Rafferty wedding, and she quickly decided he had a point.

They could live either in Oceanside or Portland or both. Ty didn't care. If Nathan wanted to stay in school with his friends, that was fine with Ty. He was congeniality personified.

As long as Rachel consented to marry him before the end of the month, which Rachel, her head spinning with excitement and confusion, did.

Nathan could come to the ceremony if he chose to, Ty and Rachel jointly decided. Nathan very adamantly chose not to. Ty made most of the necessary arrangements. Rachel invited Allison and Shawna, who both stared at her, their mouths wide circles of disbelief. They accepted, and Rachel and Ty drove to Portland where Rachel purchased a street-length soft white lace gown and a matching pair of pumps.

In three weeks every arrangement had been made—except for the phone call to the Raffertys. That Ty refused to do, and though Rachel understood why, the secrecy of Ty's actions hit a vital internal chord somewhere deep inside her, and she couldn't control the doubts that ached to be heard, the doubts that when voiced were kissed away by Ty's lips, soothed by his words of commitment.

But he never really said he loved her, and when the day of the wedding arrived with almost surreal speed, Rachel walked down the aisle with every muscle quivering with tension, every instinct screaming at her that she was making an irrevocable mistake.

And then Ty took her hand. He looked handsome in a black suit, but his normally dark face was unusually pale. The finality of the moment was getting to him, too, she concluded. For half a second she wondered if she should call it off, but then the justice of the peace began the ceremony, his sonorous voice deep and soothing—and the terrible moment passed. With Allison and Shawna in attendance, Rachel nervously repeated her vows. Ty repeated his with a cool detachment she would have reason to wonder about later.

At least that's what she remembered—or thought she remembered—later, when they were alone in their hotel room overlooking the ocean. They'd had dinner in the hotel restaurant—lobster and caviar, which Rachel couldn't even think about imposing on her fluttery stomach. Nathan was staying with the Holts again, so she didn't have to worry about him, but even so, now, alone with Ty in a luxurious suite about ten miles south of Oceanside, a bottle of champagne sweating in a bucket of ice, two enormous bouquets of flowers filling the room with their sweet, delicate scents, Rachel surfaced as if from a dream. She held out her hand and stared at the band of gold on her left ring finger, incredulous that it was there.

"I'll buy you the real thing later," Ty had promised when they'd picked out their rings two days earlier. "For now it's a symbol."

But she didn't want a fancier ring. She wanted this one. She wanted something plain and real and pure.

"What are you thinking about?" Ty sank down on the edge of the bed beside her, cupping the back of her neck and dropping a kiss on her lips. His mouth was cold from the chilled champagne. "Mmm, you taste good," he said, grinning.

"I feel strange," she told him.

"You look fabulous. My wife," he said, as if trying out the words.

"See, you feel strange, too."

"I would think feeling strange is normal," he pointed out. "How was it after your first marriage?"

Rachel smiled. "Strange."

"What did I tell you?" Ty kissed her again, his lips warmer this time, more caressing.

"I don't feel like your wife," she said thoughtfully.

He tensed. "Whatever you do, don't say you're sorry we got married. Not tonight."

Rachel gazed at him with love shining from her eyes. "You actually think that on the night of our wedding I would tell you I was sorry we got married? What a pessimist! Ty, even if I felt that way—which I don't, I just feel weird—I would never, never say that to you! Come to that, I would never have even married you in the first place. I'm here because I want to be here," she added, laying her palm across his beard-roughened cheek, pulling his mouth gently to hers.

"I love you, Mr. Rafferty," she said, the words spoken straight from her soul.

His answer was another kiss, this one while he bore her backward against the coverlet. He kissed her ravenously, his hands in her hair, his mouth searching her face. Rachel slid her arms around his back, her fingers digging his shirt from his pants, her hands sliding over the taut muscles of his back. They'd been too busy to be together these past couple of weeks. There had simply been no time or place.

Ty rolled atop her until there was no doubt that he was ready, willing and able, and Rachel smiled against his mouth. A rakish chuckle filled his throat. She slid her hands slowly over his hips. He buried his face in her hair and groaned.

"Mrs. Rafferty," he said in that low, raspy voice she found so attractive. "Do you have any idea what you're doing?"

Her hands slid over his hips to his thighs. This was as far as she could reach. "No," she lied. "Do you want me to stop?"

His mouth smiled against hers. "Not yet."

"You'll tell me when?"

"Uh-huh."

And then he didn't say anything else for a long, long time.

* * *

The honeymoon lasted all of one weekend. Nathan couldn't be cooped up with the Holt family much longer. He would wear out his welcome no matter how much they liked him. It was just best to cut the honeymoon short and hopefully make up for lost time later, so Rachel and Ty picked up Nathan Sunday afternoon and that evening the three of them sat down to their first family meal.

A memorable occasion, Rachel thought with some trepidation as she sat down between the two men, glancing from one to the other. Nathan was being purposely silent and rude. Ty's left brow was lifted in amused tolerance. Great, Rachel thought. Just great.

She'd made a pasta salad, one even Nathan liked. They ate in a kind of gathering silence. When Ty had finished about half of his salad, he looked across the table thoughtfully at Nathan.

"Nice earring," he observed.

Rachel gave Ty a speaking look. This was not a safe topic of conversation.

"I like it," Nathan said shortly. His string had been exchanged for a fake diamond. At least Rachel assumed it was fake. Lord, she hoped it was fake.

"How's the work at Tennyson's going?" Ty tried again.

"It's going."

"Rachel said they want you on the football team, but you don't want to join up."

Nathan lifted his lashes and gazed belligerently at Ty. "So?"

"So, it's okay with me. I never much liked football myself." He dug his fork back into his salad.

Nathan seemed perplexed. He shot a glance at Rachel, who just shrugged and smiled. She didn't know what to make of that. Nathan then made the mistake of turning his index finger in a circle by his ear, indicating Ty was crazy.

When he looked over at Ty, it was to encounter his ironic gaze. Nathan blushed and glanced away.

"Would you like to come to Portland and meet my family?" Ty asked in a surprisingly neutral voice.

"No."

"You're going to have to sooner or later because we're going to be spending some time there, and we can't keep dropping you off at the neighbors'."

"I can stay here alone!"

"No." Ty was calm but firm.

Rachel held up a hand, wanting to step in, not knowing how.

"You don't have to like me, but I assume you like your mother. In fact, I assume you love your mother. No, don't answer," Ty interrupted when Nathan looked ready to argue. "I know you love her. And because you love her, you're not going to hurt her any worse than you already have, are you?"

Nathan was speechless.

"You're not the only one who's been through tough times here," Ty reminded him. "Try to grow up a bit and think about Rachel, not just about yourself. She's a person with a life outside of being your emotional target. Stop treating her like she doesn't count."

Nathan shoved back his chair and stomped from the room.

Ty sat in silence for several moments. He grimaced. "Nice going, huh?"

"At least he didn't hit you."

His killer smile made her grin in return.

Ty stayed through Monday, left for Portland that evening, then returned again Friday afternoon. It felt as if a bomb was ticking somewhere just out of reach, letting Rachel know that life, as she knew it, was about to take a radical turn. For that week she went to work as usual, laughed with her friends as usual, tried to keep Nathan on track as usual.

At the school one morning before work she ran into Madeline Dayton. Rachel said hello to her, and Madeline managed a tight "hi" in return. Instead of being irritated, Rachel wanted to shout with laughter. She hugged the knowledge of her recent marriage to Ty to her chest, recognizing for the first time how much she'd let people's opinions get her down, how much she'd judged herself, how much she'd felt inadequate. Now, renewed by Ty's love, she felt strong.

And wouldn't Madeline just *die* if she knew how wealthy Ty was?

Rachel's thoughts were traveling this very path when Ty came to pick her up at the travel agency Friday evening. Allison actually started clapping when he walked in.

"So, how long are you going to let us keep her before you whisk her away to Portland?" Allison demanded without preamble. She folded her arms across her chest in mock severity.

"She doesn't want to be whisked," Ty explained, his eyes slanting her way, watching her reaction.

Rachel knew it was just a matter of time before that issue, one he'd promised he wouldn't force, was right out in front of them. They couldn't live between two cities. Not really. Rachel didn't even want to. She was willing to move to Portland. But she wouldn't upset Nathan. Not yet.

And since Nathan wasn't Ty's son, there was no way Ty could truly understand. Eventually he would get tired of playing by Nathan's rules. The bomb was ticking.

"Oh, I'll be whisked sometime soon, I'm sure," Rachel said. "As I recall, I wanted to wait to get married. You won that one."

"To sound even mildly disgruntled is blasphemy," Allison muttered.

Shawna signaled Rachel, pointing to the phone.

"Duty calls," Rachel said, picking up the receiver. "Rachel Stone, er, Rafferty," she answered.

The gasp on the other end of the line chilled Rachel's blood. *"Rafferty?"* a woman's voice demanded with rising incredulity. "Did you marry my brother?"

Oh, God. Kathleen. In desperation, Rachel turned to Ty. He frowned. "Kathleen?" she asked a bit weakly.

"Is he there? With you?" She sounded apoplectic.

"Er, yes. Just a minute." She placed her hand over the receiver. "It's for you."

There was a momentary pause, then Ty pulled the receiver from Rachel's nerveless fingers. "Kathleen," he greeted her coolly.

"Tyrrell, for God's sake, Mother will flip! Absolutely flip! Have you lost your mind? Good Lord, is this marriage legal? Why didn't you tell us? What are you trying to hide? *Ty, I can't bear it!"*

His sister's histrionics had annoyed Ty for years. Now he found them intolerable. "Mother knew what my plans were," he said shortly. A little white lie.

"And no one bothered to tell *me?* What am I to deduce from that, little brother? That you find me unimportant enough to include in your plans. This is the Rafferty name we're talking about," she reminded him. "Your heir is the Rafferty heir."

"I'm aware of that," Ty muttered testily. "Give it a rest, Kathleen."

She'd never been able to stand the fact that their father had left almost everything to Ty. It had been a cruel, chauvinistic thing to do, but Tyrrell Rafferty II had not been known for either his sensitivity or his fairness.

"Is she pregnant?" Kathleen asked suspiciously.

Ty severed the connection with his index finger. He was so angry he was speechless. Shaking his head, he surfaced enough to realize that both Rachel and Allison were staring at him.

"My sister," he said blandly. "Not one of her better days."

Rachel's hazel eyes were wide and anxious. Ty pushed her chair under her computer table and asked, "Ready?" in a gentle voice.

"For what?"

"To leave."

She nodded jerkily, signed off her computer and collected her purse, then stood quietly for several moments, as if unsure which way to go or what to say.

"Rachel?" Ty frowned.

"Are we going to Portland tonight?"

She knew they were. They'd decided to meet his family en masse to tell them the good news. "Yes," he said a trifle shortly.

Ducking her head to avoid his eyes, she made a beeline for the door. Ty, uncertain what that meant, followed her, dreading this meeting with his family more than anything he'd dreaded so far.

Kathleen was on the patio, sitting beneath the deep purple clematis, which climbed riotously over the latticework frame above. She was seated at the glass-topped white table, sipping club soda. Sybil sat ramrod stiff, drinking tea. When Mary showed Ty, Rachel and a sullen Nathan to their table, Sybil half rose from her chair. Then her gaze riveted on Nathan, who was making a point of not looking at anything except his own restless hands, and Sybil sat back down as if she'd been pushed.

Ty pulled out a chair for Rachel, who sat down gingerly against a blue-and-white-striped cushion. The chair was white wrought iron, sturdy and ornate. A bee buzzed past her ear, somnolent and unconcerned that the auburn-haired woman who'd just been seated was a complete and total wreck.

Without a word being said, Rachel could feel hurt emanating from Sybil and animosity flowing out of Kathleen. Ty's exclusion of them wouldn't be easily forgiven. Rachel could scarcely blame them, though she also knew Ty wouldn't have been able to stand it any other way.

"Nathan, would you like to sit down?"

This was from Sybil, speaking in a quiet, almost unsure tone. Rachel looked at her in surprise.

"No." Nathan shifted his weight from one foot to the other, then remembered his manners. "Thank you."

"Mary was about to serve dinner," Kathleen said. "We weren't sure you'd be here in time. Should I tell her there'll be three more?"

"No." Ty might be willing to let his mother and sister meet his new family, but he had no intention of trying to meld them together. And the way his mother was eyeing Nathan, as if memorizing every detail of his face, was beyond nerve-racking. Not to mention that it was obviously embarrassing Nathan.

"I just felt it might be necessary to stop by," Ty explained on a drawl. "We don't plan to stay."

Nathan shot him a swift look.

"Nonsense," Sybil interrupted. "You must stay. If we've seemed ungracious, please forgive us," she added, turning to Rachel with a smile. "Tyrrell takes us by surprise time and again, and we never seem to know how to handle it." She twisted her neck to include Kathleen, but her gaze strayed once again to Nathan. "Tell Mary there'll be five for dinner." When Ty looked ready to argue, she said in a voice to be reckoned with, "I insist."

\* \* \*

"What a crazy family," Nathan muttered under his breath when he was alone in the hall with Rachel some two hours later.

Rachel, who was still rubbing her arms in an effort to soothe strung-out nerves, had to fight back a laugh. "Kathleen's something else," she agreed, enjoying being on the same side as her son for once.

"What about the old lady? She keeps *staring* at me!"

"Maybe it's the earring."

"Maybe it's that she's kind of weird that way, y'know? Likes younger men."

"Oh, Nathan!" Rachel's eyes sparkled with suppressed mirth.

"Well?"

"Don't say that in front of Ty. She's his mother. Anyway, she was probably just trying to decide what to make of you. Think how long it's been since she's seen a teenager. You're an alien being."

"She's the one with the blue hair."

"It's silver. And try not to be rude," she said on a laugh.

They smiled at each other in shared amusement. Nathan's dark hair was lopped boyishly over his forehead, but his jaw had squared and was darkened with an afternoon shadow. He'd started shaving—what?—less than a year ago, but it was clear he was going to have a heavy beard. Like Ty's.

Ty, who'd been cornered by his mother for a private conversation, finally appeared from the room down the hall where Sybil had closeted him. His expression was grim. "Let's get out of here," he said tightly.

"Okay by me," Nathan answered agreeably.

Ty's lips twisted. "Let's go to my place and relax."

"Have you got a video recorder?" Nathan asked.

Rachel gazed at him in disbelief. He was actually talking to Ty.

"Yeah, I've got a video recorder." Ty was eyeing him with a mixture of distrust and some other emotion not readily identifiable to Rachel.

"Got any videos?"

"A few."

"How about a movie marathon?" Nathan suggested with a shrug. "Stay up all night. First one to fall asleep loses."

Rachel's mouth dropped open. She quickly looked at Ty, her expression hopeful and desperate. Did he realize what a white flag Nathan was waving? Did he have a clue? Oh, Lord, don't let him blow this chance!

Ty's lashes swept downward, hiding his eyes. The corner of his mouth lifted faintly. "What does the winner get?"

Nathan grinned, and Rachel's heart nearly stopped. He looked so much like Ty sometimes it was positively frightening. How could that be? Was she going nuts?

"The winner gets to choose where to live," Nathan said devilishly.

Ty grinned. "I thought you were set on Oceanside."

"Hey. A guy's gotta keep his options open. If your place is anything like this, well, I gotta see before I commit myself."

"Nathan," Ty said, "you know, it kind of sounds like you can be bought."

They were walking to the front door. Ty's gentle teasing brought Nathan up short. Rachel wanted to cry out in despair when she remembered whom he was with and how he should be acting. But instead of reverting to antagonism, he just muttered under his breath, "I don't want my mom to be poor anymore," then slipped through the door before either Ty or Rachel could react.

The phone rang halfway through the very first movie. Ty and Nathan had disagreed on what they should watch, so Rachel had chosen a romantic comedy that had made them both groan. The phone was closest to Rachel, so she picked up the receiver.

"Rachel?" Sybil Rafferty's voice asked politely.

"Yes, hello, Sybil. Would you like to speak to Ty?"

Rachel glanced Ty's way, baffled by the searing look he was sending back. She lifted her brows questioningly. He was staring at the phone.

"No, actually, I'd like to talk to you. Did Tyrrell tell you I wanted to see you?"

"Rachel," Ty said, on his feet and across the room in three long strides. His hand reached forward, as if he were about to rip the receiver from her hand.

"No, he didn't tell me," she answered, her confused eyes on Ty's face. "He must have forgotten."

"Tell her I'll call her tomorrow," Ty rasped tersely. His tension vibrated through the room. Nathan's dark head snapped around in Rachel's direction, too, his own eyes full of questions.

"I don't need to speak to Ty," Sybil insisted, her voice tightening. "But there is something you and I need to discuss, Rachel. Ty won't tell you about it. I asked him to this evening and he refused."

"What is it?" Rachel's pulse started beating thick and hard.

Ty gently pulled the receiver from her hand. "I'll take care of this, Mother," he said, severing the connection before Rachel could decide what to do next.

"Your mother wants to talk to me about something."

"I know."

"You don't think she just wants to get to know her new daughter-in-law a little better?" she asked hopefully. How silly. It was clear there was far, far more to it than that.

"Rachel..."

Sensing the powerful emotions gripping Ty, Nathan lowered the volume on the movie, unwound his lanky limbs from the couch and came to stand beside Rachel, his expression watchful.

"Maybe you'd better explain yourself," Rachel said slowly, fear creeping across her skin.

Ty gazed into her anxious eyes, seeing in them all the fears and doubts he'd worked so hard to destroy over the past few months. And now—now when he had everything he wanted!—it was all about to shatter into nothingness. His mother had pulled him aside and informed him she was going to tell Rachel the truth. For reasons he didn't fully understand, Sybil had taken a liking to Rachel. She'd insisted the only way Ty was going to make this relationship work was by being completely, totally honest. He'd begged for time. The folly of what he'd done was a constant pressure. But upon seeing Nathan, Sybil had gone all soft and grandmotherly and she wanted the two families combined as soon as possible.

"Kathleen needs to know, too," she'd insisted. "She still thinks she's going to get her hands on some of the money your father left to you. When she realizes Nathan's your son, she'll give up that silly notion and get on with her life."

"I'll give her the money! I've said so thousands of times!"

"It's not the money she wants. You know that," his mother had chided him. "It's some kind of acknowledgment beyond the grave. And she's never going to get it. It's not there. Learning you already have an heir might make her finally realize that. Plus, I want my grandson to know who he is.''

"You think I don't?" Ty had growled.

"Yes! I think you don't. You don't care if he knows he's a Rafferty or not. It's not what you care about. And you're scared to death of losing Rachel. I can see it in your eyes."

Their argument had escalated into an out-and-out fight, culminating with his mother demanding to talk to Rachel alone, Ty refusing and then Ty storming out of the room when they'd reached this tense stalemate. He'd nearly run over Kathleen on the way out—Kathleen, who'd been doing her best to eavesdrop. The look on her face said she still didn't know what in the world was going on, however, and Ty didn't enlighten her. Instead he thought hard and fast for about thirty seconds, feeling time running out with the swiftness of the changing tide.

He was going to have to tell Rachel. Tonight. First chance.

And then he'd joined Nathan and Rachel in the foyer, and for the *first time* Nathan had responded to him in a positive way. He hadn't been able to bear the thought of losing everything he'd gained. He could put off the moment of truth a little longer, he'd determined desperately. Just a little longer.

But he'd forgotten about his mother's steely determination. Truth, justice and the American way; she was a champion for right when it suited her. But didn't she know she was going to bury him in his own deceit? Didn't she have any clue to what kind of person Rachel was?

"Ty?" Rachel asked.

His heart was hammering so loudly he could scarcely think. In a blinding stab of truth he realized he loved her. Love. Pure and simple. Love. Incredibly complicated. It had all happened too soon.

"I don't know how to start," he said aloud. His gaze landed on Nathan.

"You want me to leave," Nathan guessed.

"This is between your mom and me." A lie. Another lie.

"What is it, Ty?" Rachel asked sharply. "You're scaring me."

"God—" Nathan said.

"Don't swear," Rachel answered automatically, her gaze riveted to Ty's. There was a muscle jerking spasmodically in his cheek. "Why don't you head upstairs? I'll be there in a minute."

For once Nathan didn't argue, sensing perhaps that this was bigger than he wanted to tackle. His retreating footsteps were muffled by the carpet. Ty heard the door to the stairway slam shut, then he was alone with Rachel.

"I made a big mistake." His voice was raspier than usual. "I haven't been totally honest with you."

"*O—kay.*" Rachel wasn't sure what was coming, but it was bad. Really bad. "Was the mistake marrying me?" she forced out.

"No. No. Oh, no." Ty was hot, stifling, burning up. Confession might be good for the soul, but it was sure playing hell with his internal temperature. "I lied to you about why I came to see you. I didn't need an airline ticket. I never talked to anyone about your skill as a travel agent."

"Why did you come to see me?" Rachel asked in a small voice.

"Because you were Nathan's mother. Nathan's adoptive mother."

Rachel's fingers searched behind her for some support. Her hand was shaking so wildly she could hardly grasp the arm of the leather couch. "What do you mean?"

Ty tried twice to force the words past his lips. He took two shaking breaths. This was hard, harder than he'd even imagined. The biggest risk of his life. His throat closed.

"Oh, my God," Rachel whispered, suddenly, shockingly aware of the truth. The connection slammed into her like a blow to the solar plexus. The way they looked. The way they talked. The way *Kathleen* had even reminded her of Nathan! She couldn't breathe. Tears sprang to her eyes though she'd never felt less like crying. She felt like dying.

"I'm Nathan's father," Ty said in a dry, scratchy voice. "His biological father."

## Chapter Thirteen

"The hell you are!" Nathan's voice boomed from the end of the room. Ty's head jerked up. Nathan had slammed the door to the stairs but had never gone through it.

He charged forward, but Ty yanked his gaze from Nathan back to Rachel, who was utterly still, holding on to the edge of the couch as if it was her sole support in a world gone crazy.

Nathan stopped short beside Rachel, his dark face full of rage.

Rachel couldn't think. She gazed dully at the silent television screen. Images flickered. A man and woman kissing. Both of them laughing. Rachel thought of her son— no, *his* son—and a molten fury swept through her at the enormity of his deception. Her whole body shook. She wrapped her arms around her waist, physically holding in her anger. "I knew there was a reason," she said in a flat voice.

"Nathan was the reason we met," Ty agreed. "But not why we're together. Not why we're married. I love you," he added achingly.

"You *bastard!*"

Nathan bristled at Rachel's side. He reminded her of Rex, ready to pounce but uncertain just what she wanted from him. He, too, was shaking. He looked shattered.

"Don't swear," Nathan told her, and Rachel would have laughed if she wasn't so totally sick and miserable. "It isn't true, is it?" he asked, his dark eyes swimming with emotion.

"I don't know. I—I think so."

"I hate you!" Nathan hurled furiously at Ty. "I don't believe you!"

"Rachel . . ." Ty murmured painfully.

"You tell me all of it!" she demanded. "All of it!"

Ty closed his eyes and took a deep breath. He told her. He told her about Julia. He told her about his initial disbelief. He told her about his conversation with Raintree, his realization that it might be the truth. And then he told her how he'd planned to make Nathan his son come hell or high water. He didn't leave anything out, and as he told her the whole truth, he sensed the woman he loved grow colder, more distant, as unapproachable as the North Star.

And his son pulled back in dawning horror.

When he was finished there was nothing left to say except how much he loved her, how much he loved them both. But he knew they wouldn't listen. Wouldn't believe. The hollow, overused, trite words would fall on deaf ears, so he didn't utter a one. Instead he heaved a sigh and said softly, and as ineffectively, "I'm sorry."

The apology landed like a stone in a lake, leaving ever-widening ripples of anger and misery and unforgiving fury.

"So you planned all this," Rachel finally murmured.

Ty rubbed his hand wearily across his face. "Not all of it. Some of it just happened."

"It happened because you wanted it to happen. Like this sham marriage," she said scornfully.

"I never planned to marry you for Nathan. Not at first. I would never have asked you if I didn't care for you."

"Liar!"

"I'm telling you the truth!" Ty hissed between his teeth.

"The truth," she snarled. "The truth!"

"Mom," Nathan whispered urgently in her ear, clasping her arm in a death grip.

What did he think she was going to do? Rachel wondered distantly. Murder Ty with her bare hands? She dragged her gaze from Ty's tortured features and looked at her son for the first time since this terrible confession had begun.

Nathan looked about ready to pass out.

"Nathan," she said, concerned.

"Can we leave? Please."

She nodded jerkily, but then Ty stepped forward to intervene, his masculine scent strong and addictive and thoroughly infuriating. She heard the way he breathed and felt the warm touch of his hand as he tried to steady her. She jerked back, burned, aware that he'd seen her sway and was only trying to help, angry and hysterical that he could do this to her.

"Touch me again and I'll scream!" she warned hysterically, not even looking over her shoulder as she gathered Nathan into her arms, squeezing him close, drawing support.

"Wait," Ty begged.

Rachel released Nathan and whipped around, her eyes brilliant with fury, her face flushed. She'd never looked more lovely. More remote and untouchable and...God, how he wanted to touch her again!

"You tricked me into marriage," she told him in a low, penetrating voice. "I'll never forgive you for that. Never."

"I married you because I love you."

"Stop it, Ty. You never once told me you loved me before. At least that was honest. Don't ruin it now. Don't talk to me. Don't say a word."

"You have no reason to believe me. I understand that. But I'm not lying. I do love you. I just never realized it until it was too—"

*"Can't you hear me? I said don't talk to me!"*

Rachel stumbled for the stairs. She was lost. Blinded. Ty's recreation room was on the lowest floor, and she had to climb upward to garage level.

Nathan was right behind her, his breath as ragged as her own. Rachel stepped outside, to the bridge that connected Ty's house to the cliff face. She gulped air. Shaking, she hung her head over the rail.

"I'm going to kill him," Nathan said in a cracking voice somewhere behind her.

"Oh, Nathan." She clamped her hand to her lips, and tears stormed down her cheeks.

"Don't cry," Nathan said miserably.

She turned around, leaning against the rail, fighting out a brave smile for her son. "I'm all right."

Then Ty was there. Standing silently between them and the yawning darkness of the garage. He looked lost.

Nathan eyed him for a heartbeat. He tensed, poised. Rachel opened her mouth to scream, but it was too late. Nathan's right fist swung fast and hard. The blow was lethal. Ty took it on the chin. Rachel heard the crack. Ty staggered backward and leaned against the side of the garage, his eyes closed in pain. Emotional pain, Rachel recognized.

*Let's just hope he doesn't have occasion to hit me again.*
Too late she understood what that meant.

* * *

They took a cab to a hotel. A fancy hotel, with dark wood paneling and velvety carpeting in some elegantly muted flowerlike pattern that flowed through the massive lobby and around huge plotted plants. A string quartet played quietly in one isolated corner. The place was posh and so different from what Rachel was used to.

She didn't even notice until the following morning. All she remembered was that terrible moment outside Ty's home. His tormented silence. Nathan's simmering fury. Her own state of suspended animation. She'd felt separated from the drama, then and now. Part of the scenery.

Ty had demanded to know where they were going. He'd wanted to take them. Rachel couldn't let him. He'd said other things as well, important things, Rachel supposed. But her mind had been so completely filled with his perfidy, she couldn't listen. All she'd wanted to do was crawl into a hole and die.

Now, twelve hours later, she let the hot sting of the shower remind her that she was alive and kicking. None of her wounds had been mortal, apparently, though she'd been uncertain about that last night when she'd woken up soaked in sweat, a cry of anguish on her lips. How could he be so cruel? How could he?

And she'd married him!

Toweling her hair dry, Rachel stepped into the main room of her suite. Nathan's was adjoining. This whole setup was costing a fortune. Costing Ty a fortune, since she'd had to pay for it using his credit card. She wished that the cost would hurt him. She wanted a little of her own back. But from all accounts Ty could rent the Taj Mahal and it wouldn't affect the massive Rafferty fortune.

"Damn, damn, damn!" She flung the towel onto the floor and flopped on the bed. A knock sounded on the adjoining door. "Come on in," she invited, and Nathan, appearing rumpled and a little under the weather, stepped into her room. He wore the same black shirt he'd had on the night before, and the same pair of worn jeans. Even his taste in clothes was similar to his father's, Rachel thought with a rush of injustice.

"Is Ty going to pay for this?" he asked, looking around the room.

"For the time being. But I'm going to pay him back. Every blasted penny," she muttered through her teeth, then realized the absurdity of that remark. Like it or not, she was a Rafferty now, and Ty, gentleman that he was, hadn't even mentioned a prenuptial agreement. She was wealthy now, too, and if she was so inclined she could take him for every cent he had.

She wished she wanted to. She wished she could convince herself that would make her happy. As it was, all she wanted to do was go home and cry.

"Mom?"

"Huh."

"What are we going to do?"

Rachel had been giving the immediate future some serious thought. "We're going to rent a car and drive back to Oceanside."

"Okay." He waited about a minute. "When?"

"As soon as I feel like driving."

Rachel was growing stronger. She could feel herself accepting the truth even if she was still shying away from the ultimate results. She would divorce Ty. All she would ask for was custody of Nathan. No money. Nothing. Surely any judge with an ounce of intelligence would realize that she'd been tricked and that she was the more worthy parent. Besides, Nathan wanted nothing to do with Ty. Surely that would count, too.

The phone rang. Rachel stared at it, actually considered answering it. It had to be Ty. No one knew she was here, not even Ty, but she knew if he wanted to find her, he could.

"Don't answer it," Nathan said anxiously.

Rachel closed her eyes. She'd thought Ty was the answer to her dreams!

The phone ceased buzzing. Silence fell like a blanket. Nathan heaved a sigh. "You think I broke his jaw?" he asked.

*I wish,* she thought, then wrinkled her nose. "No. And you shouldn't have hit him. That's twice now you've come at him swinging. It doesn't help anything, Nathan. You're lucky Ty didn't choose to fight back because, like it or not, he's stronger and bigger than you are. I know it's tough, but you've got to control your temper—find some other way to deal with stress—or else you're the one who'll end up getting hurt."

"I wanted to hurt him."

"I know. And I think you did."

"He's not my dad. He's not."

Rachel lifted a shoulder, unsure how to answer him.

Nathan sighed several more times. Rachel looked at him, realizing he was working up his courage to tell her something.

"What is it?"

"I think I broke my hand."

Rachel's heart constricted. She scrambled off the bed, then sank down on her knees beside her son, gingerly examining his right hand. It was terribly swollen. "Oh, Nathan."

"I'm sorry."

"No, no. It's not your fault." Rachel raked her fingers through her hair in disbelief. "We'll have to get you to the emergency room."

With help from the front desk, Rachel rented a car and found her way to the nearest hospital. Within the hour she and Nathan were being attended by a young doctor whose first question was, "What's the other guy look like?"

Nathan, in an unwitting and scary imitation of Ty's matter-of-fact tone, said, "Actually, he looks a lot like me."

A cast was placed over Nathan's hand and forearm. He had indeed broken one of the bones in his hand, the most usual one for the kind of blow he'd inflicted.

"Maybe Tennyson'll take pity on me," he said with a return of humor as they drove back to Oceanside. "No more sweeping."

"I'm sorry for being so stupid. So gullible."

Her son actually smiled at her. "It's okay. At least I know who my dad is now. I kind of always wondered."

Rachel felt heartsick. Her expression must have said as much, because Nathan started trying to cheer her up, get her mind of Ty.

"You know, maybe the earring wasn't that great of an idea," he said, fingering the diamondlike gem. "I guess I've done some pretty stupid things."

Rachel smiled halfheartedly. "If this is a confession, I don't think I'm up to hearing it."

"I thought you always knew how stupid I was."

"I knew how smart you were. You just didn't know it."

Nathan snorted and subsided into silence, apparently lost in thought.

Home had never looked so good to Rachel. Why had she ever thought she could leave this place and make her way in Ty's world? She didn't even want to. He'd just been such a powerful force that she'd thought she wanted to.

It was nearly twilight before the phone rang again. This time Rachel answered. It wasn't Ty. It was Sybil.

"I'm not ready to talk to you." Rachel said with false calm.

"I understand." Regret tinged her words. "But when you are, please call. I'd like to know my grandson."

"Yes," she said, not certain quite what she was agreeing to, feeling it was necessary to say something.

Sybil hesitated. Rachel sensed her searching for the words that would somehow absolve Ty. "Don't," Rachel burst out, but it was too late.

"My son's in absolute agony. I've never seen him like this."

A storm of hot tears filled Rachel's throat. She had to count to ten before she could respond. "I'll call later."

"Thank you, Rachel."


The construction site smelled of mud and muck. Rain drizzled depressingly, making even the bright, mustard-yellow machinery seem dull. Big Jim Carlson stood with his hands on his hips, oblivious to the rain pinging gently against his hard hat.

Ty stood beside him, the collar of his jacket turned up against his neck. "What do you think?"

"About what?" Big Jim asked.

"The work," he answered testily.

"Well, we're a little ahead of schedule. Nothin' great, but it's good. It's rainin'," he added, as if that had anything to do with the price of tea in China.

"At least all the concrete work's done on this project." Ty gazed up at the gray heavens, rain spattering his face.

Big Jim sent him a sideways look. "You gonna tell me how you got that bruised-up face, or not?"

Ty flexed his jaw. Pain shot into the joint whenever he moved it. He was lucky it wasn't broken. The kid was a killer. "Or not," he said firmly.

"Hmm." Big Jim shook his head.

"Ever done anything you really regret in your life?" Ty asked. "I mean, really regret. Enough to make you want to sell your soul to change it."

"Nope."

Ty expelled a sound somewhere between a laugh and a swearword. "I should have known."

"I don't know whatcha did, Ty, but if you make the kinda mistake you're talkin' about, you just gotta fix it."

Big Jim was a couple of inches taller than Ty but a bit stoop shouldered, so that Ty's gaze was level with his. Big Jim had friendly, honest eyes. Ty had seen him get mad only once, when one of the workmen had endangered the life of another out of pure negligence. Big Jim had lifted the man by the lapels and shaken him until the fellow's teeth rattled. Then he'd stood him on his unsteady feet and fired him. That was that. Justice done.

"What if it's unfixable?" Ty asked, feeling a little like an errant child.

"Nothin's unfixable. You ever really think you can't fix somethin'?"

"I'm damn close," he muttered savagely.

Big Jim just shook his head and pulled a dirty, coffee-stained paper from his back pocket, his daily checklist. Ty watched him slop through the mud to where two men were carrying on an animated discussion about the flaky framing crew who'd missed showing up for work three days running. Normally Ty liked to involve himself in the day-to-day responsibilities, but he was currently so filled with self-loathing and remorse and, yes, fear, that all he wanted to do was hole up in the trailer and swill the strongest, most bitter coffee he could find.

Which is what he did. Until four o'clock, when he accidentally poured his latest cup over a set of blueprints. Bellowing furiously and turning the air blue in the process, he swept the blueprints from his messy desk along with three pencils, an ashtray and the city building permit.

The phone rang. "Hello," he growled furiously.

"You're sure in a great mood."

Ty silently uttered three more swearwords. It was Kathleen. "I'm always in a great mood when you call."

"Ty, please. I don't want to fight. Mother told me—everything, and I think she feels responsible. She wants—"

"I don't care what she wants. Nor do I care what you want."

"Acting with the brain of a prepubescent male isn't going to help!" Kathleen declared with a return of her usual spunk. "If this boy is really a Rafferty, then he should be with us."

"Stay out of it, Kathleen!" Ty yelled at the top of his lungs. *"Out of it!"*

"And I actually thought you'd be glad that I'm willing to accept Nathan," she said in a hurt tone, slamming down the receiver before Ty could deliver another scathing response.

"Oh, hell," he growled in frustration, punching Raintree's phone number. As soon as Gerald came on the line, Ty said, "Well, it hit the fan. And you were right. It couldn't be any worse."

"Too bad you don't drink martinis," Gerald answered on a sigh of sympathy. "Meet me at the bar. We'll talk."

"There's nothing you can do to make it better now," Gerald explained for the fourteenth time. "Leave it alone. Let it heal. Give her a chance to think things over."

"How long?" Ty asked dismally.

"I don't know. A few weeks. A few months...."

"Nope." He shoved his latest beer aside and gave his worried friend a pain-filled smile. "A few weeks is all I'll be able to bear. If she doesn't call me by the middle of October, I'm heading to Oceanside.''

"She might push you away farther.''

Ty dropped some money on the table and pointed out fatalistically, "It couldn't be any farther than this."

Oceanside looked uncommonly gloomy under the blanket of rain. Shades of gray: gray sky, gray buildings, even the finish on the brightest-colored automobiles seemed to be overlaid with gray.

It was dusk as Ty drove through the city center. Rachel was probably home. It was two weeks since she'd left. Two weeks of wondering about her, of either phoning and receiving no answer or having her advise him coldly, "I have nothing to say to you,'' when she heard his voice.

Well, okay. She was ticked off. She was wounded and furious. But she was his wife now, and this limbo couldn't go on forever.

There were lights on in the kitchen as he pulled in to her driveway. The front of the house was dark, the living room empty. As he cut the engine he saw Nathan's silhouette walk from the kitchen toward the bedroom end of the house. Then Rex set to howling and growling, announcing Ty's arrival better than a siren.

The porch light flicked on.

Ty climbed out of the car, steeling himself, but it was Nathan, not Rachel, who came out onto the porch.

Nathan watched him steadily as he walked toward him. Silence. At least he's not screaming for me to leave, Ty thought, resorting to taking the least little break as a good sign.

"She's not here,'' Nathan declared bluntly. His gaze fell on Ty's jaw with something akin to amazement. The worst of the swelling was over. Even the bruises had passed through their purple, green and yellow stages. But there was still a brown circle on his cheek that couldn't be disguised.

"I'll wait for her," Ty said, eyeing the cast on Nathan's forearm in turn. From the punch? Ty gazed at his son, his eyes full of questions.

"You can wait in your car," was Nathan's angry response.

"Nathan, don't push me." Ty was testy. "I'm tired and it's kind of taken the edge off my good humor. I'm going inside and I'll wait in the living room. But let's get one thing straight—take another shot at me, and I'm going to defend myself. I don't want to hit you, but I'll be damned if I'll settle for being your target anymore."

He hadn't really known what he was going to say. He'd just said it. And he'd never once considered what Nathan's reaction might be; to hell with it, he figured. Still, he was surprised when Nathan let him push his way inside.

"You're not my dad," Nathan snarled. "I hate you. I hate you for what you've done. You've ruined my mom's life and mine, and nothing you can do will fix that now!"

"I know." Ty was sardonic.

"I mean it!"

"Nathan, I know."

Ty stared regretfully at his son. Nathan glared at him, his throat working. Then he stormed down the hall to his room, slamming the door behind him.

Taking a breath, Ty sat down in front of the TV. He didn't turn it on, nor did he switch on the lights. He just waited.

He didn't know where Rachel was, and he didn't feel like pounding on Nathan's bedroom door, where rock music was now blasting away, and asking. Rachel's car was parked in the driveway, so she was either out with someone or down on the beach.

Out with someone? His mind flicked to images of her with another man. Angrily he shook his head. That wasn't the problem between them. Hell, if he had a choice he would rather have that be the problem! Another man was something he could battle. But Rachel's complete and total rejection, her lack of trust, of faith, was an insurmountable reality.

"No one to blame but yourself," he told the darkened room.

The back door to the kitchen squeaked open. Ty tensed. He knew it was Rachel even before he heard her tired sigh. Twisting his head, he could only see the edge of the door frame from this angle. A section of Rachel's hair came into view, tied back in its ponytail. She was sitting on the floor, taking off her shoes. She'd been running.

He would inadvertently scare her if he said anything. It was clear she didn't know he was there. Night had fallen and she obviously hadn't seen the black Porsche parked behind her car. Probably hadn't even looked.

But he couldn't wait in the darkness forever.

"Rachel."

She nearly jumped from her skin, shrieking with fright. Ty walked into the kitchen and she spun around, her hand at her throat. She was standing in her stocking feet. He'd forgotten how small she seemed without shoes. Her eyes were full of smoldering anger.

"Who let you in here?" she demanded.

"Nathan."

That stopped her for a beat, but then she went on. "Just leave. I don't want to talk to you."

"You're going to have to talk to me sometime. We're married."

She wore a dark green T-shirt and black sweats. She was breathing hard and the T-shirt was wet with rain. Her hair was wet with rain, too. The red-brown strands had dark-

ened, making her face seem paler, and her eyes greener.
"I'm going to divorce you."

"For God's sake, Rachel, get over it a minute." Ty's
temper got the best of him. "I need to talk to you. I don't
want to hurl insults and demands and accusations back and
forth anymore."

"Too bad. I do. I want to tell you what I think of you,
and it's not pretty. If you stay here, you're going to hear it
all!" Her chest heaved with emotion. Ty had to forcibly
control the direction of his gaze lest he antagonize her further by being irresistibly drawn to the distraction of her wet
T-shirt and the soft, lush outline of her breasts.

"Okay, fine." He raised his hands in surrender. "Hit me
with both barrels. There are some things I need to say, too.
Some things we need to decide. Go ahead and get it over
with, so we can move on."

Rachel drew a deep breath into her lungs. Her emotions
were in such turmoil she didn't trust herself to speak right
away. How could he stand there and look so appealing?
How could *she* feel *anything* for him?

She suddenly felt unprepared. While she dripped rain
over the linoleum he appeared calm, unmoved and in control. His face was hard and alien with its faintly bruised
jaw. She wanted to reach out and touch him. She wanted to
feel those lips on hers. He looked *good*. The shoulders of
his brown leather bomber jacket were damp, just like the
night he'd rescued her. Rescued her? She nearly choked on
the thought.

"I'm not your wife," she told him unsteadily. "You
never really wanted a wife or you would have married Barbara. You wanted Nathan."

A muscle worked in Ty's jaw but he didn't deny it.

"I don't want anything from you—not a dime of your
fortune! I just want out," she went on tautly.

"You want something else, too."

Rachel's brows drew together.

"My son."

"Ohh..." Rachel turned away, filled with a misery and betrayal so huge she couldn't speak. Ty made the colossal mistake of grabbing her arm. She whirled on him, all fire and spite. "Let go of me!"

"And I want you," he said urgently on the breath of a whisper.

"Ty, so help me, if you don't let go of me, I'll scream."

She was trembling so violently that he believed her. Reluctantly he released her. Rachel stumbled toward the bedroom. He heard the door close quietly behind her. Too quietly. She was fighting for control.

He looked down at his own hands, mildly surprised to realize they, too, were shaking from a tremor that seemed to have him in its breath-squeezing grip. He heard Gerald's warnings run through his mind, over and over. *That woman is never going to forgive you. She's going to come after your hide when she learns you've had an ulterior motive all along. She'll make your life a living hell.*

Reluctant footsteps sounded in the hall. Nathan's footsteps, not Rachel's. His son appeared in the kitchen aperture. Ty stared at him, and he stared right back.

"What?" Ty asked.

"She's crying."

Something inside Ty broke wide open. He'd never really seen Rachel cry. He'd forced tears to stand in her eyes—an anguish he lived with daily—but she'd never cried. He'd somehow thought she handled her problems like he did, alone and deep within herself. He'd been wrong. Again.

He realized Nathan was watching him. Ty focused on him. Nathan's expression was less antagonistic, more thoughtful.

"If I—if I said I'd—come live with you. Would you leave her alone?" Nathan asked solemnly.

Ty sighed wearily. "Nathan, I don't want to split you and your mother up."

"But that's what you've been trying to do."

He shook his head. "No."

"Yes, it is." Nathan turned away in disgust.

Ty grimaced. The kid was too smart to lie to, and that's what he'd been doing—lying. Funny. For years he'd avoided lies, scorned the weak who resorted to them. But since he'd met Rachel, lying had become almost second nature, an old friend.

He drew another fortifying breath and followed Nathan down the hall. It was time to go back to the plain, unvarnished truth, even if it meant laying himself bare to the pain of Rachel's rejection once more.

"Mom? Mom?"

Rachel sat on the edge of the bed, her hands clenching the spread. When she'd first heard the knock she'd thought it was Ty. But it was Nathan's soft voice calling her, pleading with her.

She opened the door. She'd changed from her running clothes. She'd taken a shower. She'd cried. Now she wore jeans and a black sweater, her hair wet and combed to her shoulders. She felt calmer.

Nathan's eyes were two dark pools in his white face. "I gotta tell you something," he said in a voice so low she could scarcely hear it.

"Is he still here?"

Nathan nodded, closing the door behind him. "You know the money? The five hundred dollars?"

Rachel's mind felt numb. She couldn't grasp where this was going. She wanted to assure herself about Ty. "Yes. Is he leaving, or is he waiting for me to come out?"

"I don't know. Mom, listen, I put the money in your account. Matthew helped me. He's made deposits for his mom before. He told me what to do, so I took one of those little white papers from your purse and handed it to the lady at the window with the money. I wanted you to have it.''

Rachel was stunned. Speechless. She blinked at him.

"I just didn't want us to be broke.''

"Nathan, how? What? Where did you get the money in the first place?''

He swallowed hard. "We sold some stuff.''

"Sold some stuff? Stolen property?'' Rachel choked out.

His eyes were filled with terror and remorse. He nodded jerkily.

It was too much to absorb. Dully, Rachel knew she wasn't handling this right. Her emotions were too raw. Hot waves of despair washed over her. She battled them back, closing her eyes, counting her own heartbeats. "Okay," she murmured, for herself or Nathan, she neither knew nor cared. "Okay. Let's talk about this later. After Ty leaves.''

"I—I want to leave with him.''

Rachel's intake of breath was a gasp.

"I don't want to be in trouble," Nathan hurried on. "I don't want to steal. I'll go with him.''

"What are you saying?'' she demanded half-hysterically.

"I'm going to go live with him.''

*"Nathan!"*

"He can take care of me. And I—'' Nathan stumbled over the words, as if he found them too cruel to utter ''—can have whatever I want.''

Rachel was appalled. She didn't believe him for a minute. "Why are you saying that? It's not what you mean! Did he talk you into this?'' she demanded, zeroing in on the only answer.

"He said he doesn't want to split us up—you and me,'' Nathan admitted quietly.

But Rachel didn't listen. Like an avenging angel she swept past Nathan to the kitchen where Ty was now standing by the sink, gazing through the window to the black and purple shadows outdoors. He turned at her approach, wary. As well he should be, Rachel thought intolerantly.

"You leave Nathan alone!" she ordered in a shaking voice. "He's not leaving with you. He's staying here. And if you think you can win him in court, guess again! I'll fight you and all your Rafferty money! I'm going to make your life miserable, just like you've made mine! You've ruined your chance, Ty. It's over. It's your fault. And you'll never, ever be able to change my mind!"

## Chapter Fourteen

Rachel stared at the glowing green letters on her computer screen. What did YCHX38 mean, anyway? Was that a child's fare? She doubted it was any cheaper than an adult nonrefundable ticket.

Concentrating hard, she checked prices, absorbed in a world with easy answers. She didn't want to think about her personal life. She'd lost too much.

She'd lost Nathan.

With practiced skill Rachel ordered the ticket for one of her business travelers and listened to it rattle off the ticketer. Her mind felt weary. She'd lost that battle with Ty. All her threats had been for nought. She'd lost because she'd guessed wrong. Nathan had *wanted* to leave. Ty hadn't pressured him. He'd pressured Ty!

He wanted to live with his father, he'd told her. She hadn't believed him, but he'd insisted he wanted to attend school in Portland and straighten himself out. Oceanside was too small. He'd made too many wrong choices here. It didn't mean he didn't love her, he just knew this was the right decision for now. As long as the judge was willing to allow his community service work to be suspended or changed, would it be all right with Rachel if he left?

Of course, she'd agreed, she'd had no choice. She hadn't believed she could be hurt more than Ty had hurt her. Nathan came damn close.

She'd had no choice but to let him go. Though she didn't fully believe him. No one, and especially not Nathan, could change so radically so quickly. But he was adamant, and with Ty and Nathan on the same side she was powerless. She wasn't sure what the right answer was any longer, so she'd let Ty take Nathan away. Not custody. No sirree. This was just a trial period, to see if being with Ty was what Nathan truly wanted and needed.

Swallowing back her pain, Rachel tried to concentrate on her work. The letters and symbols on the screen seemed to suddenly be a wash of green liquid. Who would have guessed her son could be bought? Her son, who'd vehemently hated Ty until he'd learned they were father and son. Her son, who was more like a Rafferty than Rachel could ever have suspected.

Her son whom she missed with all her heart. And he'd only been gone six days!

Rachel blinked rapidly, battling an almost overwhelming despair. She'd talked to Nathan three times; she'd phoned twice, Nathan once. It had been all she could do to keep from begging him to come home. Why did he want to stay away? *Why?* She couldn't believe it was money. Nathan was as mercenary as any teenager, but he had ethics. Why was he doing this to her?

And why was she letting him?

Abruptly she rose from her computer and walked into the photocopy room. Someone had just made coffee, and it was dripping in a small brown stream through the filter and into the glass pot. The photocopy machine was running off copies and the papers were stacking neatly, automatically, falling softly into place. A brochure of London lay forgotten on the coffee counter. Big Ben had a coffee ring covering its face.

Rachel gritted her teeth. It was interesting. She had no desire to see faraway places with strange-sounding names. She wanted to stay right here, with Nathan, and—

With Ty.

Okay, call me stupid, she told herself with ruthless honesty. But I still love him. He doesn't care a damn about me, but I still love him.

"Rachel?" Shawna peeked inside the door. Today her lipstick matched her nails, so red it looked surreal.

"Yeah?"

"Your—er—husband is on the phone."

Rachel snorted, consumed with an emotion she couldn't begin to describe. "Tell him I'll be there in a minute," she said after a moment's hesitation.

Shawna saluted and left. Rachel took her time getting her coffee. She decided to treat herself to cream and sugar today, something she almost never did. By the time she punched the flashing light on her phone, a full ten minutes had passed.

"This is Rachel Stone," she said deliberately.

"This is Tyrrell Rafferty," he answered just as deliberately, his voice edged with impatience. Score one for me, Rachel thought, finding no joy in the small victory. "Have you talked to Nathan?"

"You mean today? No." Rachel's gaze turned to the clock. "Isn't he in school?" She bit down hard on her lip, fighting back the urge to jab Ty about the private school his family had enrolled her rebellious son in. She predicted he wouldn't last long.

"Apparently not. They called me, looking for him."

"He's *skipped?*" Perversely, she was almost glad Nathan was up to his old tricks. It would give Ty something to think about. There were minuses to fatherhood, too.

"I'd say that's a fair assessment." His tone was dry.

"What would you like me to do?" Rachel asked.

"Be somewhere where I can reach you, just in case."

Just in case of what? She didn't say it. Instead, she murmured, "I'll be home after work," hanging up before she lost the threads of her control.

Worry followed her home like a dark thunderhead. She'd taken the news of Nathan's disappearance like a selfish child, glad that Ty was the one responsible, the one who had to make choices. But if Nathan had been living with her she would have gone through the roof. Where was he?

When Ty hadn't phoned her by nine o'clock that night, Rachel couldn't stand it anymore. She called his house, listening to the four rings before his answering machine picked up. She also listened to his voice, low and sexy and drawling with that touch of self-deprecation she found so attractive as he asked her to leave her name and number so he could call back later.

She hung up without leaving a message.

Needing to think of something else, she reflected on the week. She had turned the five hundred dollars over to Nathan's truant officer, who was in the process of questioning Matt, Jessica and Nathan about what they'd stolen and who should be reimbursed. She should have expected the hysterical call she'd received from Madeline Dayton, but she didn't, and when the woman had started shrieking long and loudly about Nathan, what a ruination he was, what a shameful waste of an intelligent boy, Rachel had told her, quite plainly, that Matt, who was no angel himself, was lucky to have turned out as well as he had considering his parental influence.

That had effectively ended that conversation.

Rachel hadn't received any further calls from Sybil. Ty's mother was an excellent strategist. She'd left her plea and those terrible words, "My son's in absolute agony," for Rachel to reflect on. Which she did. Hourly. But so far Rachel hadn't cracked, mainly because she believed Sybil was wrong. Ty was a bit remorseful, true. But only a person who truly cared would be in agony, and she knew he didn't care at all.

By eleven o'clock she could stand it no longer. She phoned Ty's home, slammed the receiver down at the sound of his answering machine, then called the Raffertys. It sounded to her fanciful mind as if the ring of the telephone became hollower, colder, more refined. Blast them all.

*The only way to deal with pretension is ignore it. Drives them crazy.*

Oh, Ty, she thought miserably.

"Hello?"

It was Mary, the housekeeper. Rachel exhaled in relief. "Hi, Mary. It's Rachel. Er—Ty's friend." Lord, this was ridiculous.

"Is he with you?" Mary asked urgently.

"Ty?" Rachel asked dumbly.

"Nathan!"

Her heart started beating hard. So hard it ached right down to her stomach. "He's still missing," she said through a dry throat, knowing the answer.

"He hasn't come home," she said brokenly, "and Tyrrell isn't here, either. Mrs. Rafferty's pale as death and Kathleen talks and talks and talks, she's so scared. I thought you was—were—the police, maybe. I don't know."

"Where is Ty?" A strange calm fell over Rachel.

"Out looking."

"Where?"

"I don't know. He doesn't tell us much."

"Thank you, Mary. I'll call back later."

Rachel walked into her bedroom and sat in the dark, thinking. Don't panic. Nathan's done this kind of thing before. Not exactly this kind of thing, but close enough. It was rebellion. He hadn't wanted to go with Ty no matter what he said. And being typically Nathan, he'd run away.

Run away to where?

Rachel's heart jolted. She hurried down the hall to the front porch and turned on the light. Nathan was a smart kid. Resourceful. Her spirits lifted in her eagerness to believe. It helped her get over her panic.

He *was* coming home after all, she told herself. Home to her.

He showed up at three in the morning. Rachel heard the lock on the back door rattle. She was awake, or at least half-awake, and stretched out on the living-room couch. Throwing off the old afghan, she jumped to her feet, still in her jeans and sneakers. As she heard the scrape of Nathan's hand searching for the key hanging inside a knothole in the porch rafters, she stumbled to meet him. A second later he was in the kitchen. Rachel flipped on the light.

Nathan gasped. "Mom!" he cried, taking a step back.

Rachel grabbed him and held him tight, resting her chin against the scratchy peach fuzz decorating his jaw. Her eyes burned, and she squinched them closed.

Nathan hesitated only a second, hugging her so hard she had to laughingly gasp, "Are you trying to squeeze the life out of me?"

"Sorry," he mumbled, easing up.

"Oh, Nathan. I've been so scared. You're going to be the death of me one way or the other." When he didn't respond, she asked, "How did you get home?"

"Truck driver. I had to walk quite a ways."

"I'm not even going to ask why you left. I know why. But just because you ran away doesn't mean the Raffertys won't come after you."

"You've talked to them." He sounded worried.

"Of course I've talked to them. We've all been wringing our hands, wondering what happened to you." Rachel focused on the kitchen clock, hating the thought of calling Ty at this hour, knowing she had no choice. "Hitchhiking isn't exactly the safest method of transportation," she pointed out, though Nathan was well aware of her feelings on that subject.

"I couldn't stand it there," he said simply. "I wanted to, I mean, I knew it was best and all. I just couldn't stand it."

Rachel held him at arm's length to see his face. "Best for whom?"

"For you."

"For *me?* Nathan, you knew I didn't want you to leave!"

He shifted his weight uncomfortably and eased from her embrace. A shock of black hair fell over his forehead as he looked at the floor, frowning. His lashes lay thick and straight, casting shadows on his strong cheekbones. Either she was simply more sensitive to the resemblance, or Nathan was looking more like Ty with each passing day.

"I know I'm a lot of trouble," he mumbled so softly she could scarcely hear. "I didn't want to do that anymore."

"Do what?" she asked.

"Cause you trouble." He glanced up, his dark eyes full of rebellion once more, as if he knew she was about to argue with him—which she was. "Ever since Dad died. I mean my adopted dad. Richard," he clarified in some confusion. "Everything's been a mess. You were unhappy and I didn't want to be around you."

"Nathan." Rachel was certain she didn't want to hear this.

"It was mean of me. But I couldn't stand it. I just thought you were sorry that I was still there."

"Nathan, I love you. I always have. You know that." She groaned with the knowledge that she was going to have to be painfully truthful. "I loved you more than I ever loved Richard, and that's one of the reasons I was so unhappy. I felt bad that I hadn't been the wife Richard wanted. My reasons for marrying him were all tangled up with him being like a father to me, and me wishing things were different. But it had nothing to do with my feelings for you, unless you count the reason I went through with the marriage in the first place was because I knew I'd have you."

"But I took that money." Nathan was determined to paint himself black. "I stole."

"And believe me, I've had some bad nights over that," Rachel assured him.

"Why didn't you come down on me? Why've you been so understanding?" he demanded suddenly.

"What good would it do? Would my yelling at you have improved matters? My God, I wanted to shake the living daylights out of you a time or two! But Nathan, parents aren't stupid, you know. No matter what you've heard to the contrary. Stealing was a symptom, not the problem. Even as bad as our financial situation has been, I knew you were stealing because you were fighting back. Fighting against fate." Rachel stopped to take a breath, slightly surprised that she was putting into words all she'd felt, slightly surprised she expected Nathan to suddenly understand. "I figured you would stop, sooner or later. I just hoped you wouldn't get into serious trouble first."

Nathan fiddled with the zipper on his parka. Zipping it up and down in short flurries of motion. "I won't do it anymore."

"Good." Rachel smiled.

"Do I have to go back?"

"No-o-o-o."

He darted her a look. "You don't sound too sure about that. I promise I won't get into trouble again. Really. I'll— I'll do extra work. I won't complain," His words tumbled out in a rapid, heartfelt plea. "I'll apologize to Mr. Tennyson. I mean, really apologize. I'll even work *extra* hours beyond what I'm supposed to."

"Nathan, you're selling the wrong person. I'd do about anything to keep you with me. But Ty's not going to feel the same way."

Silence fell sharply. Nathan's urgent speech was cut off as if she'd doused flames with water. Rachel sighed. "We've got to call him."

"Let's wait," Nathan said, his eyes widening. Perhaps he feared retribution. Rachel couldn't blame him. He'd probably given the Raffertys more to think about in one evening than they'd had to worry about in five years.

"That'd be cruel." Rachel was already dialing Ty's number. "Ty needs to know you're safe."

"Are you going to divorce him?"

She turned toward him, momentarily distracted by his fearful tone. "I—" she started, then Ty's answering machine clicked on. She waited for the tone, then said quietly, "Ty, it's Rachel. Nathan's here with me. He's safe."

There was a lot more she could have said, but Rachel stuck to the basics. Ty would be able to read between the lines, anyway. He understood her too well not to. And she wished suddenly, foolishly, that that wasn't so. She wished that she was a mystery, someone he could have really been attracted to, really fallen in love with.

Someone he wouldn't have been able to use.

It was five-thirty when Ty drove into Oceanside. Vacancy signs abounded along the main street, glowing pink or blue or green, cutting through the cloud cover and looking like misplaced party favors, cheery but not quite right. He rolled down the window and inhaled the brine-scented air. He felt sweaty and tired and depressed. Failure had never been an aspect of his life, but he'd learned its taste well these past few weeks and it was bitter.

If Nathan hadn't come back to Oceanside, Ty didn't know what he'd tell Rachel. Rehearsed speeches had crossed his mind dozens of times. There was no way to say "I'm sorry" and come off as if he meant it. No way words could make up for the turmoil he'd forced upon her.

But Nathan had to be here. He had to.

But if he was, his mind argued in endless circles, Rachel would have called and told you.

Yanking the wheel, he pulled to the side of the road. A few trucks rumbled by and several RVs. It was quiet, except for the dull ocean roar, which from this point sounded like background static on the radio. His mouth was dry. Selfishly he thought of seeing Rachel, of dragging her against him, burying his face in her lush hair, inhaling her scent, drowning in her. Self-loathing followed. How could he think about what *he* wanted, when he'd ruined everything for *her?*

"God." He raked his hands through his hair, switched on the engine with restrained fury, threw the Porsche into gear.

Her driveway came up so quickly he almost missed it. There was no newspaper in the box. He was too early.

Too early. Should he wait to knock on her door? Yes. No. Maybe.

Indecision. A person could go crazy second-guessing himself.

Ty drove right to the front door. For reasons that escaped Ty, Rex didn't set to his usual barking. Instead, he stood on all fours, his tongue lolling in a friendly manner, his tail gently swaying to and fro. It baffled Ty why the dog should choose to accept him now, when Rachel and Nathan—no matter what the kid had tried to say to the contrary—considered him their number-one enemy.

He took the dilapidated front steps lightly, feeling better now that he was here. Why? God knew. His last few encounters with Rachel hadn't exactly been winning ones. But action was better than waiting. He was terrible at waiting.

The porch light had been left burning, golden in the dense morning air. Ty pushed the button and in the depths of the house, somewhere near the kitchen he suspected, the doorbell rang. It was a buzzer, the kind you could hold your finger on and keep it blasting away as long as you liked. Ty gave two quick rings and waited.

And waited.

And waited.

Okay, not good enough. He held his thumb to the bell and it buzzed furiously, like an angry bee. A loud angry bee. A door banged open. Footsteps shuffled. *Thud.*

Ty craned to look through the windows. It sounded as if someone had run into a wall.

The front door cracked open. Nathan squinted through the fog, focusing on Ty. "Oh," he greeted him, rubbing his face.

He'd been here all along!

"Where's Rachel?" Ty demanded in a flood of rage. How could she? How *could* she? He'd been half out of his mind with worry and she hadn't even bothered to call!

"In bed," Nathan answered. "It's kinda early."

"Where the hell have you been? How come you ran off? No, don't tell me, I already know. The question I should be asking is why you came with me in the first place."

Ty was through the door, marching steadily down the hall in such long, ground-devouring strides that Nathan, half-asleep, had to run to catch up to him. "Wait! Wait!"

But Ty was too angry. He was fueled by adrenaline. And hurt. He flung open Rachel's bedroom door, took two steps into the room and stopped short. Nathan careened into him from behind.

Rachel was sound asleep, facedown, her hair a glory of dark reddish brown, her back bare where her nightshirt had fallen over one shoulder. He could see the tip of her up-turned nose and the shape of her lips beneath the curtain of hair.

"She's sleeping!" Nathan hissed under his breath. He was fully awake now and ready, willing and able to defend his mother.

"I can see that."

Nathan was forced to one side as Ty backed out of the room. Ty closed the door, thinking hard. Nathan watched him.

"Look, I'm sorry I left," Nathan said as a kind of backhanded apology. "I'm going back to bed. Make yourself some coffee or something," he added on a yawn. "Mom'll be up later. Don't wake her."

"I won't," Ty assured him testily.

Hesitating, Nathan suddenly tossed up his hands in surrender, apparently anxious to leave the complicated world of man/woman to these two crazy adults who couldn't seem to decide what they felt about each other.

Rachel opened her eyes and groaned. It was early, the daylight still pale. She didn't want to get up but she had to call Ty again and make certain he'd gotten the message about Nathan's whereabouts.

Climbing from her tangled bed, she grabbed a robe, flung it over her nightshirt, then headed for the kitchen. Combing her fingers through her tousled mane and yawning, she nearly ran into a wall of flesh when she rounded the kitchen corner.

"Ty!" she yelled on a stifled scream. His hands were on her shoulders, steadying her. She jerked backward. "What are you doing here? How'd you get in? How long have you been here?"

"I'm the one who deserves some answers. Like how long has Nathan been here? And when were you going to tell me?"

"Tell you?" Rachel glared at him. "I already told you! Nothing gives you the right to just waltz into my house like you own the place!"

"I'm your husband," Ty pointed out dryly.

"The hell you are."

"Okay, fine. I'm not getting into that with you. I don't have time for it." He regarded her broodingly for several moments, supremely conscious of her unaffected allure. The bathrobe was too big, the arms falling over her wrists. Rachel kept pushing the sleeves up to her elbows, her beautiful eyes wary and flashing fire. "You could have picked up the phone," he pointed out, focusing on the one issue where he knew he was in the right. Everything else was too cloudy. "No matter what you think of me, you could have called."

Rachel regarded him thoughtfully. He hadn't gotten the message. "I left you a message on your answering machine."

"When?" he bit out.

"Last night. About three o'clock. When Nathan showed up here."

Ty nodded slowly. "I can check on that."

"Do that!" Her temper skyrocketed. "Why don't you go do it right now, in fact!"

"Rachel, look—"

"No, you look. This is nuts. I'm—I'm seeing a lawyer today to start divorce proceedings," she manufactured, lifting her chin. "As far as Nathan's concerned, he wants to stay with me. He only went with you because he thought he was being a burden to me, but that's all resolved now. I know you're his father and I won't keep you from him. But don't expect me to like it."

"Damn it, Rachel—"

"We've gone over this ground enough. It's over. We made a mistake. Let's leave it at that. You don't love me, and I don't really love you, either." Her voice lowered on the lie. "All we have in common is Nathan. Let's concentrate on making him happy."

Ty looked past her. A strange sense of acceptance enveloped him. This was as good as it was going to get. The most he could hope for. It wasn't enough, but it was all there was. "Okay."

Rachel wasn't certain she'd heard correctly. With a wrench of her heart she realized how much it had cost him to agree with her. Perversely, she wished he'd argued more. He looked terrible. His eyes were red rimmed from lack of sleep, and a heavy five o'clock shadow darkened his chin. Even so, it couldn't mask his masculine appeal, and emotion stirred inside Rachel, unwelcome but existing nonetheless. There was something piratical about his appearance, piratical and raffish and vulnerable.

"Okay?" she repeated tentatively.

"If Nathan wants to live with you, then okay. He didn't exactly take to my mother's choice for education. I don't blame him. And since there's no chance of you and me reconciling, he can't live with us both." He was leaning against the counter, his fingers curled tensely along the edge. Now he pushed himself to his feet. "I never thought I'd say this, but he's yours, Rachel. Your son. You raise him as you see fit. I'll be a weekend father."

"Ty..."

He brushed past her, but Rachel, reacting on instinct, reached for his sleeve, surprising both him and herself that she would do such a thing. Ty stopped dead in his tracks. He looked down at her for a long, drawn-out moment. He must have seen in her face everything she was trying to conceal—her need, her love, her desire—because his hand suddenly cupped her chin, lifting it, forcing her to meet his hard gaze.

"I don't—" Rachel began, but Ty pulled her to him, crushing her mouth to his in a thrilling way. Rachel stiffened. She cautioned herself not to feel anything, but it was impossible. Her body melted. She clutched his arms, felt his weight bearing her backward, crowding her against the wall. Her knees weakened. She returned the ardor of his kiss; her mouth hungrily demanded more. She wanted to absorb him inside her one last time. One last time. She wanted it so badly she was shaking, afraid his mouth might stop ravaging hers, his urgent hands might stop convulsively kneading the muscles of her back, her breasts, her hips.

"Rachel," he groaned. His palms cupped her bottom, pulling her upward, against the hard, hot pressure of him. Her arms were slung over his shoulders, needing his support. Their intimacy wasn't enough. She wanted to rip his clothes off. Her breath escaped on a soft moan as his fingers grabbed the hem of her nightshirt, bunching it into a fist. Then her breasts spilled into his warm hands.

He smelled so good, felt so good. Rachel pressed her face into his neck, loving the heat and taste of his skin against her mouth. Ty's breathing was tense and ragged. His thighs pinned her tightly, deliciously against the wall. Rachel, who for years had never understood the torment of frustrated desire, understood it now. There was no way she could make love to him. Not here. Not with Nathan right down the hall. Not with Ty's treacherous plan exposed to her.

Yet she wanted to. She *wanted* to. For a wild moment of pure selfishness she actually considered it. Let me make love to him once more and damn the consequences. Her hands moved of their own volition, sliding beneath his jacket, holding his hips against hers, making him feel exactly what she wanted.

"God, Rachel," Ty muttered, his breath tickling her ear.

Please, please, please, she thought. She wanted to close her mind to the clamoring voices that screamed at her to wake up and salvage her pride. He'd hurt her too much. This wouldn't solve anything.

Why, then, did it feel like salvation?

His touch grew bolder, one hand traveling downward to where their bodies were joined. Rachel gave a soft whimper, her head arching back.

Ty was at the edge of his control. "Rachel, I love you," he ground out through his teeth, as if the more furiously he told her, the easier it would be for her to believe.

"Shh."

"I want to make love to you," he murmured against her lips. "I want you to stay my wife. I want everything!"

He was stroking her to mindlessness. He was doing it on purpose. She dragged her mouth from the marauding power of his, where his tongue was persuasively imitating the act of possession she ached for. No, no, no!

"Tell me you want it all," he ordered urgently. "Tell me."

She shook her head. A wave of anguish was replacing desire. It was ending too soon. Too soon.

Ty lifted his head to look into her eyes. His hands were planted on either side of her head, molten desire flaming in his dark gaze. "Tell me!"

Rachel drew a shaking breath. She bit into her lower lip. She wanted to lie to him, but she couldn't.

His gaze drilled into hers. Mouth twisting, he shoved himself away from the wall. "If I can't have it all, I don't want any of it!" he declared bitterly.

And then he walked away.

"Ty, wait!"

He turned at the door, one hand on the knob. When she didn't say anything further, he asked, "For what?" and slid her a faint smile, one she was beginning to associate with him each time he drew beyond her reach. "I'll talk to you later, Rachel. Oh, and I plan to help pay for Nathan's expenses, no matter how long and loudly you argue about it. See you later."

"Ty..."

But he was already out of earshot. Through the window Rachel watched him roar away. She ached inside. She was soul sick. But she had no other choice. No other choice.

## Chapter Fifteen

"The temperature is going down, down, down," the DJ announced in a voice deepening by degrees. "Hey, we might even see snow by this evening. Wouldn't that be a trip? The beach covered in white stuff. When's the last time any of you saw snow around these parts, huh? We should have a real Friday-night party. Yeah! Let's all meet after work down on the sand and limbo in the snow!"

Rachel switched off the radio with an impatient snap. She didn't like to be reminded of the passage of time. It was December. The trees were starkly naked except for the firs, which seemed to bush out blue green with good health. Just in time for Christmas trees.

Thanksgiving was over, thank God. The Raffertys had politely asked that Nathan spend the holidays with them, and Rachel had practically had to pry Nathan's fingers off the porch rail and tie him to the car seat to get him to go. It both saddened and amused her. The main reason Nathan was resisting the Raffertys so hysterically was for her benefit. Oh, sure, they bugged him. Sybil was too much of a matriarch. Kathleen was a master at the double-edged remark, and Ty... well...

Rachel turned into the parking lot of Neptune Travel, her mind shying away from Ty. Thinking of him made her brain weary. And it didn't help that since that last scene with him, Ty had pulled on this good-guy role of weekend father as if it were a second skin. He was incredibly understanding. Patient. Willing to meet her more than halfway where Nathan was concerned. Okay, the few times she'd seen him he'd looked a little tense, but nothing in his demeanor suggested he was suffering over their ill-fated love affair like she was.

And she was definitely suffering. She ached for him at night and thought about him all day. But she'd be damned if she'd crawl back to a man who'd set her up and used her.

The only hope she harbored that he still cared at all was that he hadn't filed for divorce. Neither, as it happened, had she. Just thinking about seeing a lawyer numbed her mind. She *was* going to do it, just not yet.

Rachel sat down at her computer, giving Shawna and Allison and the others in the office a perfunctory hello. She was in a bad mood. Another sleepless night courtesy of Tyrrell Rafferty III. Having to see him at all made her crazy. Salt in the wound. Her fingers itched to touch him. Her eyes traced the curve of his mouth. Her flesh broke out into goose bumps at the raspy sound of his voice.

And though he didn't smile often these days, when he did, well...

Rachel muttered furiously, directing scathing comments at herself. Why should it bother her that he never touched her, never even made a move toward her? She should be happy, elated that he'd taken her at her word. What they'd shared was over. Kaput. *Finito.* Ty knew it, and so did she.

Sort of.

"Damn!" The computer beeped at her in outrage. Rachel resisted banging the top of the monitor. Blasted thing. If you made one tiny mistake it nagged you.

"Pace yourself, you've got the whole day ahead of you," Allison drawled.

Rachel made a rude comment that made Allison snort with laughter. Her friends had been good to her throughout this whole mess, Rachel realized. They'd supported her and tried not to ask too many questions over the strangeness of her marriage to Ty. They'd helped her get through each day, when so many times she wanted to stay in bed and hold the covers over her head. They'd made life bearable for her.

At five o'clock Rachel glanced up from her bookings. The DJ's weather prediction had come true. Tiny snowflakes were swirling furiously past the windows, driven by the wind. "Let's go have a hot toddy," Allison suggested from behind her.

"Sorry, not tonight. Nathan's finished with his community service work. We're celebrating his parole."

"Tell him congrats."

"The only good thing about it is I really think he learned a lesson. And you know, that old grouch Tennyson actually offered him a job after school?" Rachel signed off her computer and reached for her purse.

"You're kidding."

Rachel chuckled. "Nathan doesn't know whether to be pleased or insulted. But at least it's progress."

Progress. As Rachel walked through the chilly, snow-dusted night, she considered her own situation. She wasn't making progress. She was treading water.

"Rachel."

Her name on his lips made her gasp. She squinted through the driving snow to the black Porsche parked kitty-corner from her wagon. She should have noticed him even though night had fallen and the snow was delightfully distracting. Her radar, where Ty was concerned, should have picked him up. She needed to be in charge and strong and sensible. She couldn't be off balance. She was too afraid of herself.

He was leaning against the car's hood. In one millisecond her brain recorded every detail: the way he slouched inside the brown leather bomber jacket, the way his black hair lay wet against his forehead, the way his hips thrust forward in his negligent position, the way his battered jeans caressed his legs.

Rachel's shell of composure wasn't in place. In a kind of slow-motion dream she watched him walk toward her. She was raw and vulnerable, her emotions plainly visible on her mobile face.

"Ty," she said, swallowing. "You scared me. Are you trying to terrorize me, or does it just come naturally?"

"It probably just comes naturally."

She instantly regretted the flip remark. He sounded so...so inured to it, she wondered how many she'd made. "Sorry," she mumbled. "Um, Nathan just got back Sunday. Did you want him for this weekend, too? He doesn't know that and I don't think he's ready to—"

"I didn't come to see Nathan. I came to see you. I thought it was time we talked over a few things."

"Such as?"

"How long are you going to leave me in this purgatory, Rachel?" he demanded, losing control. "I can't stand it. Maybe you can, but I can't! I told myself I wouldn't pressure you, but, damn it all, I'm no good at biding my time. I can't do it. I love you, and I want you, and whatever it takes, just name it and I'll do it! Just stop this—waiting."

Snow melted against Rachel's cheeks, stinging cold. She blinked against the flakes gathering on her lashes. Her initial impulse was to throw herself into his arms. She just barely stopped herself, then was baffled at how difficult it had been to do so. She'd forgiven him, she realized, the truth dawning slowly. Somewhere in the past few weeks she'd forgiven him. *And I even believe he does love me!* she thought incredulously.

Her silence aggravated Ty. He clenched his hands to keep from grabbing her by the shoulders and shaking her. "I've done this all wrong," he said. "Nathan. You. Everything. And you're right, I didn't love you in the beginning. At first you were a means to an end. A very attractive means to an end," he amended, the corner of his mouth lifting. "I never expected to fall in love with you. I didn't even recognize it when it happened. All I knew was that every day it got worse—the worry about when you'd learn the truth. I knew you'd hate me. I knew I'd lose you, but I thought I'd win you back. Somehow."

Rachel's chest tightened. It hurt to take a breath.

"I thought if I married you, it would be harder for you to leave. I thought that was why I married you, but it wasn't. I love you. *You,*" he repeated intensely. He couldn't stand it any longer. He grabbed both of her icy hands and held them tightly. "I've never said that to anyone. I couldn't even say it to you until I knew it was the truth. You want to live in Oceanside, we'll live here. You want to move to Portland, or Los Angeles, or Caracas. Fine. You want to live apart—no can do. I simply...can't...bear it." He enunciated each word heavily. "So speak up, Rachel. Make your demands. I don't believe you really want a divorce or you would have gotten one by now. Tell me what you do want. Just say it."

"I want you," she admitted softly.

"Excuse me?" Ty peered closely into her face, certain he'd heard wrong. The last thing he'd expected was complete surrender. He didn't dare believe his ears.

"I want you." Rachel grinned at his stupefaction, her spirits lifting. She laughed aloud, gloriously happy. "I want you!"

He cupped her chin, staring down at her, his expression fierce. "Rachel, if this is some kind of game..."

"I don't play games. You know that, Ty." She watched a snowflake melt against his cheek. "You're not the only one who's been miserable, you know. It's been hell trying to do the right thing."

"The wrong thing," he quickly pointed out, a smile forming on his lips.

"The wrong thing," she agreed. "I want you and Nathan. We don't have to make any rules about where we live or what we do. As long as we do it together."

"Rachel, Rachel," he murmured, dragging her close, molding her curves to his masculine angles. "I can't believe you're saying this."

"I lied, Ty," she said in a small voice. "I said I'd never forgive you."

He laughed against the damp glory of her hair, burying his face in its shampoo-scented richness. "I've done my share of lying over this whole mess, too. I even lied to myself over why I was romancing you. I thought it was all for Nathan, but it was all for you." He brushed her hair back, smiling into her eyes. "I love you, Rachel."

"You know something, Mr. Rafferty? I actually believe you."

"You know something, Mrs. Rafferty? It's high time you did."

And with that he clasped her hand and dragged her into

# Silhouette Special Edition

## COMING NEXT MONTH

**#703 SOMEONE TO TALK TO—Marie Ferrarella**
Lawyer Brendan Connery was dreading the long-overdue reunion
with his ailing father. But then nurse Shelby Tyree appeared by
Brendan's side, offering to help him heal the wounds of the past....

**#704 ABOVE THE CLOUDS—Bevlyn Marshall**
Renowned scientist discovers abominable snowman.... Was it genius
or madness? Laura Prescott sought to save her father's reputation;
newspaperman Steve Slater sensed a story. On their Himalayan hunt
for truth, would they find love instead?

**#705 THE ICE PRINCESS—Lorraine Carroll**
To DeShea Ballard, family meant pain; to Nick Couvillion, it meant a
full house and kisses on both cheeks. An orphaned nephew united
them, but could one man's fire melt an ice princess?

**#706 HOME COURT ADVANTAGE—Andrea Edwards**
Girls' basketball coach Jenna Lauren dropped her defenses once
boys' coach Rob Fagan came a-courting...again. Familiar hallways
harkened back to high school romance, but this time, love wasn't just
child's play....

**#707 REBEL TO THE RESCUE—Kayla Daniels**
Investigator Slade Marshall was supposed to discover why
Tory Clayton's French Quarter guest house lay smoldering in ashes.
Instead, he fanned the flames... of her heart.

**#708 BABY, IT'S YOU—Celeste Hamilton**
Policeman Andy Baskin and accountant Meg Hathaway shirked
tradition. They got married, divorced, then, ten years later, had a
child. But one tradition prevailed—everlasting love—beckoning
them home.

## AVAILABLE THIS MONTH:

**#697 NAVY BABY**
Debbie Macomber

**#698 SLOW LARKIN'S REVENGE**
Christine Rimmer

**#699 TOP OF THE MOUNTAIN**
Mary Curtis

**#700 ROMANCING RACHEL**
Natalie Bishop

**#701 THE MAN SHE MARRIED**
Tracy Sinclair

**#702 CHILD OF THE STORM**
Diana Whitney

# "INDULGE A LITTLE" SWEEPSTAKES

## HERE'S HOW THE SWEEPSTAKES WORKS

### NO PURCHASE NECESSARY

To enter each drawing, complete the appropriate Official Entry Form or a 3" by 5" index card by hand-printing your name, address and phone number and the trip destination that the entry is being submitted for (i.e., Walt Disney World Vacation Drawing, etc.) and mailing it to: Indulge '91 Subscribers-Only Sweepstakes, P.O. Box 1397, Buffalo, New York 14269-1397.

No responsibility is assumed for lost, late or misdirected mail. Entries must be sent separately with first class postage affixed, and be received by: 9/30/91 for the Walt Disney World Vacation Drawing, 10/31/91 for the Alaskan Cruise Drawing and 11/30/91 for the Hawaiian Vacation Drawing. Sweepstakes is open to residents of the U.S. and Canada, 21 years of age or older as of 11/7/91.

For complete rules, send a self-addressed, stamped (WA residents need not affix return postage) envelope to: Indulge '91 Subscribers-Only Sweepstakes Rules, P.O. Box 4005, Blair, NE 68009.

© 1991 HARLEQUIN ENTERPRISES LTD.      DIR-RL

---

# "INDULGE A LITTLE" SWEEPSTAKES

## HERE'S HOW THE SWEEPSTAKES WORKS

### NO PURCHASE NECESSARY

To enter each drawing, complete the appropriate Official Entry Form or a 3" by 5" index card by hand-printing your name, address and phone number and the trip destination that the entry is being submitted for (i.e., Walt Disney World Vacation Drawing, etc.) and mailing it to: Indulge '91 Subscribers-Only Sweepstakes, P.O. Box 1397, Buffalo, New York 14269-1397.

No responsibility is assumed for lost, late or misdirected mail. Entries must be sent separately with first class postage affixed, and be received by: 9/30/91 for the Walt Disney World Vacation Drawing, 10/31/91 for the Alaskan Cruise Drawing and 11/30/91 for the Hawaiian Vacation Drawing. Sweepstakes is open to residents of the U.S. and Canada, 21 years of age or older as of 11/7/91.

For complete rules, send a self-addressed, stamped (WA residents need not affix return postage) envelope to: Indulge '91 Subscribers-Only Sweepstakes Rules, P.O. Box 4005, Blair, NE 68009.

© 1991 HARLEQUIN ENTERPRISES LTD.      DIR-RL

## INDULGE A LITTLE—WIN A LOT!

### Summer of '91 Subscribers-Only Sweepstakes

# OFFICIAL ENTRY FORM

This entry must be received by: Oct. 31, 1991
This month's winner will be notified by: Nov. 7, 1991
Trip must be taken between: May 27, 1992—Sept. 9, 1992
(depending on sailing schedule)

**YES,** I want to win the Alaska Cruise vacation for two. I understand the prize includes round-trip airfare, one-week cruise including private cabin, all meals and pocket money as revealed on the "wallet" scratch-off card.

Name _____

Address _____ Apt. _____

City _____

State/Prov. _____ Zip/Postal Code _____

Daytime phone number _____
(Area Code)

Return entries with invoice in envelope provided. Each book in this shipment has two entry coupons—and the more coupons you enter, the better your chances of winning!

© 1991 HARLEQUIN ENTERPRISES LTD.          2N-CPS

---

## INDULGE A LITTLE—WIN A LOT!

### Summer of '91 Subscribers-Only Sweepstakes

# OFFICIAL ENTRY FORM

This entry must be received by: Oct. 31, 1991
This month's winner will be notified by: Nov. 7, 1991
Trip must be taken between: May 27, 1992—Sept. 9, 1992
(depending on sailing schedule)

**YES,** I want to win the Alaska Cruise vacation for two. I understand the prize includes round-trip airfare, one-week cruise including private cabin, all meals and pocket money as revealed on the "wallet" scratch-off card.

Name _____

Address _____ Apt. _____

City _____

State/Prov. _____ Zip/Postal Code _____

Daytime phone number _____
(Area Code)

Return entries with invoice in envelope provided. Each book in this shipment has two entry coupons—and the more coupons you enter, the better your chances of winning!

© 1991 HARLEQUIN ENTERPRISES LTD.          2N-CPS